Death at the Wharf

Death at the Wharf

A Mrs. Kelly Mystery

Jolie Tunnell

TULE
PUBLISHING

Dedication

To the real Becky, my sassy and saucy ride-or-die
who would (probably) eat the eels.

Chapter One

M ISS REBECCA SMITH had stamina; I had to give her that. An early morning rise, a whipping chill in the air, and my own silent determination to not lose our way left her to chatter nonstop about everything and nothing.

The girl had yet to surface and take a breath.

A breakfast of scalding coffee taken directly from the hotel kitchen had settled my stomach for the first half hour. The rest of our ride to the shore was punctuated with seagull cries and a rumbling from the exact center of my corset. That Becky heard neither did not come as a surprise.

"She stood there, saucy as you please, and demanded I give the money back." Becky tossed her chin and the feather in her bonnet brushed against the open parasol above it. "She's the one ruined the gloves. Why should Dr. Park be held responsible? I tell you, Mrs. Kelly, she has enough money to be Midas."

Becky was pale to the point of invisibility. Her hair was not the deep blonde I carried from my Norse ancestors, but a washed-out version of straw. Where my blue eyes snapped, hers grayed to a colorless murk. The autumn winds had chapped some color into my cheeks, but Becky remained on the sallow side. All this to say that when she waxed eloquent on an opinion for the better part of an hour, it was reassuring.

The girl did not choose to be wallpaper.

Despite my careful navigation, a wagon wheel bumped through a deep hole in the road, and she loosened her grip on her shawl and took hold of the seat we shared. The woolen shawl dropped from her shoulders, revealing a spotless white shirtwaist over a proper gray skirt with only a suggestion of ruffles. The uniform of a shopgirl was attractive in its simplicity. Serviceable. I had learned not to judge this book by its cover.

I clucked reassuringly at the horse and drove us through a soft spot of sand. The streets of San Francisco were paved with cobbles for the most part, and our journey from the Palace Hotel along Market Street to the Bay had been uneventful, if congested, with Monday morning traffic. Once the Ferry House was in sight and the houses turned to hotels and factories, we'd turned left and headed north along the wharves and docks.

The Bay swirled deep enough to hold entire cargo ships. The crowded terminal directed traffic not only for the daily commuting ferry boats, but giant schooners from Australia and steamers headed for Hawaii. Paddle boats and sailing vessels and cross-continental trains connected passengers and baggage with exotic ports around the world.

San Francisco's golden gateway to the Bay presided over wealth untold. Gold dust from the distant hills had once filled our city with men. Now men jostled for an inch of town and dug for gold in each other's pockets instead.

Becky exclaimed over each ship we passed, although her words were lost in the screeches of gulls and the whistles and shouts of the laboring men and lines of travelers thick along the docks, cable cars, and warehouses.

Although the noise did not diminish, the scent of tar and lumber gradually gave way to one of salt and fish as we continued the curving road that soon became dirt that mingled increasingly with the white sand on which our peninsula was built.

Telegraph Hill rose on our left as we meandered north, Broadway cutting a direct line from our nebulous road past its very feet and on across to the Pacific Ocean, following the sun as it rose and fell over the city.

Another squint down Broadway convinced me I couldn't see the jailhouse from here.

I returned to the task at hand as Becky said, "I gave it to her, of course. Dr. Park always says to humor the ladies so they'll keep coming back, but the skinflint is only in twice a year." Her eyes darted to mine. "I shouldn't have said that."

"It's our day off, Miss Smith," I said. "Whatever you have to discuss today will never reach the ears of your venerable Dr. Park."

She grinned back at me. "The right glove had a tea stain on it. I could tell she tried bicarbonate before giving it up as lost." The wagon bucked again, but she regathered her shawl. "They happen to be my size. And I happen to know how to properly clean a glove."

I chuckled and her pale blue-gray eyes widened. "We're

here! The air is so thick with fish, you can taste them."

"I should hope not," I muttered, pulling up to a bustling wharf.

Securing the reins, I pulled the slip of paper from my reticule and rechecked the name. Which fisherman was the correct one?

Becky and I weren't the only early shoppers at the Filbert Street wharf. Wagons vied for positions along the boardwalk, some painted with the names of restaurants on the sideboards, others destined for the myriad of shops in the city. Shrill demands from hunched women with baskets on their arms and provocative calls from younger women swathed in colorful shawls were answered with encouraging shouts or barked words as the morning's catch was purchased as fast as it could be unloaded from the docked boats.

At least three different languages mingled over the crates of ocean harvest.

"We need Hiram," I said. "Hiram Paiva."

But Becky was already over the side, parasol closed and stowed. Her eagerness was a good balance for me. I had yet to understand the meaning and good use of a day of rest. I'd only agreed to drive us to the wharf because the Palace Hotel had a standing order on Mondays and offered the loan of the wagon if I fetched it for them.

We needed a barrel of salmon and another of anchovies. Becky's tastes obviously ran to the exotic. She was leaning, spellbound, over a tub of water snakes before I caught up with her.

With a gasp, I pulled her back.

"Mrs. Kelly." She laughed. "They're eels. You eat them. They don't eat you."

"I refuse to go near anything that isn't a good, honest fish," I said. "And a crab is a creature more fit for nightmares than dinner plates." I shivered. "This Mr. Paiva is going to load the wagon for us. If we can find him."

A woman had her limits. I'd been running a dairy farm in Minnesota not four months ago and though the sea intrigued me, I had no interest whatsoever in touching it. Or the things that slithered in its depths.

Becky took my elbow and steered us past a long dock crowded along both sides with small fishing boats. A tall rail ran down the center of the dock, draped from end to end in sprawling nets. Women picked their way through it all, refastening colorful floats or pulling at bits of seaweed or retying a knot.

"Let's try the other side," Becky said, tugging us into the crowds. I put a hand to my hat and reassured myself it wouldn't come off with a gust of wind or an errant flying fish. We had neither basket nor parasol to break a path forward with, and only my fashionable bustle flailing behind, so I tolerated a certain amount of bodily crush as we fought our way toward the larger crates and the burly men who presided over them.

"Mr. Paiva!" I called, and the closest man glanced our way with heavy, rheumy eyes and a gray-streaked beard stained by years of tobacco juice. He grunted and jabbed his fat thumb over a shoulder.

"There." Becky and I pushed onto the wooden planks

and moved carefully toward another row of crates, picking our way around coils of rope, long barbed poles, and barrels of salt. One fisherman wrapped a huge fish in a sheet of newspaper while the other took coins from a woman in a yellow shawl.

"Mr. Paiva!" I called, hoping we were getting close to our quarry.

The second man squinted at our approach and dropped the money into one of the deep pockets of his canvas apron. His hairy arms were bare nearly to the shoulder, thick with sinew and muscle that rolled with indecent masculinity. Becky stared at the anchor tattoo on his forearm, gripping my elbow until I peeled her fingers free.

"I'm with the Palace Hotel," I said, arresting my hand before it had extended far enough for a handshake.

He was smeared in a cocktail of scales and blood. The woman in the yellow shawl pushed past us with her purchase.

"Here to pick up the Monday order," I said. "For salmon and anchovies."

I could understand his apparent confusion. In my soft violet dress, fashionably cut for an afternoon outing, gloved and bustled and hatted, I hardly passed for a delivery boy. Even Becky was obviously one step up from a domestic servant in her tidy skirt and boots.

Next to us, a heavily bearded man began a heated conversation. I held out the slip of paper, hoping it was enough. Mr. Paiva accepted it and stared at the words, and I pointed back toward the wagon.

"I can bring it closer," I said, "but not nearly close enough. Can you load the order for us?"

He frowned at the paper for another moment and I felt the crush into my bustle as a fisherman bumped by with a basket of sloshing water.

"Here, Mrs. Kelly," Becky said. "Stand to the side before you're drenched."

I found myself on the edge of the dock and took hold of a raised piling in case anyone else came sideways at me.

"We will wait here," I said to Mr. Paiva.

It seemed the normal Monday fish order came with plenty of chaos and the responsibility of getting it correct kept my feet glued in place.

"Are you sure he's the right one?" Becky looked anxiously from the fisherman to the shore and back.

But Mr. Paiva—if that was who he was—tucked my paper into his pocket and trudged off down the dock.

"I can't help but think he's illiterate," Becky said behind her hand.

"Portuguese," a deep voice said.

The voice came from a bald Goliath of a man with his face hidden behind a huge, sloshing basket on his shoulder. His hands and arms were black as pitch and held the burden with ease.

For the first time in my life, I felt diminutive. As though my sturdy frame and square farmer's hands had become magically dainty and delicate.

Becky blushed.

"He speaks Spanish," the man continued. "Italian." He

shifted the basket and brought his deep, dark eyes to mine. A small gold hoop glinted in one ear. "And English."

"Thank you," I said, regaining my senses. "I imagine you all do. For business. Of course."

When he smiled, his teeth gleamed. "I hail from Barbados, darlin'. For me, it is only the French. *Oui?*"

Becky stared hard at the wooden planks beneath her boots and I looked frantically around for our fish order. With a wink, the man was gone.

"It's more than I was expecting for a lark to the beach," I muttered.

"I'm so pleased you agreed to this little jaunt." Becky giggled and glanced at the water. "It's ever so much better than waiting on ladies in my stuffy little shop."

"By all means, enjoy yourself, then." I kept my hand firmly on the piling, but turned away from the bustling people, determined to avoid another embarrassing commentary but unwilling to diminish the girl's fun. Becky launched into a sermon on the varieties of fish before us.

The water glimmered in the morning sunshine and it felt as though we could reach out and touch the island of Yerba Linda. Beyond the Bay, the mainland mountains shimmered in the golden hues of dried grasses painted with a summer-bleached brush.

A brief dizziness washed over me, and I brought my gaze down to my feet, blinking.

"Becky. Look there." A rope floated below us, nearly out of sight beneath the dock. "It might be…"

"Someone lost a net," Becky finished. "I suppose it happens."

"There must be a float of some type on it." I recalled the nets drying across the way.

"What if someone lost their catch?" Becky was already reaching for a pole.

"I'm sure such a thing would not go missing for long. Leave it be, Becky."

She paused, and we considered the pole in her hands. It was more of a javelin with a wicked-looking barbed hook at the top and soared a good five feet above her head.

"Goodness," she said. "I feel like Captain Ahab."

The image of Goliath wielding such a thing on the open sea like Neptune had me looking down again, and I took a renewed interest in the floating rope.

"Let me see it," I said, holding out my free hand.

Visions of Odysseus and the Vikings of my childhood bedtime stories flashed in my head, and I tipped the top-heavy pole into the water. "It's an awkward thing, isn't it?" I mumbled, poking at the rope.

"Oh, you've caught it." Becky clapped her hands. "That makes you a fisherman. Or fisher woman."

"I didn't mean to." It was impossible to untangle the rope from the end of my pole with one hand, and I didn't trust myself to release the piling. I certainly wasn't going to let Becky do it.

"Careful." Becky leaned out to see.

Her ear-piercing shriek forced the issue. She wobbled at the edge of the dock. I grabbed her instead of the piling, and to prevent us both from falling headfirst into the water, I pulled us directly down to the planks and landed hard on my backside.

The result was a heavy leveraging on the pole that dragged the tangled net, for net it was, out into the open.

Someone yanked the pole away from me, but my eyes were fastened on the scene below.

"Mrs. Kelly." Becky's whisper filled the space of everyone's collective inhale.

And then we were surrounded with shouts. Fishermen and shoppers alike swarmed around us as I pulled Becky close.

A hand had appeared first. White. Wrinkled. Curled. A gold ring adorned one finger.

Once stronger backs than mine applied themselves to the task, the hand was quickly followed by an arm, a torso, a long dress wrapped around a body in high-button shoes. Her long hair had drifted down and covered the face, brown but shot through with gray, telling that an older woman had tangled in the net. A fairly well-to-do female by the cut of her jacket and buttons that still lustered like pearls.

By the time the body was pulled onto the dock, the pandemonium reached fever pitch. I struggled to my feet, dragging Becky with me, trying to keep us from being trampled. Our skirts were ruined.

Water spread over the planks as eager hands pulled at the tangled netting around the dead woman.

"Mrs. Kelly," Becky said, teeth chattering.

"Wait, Becky." I patted her back, watching. Knives came out to get the job done faster, and no one protested the ruin of the net.

The woman's face was bloated and bleached, and I

stepped closer as they peeled hair from it. "They shouldn't be touching her," I said.

Not that anyone heard me.

An exclamation brought the men to a halt. Several stood upright and more backed away quickly.

It was my fisherman. Our Mr. Paiva. With a scowl, he held up a little, dripping book and the crowd dispersed with oaths in several languages.

"It's..." Becky blinked. "It's a Bible, Mrs. Kelly."

Chapter Two

"*SACRILEGE.*"

Aunt Mary's voice whispered in my ear. She always managed it at the worst times, and from her Minnesota grave no less, but as she was the only one of my relatives who knew where I was, I'd accepted her presence in my head whether it was welcome or not.

It very generally was not.

Mr. Paiva had replaced the Bible next to the dead woman in her net and stood nearly alone in his uneasy vigil, hands on his hips. Becky tugged my sleeve and made a move in the direction of our wagon.

"And where is it you think you are going?" Goliath asked. He effectively blocked our path, legs wide, arms crossed, a most unpleasant scowl on his swarthy, clean-shaven face.

"Let us by," Becky pleaded. "I'm unwell."

Her pale face was convincing on any day, but the man shook his head before her words were finished.

"The police are coming," he growled. "As you fished her out, maybe you know her, hm?"

I straightened and brushed at my sleeves. "Nonsense.

We've come from the Palace Hotel. To collect the fish order." Even I had to roll my eyes. "You can ask Mr. Paiva, there. Our wagon is at the boardwalk and the hotel's insignia is clearly marked."

Becky swayed and I threaded an arm around her waist. "At the least, allow us to sit while we wait."

Our position on two upturned barrels next to Mr. Paiva's fish wasn't much better, but it gave me a moment to collect myself and prepare for the inevitable.

The arrival of Police Detective Maximilian P. Fisher.

His officers, and even his supervisor, Sergeant Ross, would be a welcome addition to this morning's affair, but I had not seen Detective Fisher since a debacle involving Chinatown two months ago.

Apparently, my sharp wits were good enough to help District Attorney Samuel Merrill install a call box from Chinatown up to the jailhouse on Broadway, afterward. In return, Sam spent some time training me in the use of my new derringer revolver. I'd managed a new job in the Palace Hotel kitchen, a shared apartment with my new friend Miss Rebecca Smith above her glove shop in the Palace building, and some new ideas of what a day off might entail.

But I was not forgiven for my interference in Detective Fisher's investigation. Or for the fact that I now carried the personal protection of the Chinatown tongs. And refused to identify said benefactors or where they might be located. For a man who'd built a career earning such information, it was altogether too much for him to stomach.

It would never do for him to find me bending over a body.

I startled as a Chinaman passed, balancing two large baskets of oysters on a pole and calling out to another in Cantonese.

Mr. Paiva stared openly at me.

"Did you at least have the order loaded into our wagon?" I asked.

He jutted his beard toward a distant fisherman. "Luigi did."

"Thank you." I glanced at the body. "She was a God-fearing woman. Why is everyone afraid of her?"

Goliath snorted through his sizable nose. "The skirt. The book. Clergy are terrible bad luck."

"A woman wouldn't be clergy," I pointed out.

"Jonahs come in all shapes and sizes," Mr. Paiva said. "None would chance it."

"A woman is bad luck all on her own account." Goliath looked over his shoulder as shrill whistles accompanied the fast-approaching footsteps on the wharf. "We need to send her away."

"Superstitious nonsense," I said. "How can you go fishing without a dozen silly ideas blocking your way?"

He turned and flashed his smile. "The sea is our mother. She feeds us and rocks us to sleep at night. Why would we anger her?"

"You'd think she'd manage," I said, "woman to woman."

But I was already ignored. Police officers gathered around the body, and I strained to hear a familiar voice as I arranged my skirts, trying to minimize the obvious dark boot prints adorning the hemline.

"Mrs. Kelly," Becky whispered, leaning in. "Do you know the woman?"

I shook my head. "But she must be a resident if no sailor brought her into the Bay aboard a ship."

"From one of the churches," Becky said. "But how did she end up in the water, poor thing?"

"Excellent question."

We looked up into the steel-gray eyes of a lean man in a business suit. A bowler hat set off the clean lines of his jaw, and his sandy-brown mustache bristled in recognition. He did not look happy to see me.

"How do you do, Detective Fisher?" I offered my hand.

He ran a thoughtful knuckle over his chin before reaching out and rendering a quick shake with two fingers.

"This is my friend, Miss Smith," I continued. "We came on behalf of the Palace Hotel. For their fish order."

Becky shrank in on herself as Detective Fisher took in every detail of our trodden state. Then he looked up at our companions.

"Paiva, is it?" he asked. Both men behind the fish crates nodded as one.

"And Captain Shorey, I believe?" Detective Fisher held out his hand and how Goliath didn't crush it with his was a mystery. "You docking for the winter this early?"

Captain Shorey rolled a massive shoulder. "It was a good run. The best of luck." He cut a quick look at me. "We're offloading five tons of whale oil from the *Alexander*. Ten of baleen. When we finish at Arctic Oil, she'll get an overhaul at the Iron Works. She earned it."

"How long have you been in town?" Detective Fisher asked.

"A week, sir. Early ships get best prices, you know."

Firm steps caught their attention. A barrel of a man approached, sporting a neatly trimmed gray grizzled beard and mustache combination that flowed into bushy side whiskers and up to form a perfect halo around the back of a balding head. His suit was pristine, if a year out of fashion, a checked cravat kept his throat out of the breeze, and a watch chain spanned the vest tightly buttoned over his paunch. His hat was in his hand.

Only his swaying gait betrayed his profession. Hooded eyes, a bulbous nose, and a grim mouth conveyed a man not to be trifled with, and the sailor in his wake hurried to keep up with him. He sized up the man in charge immediately.

"Captain Carroll," he said, extending his hand to Detective Fisher. "What's this all about?"

"Detective Fisher. Carroll?" Detective Fisher pursed his lips. "You in port, too?"

The two captains spared a glance at each other. Where Captain Carroll was dressed for the city, Captain Shorey wore the battered trousers and rolled sleeves of a dock worker.

"Pirate," Aunt Mary whispered.

"The *Hidalgo's* been in port for two weeks, sir." Captain Carroll glanced at the dead woman. "I was at the barber's when word spread down Broadway about this…" His brows came together. "Situation. Tragic."

"Do you have reason to be interested?" Detective Fisher

reassessed the man. "Fair piece of walking to get here from Broadway. I just came from there myself."

"My men are all over town," Captain Carroll replied. "Not much gets past them if it happens in the water. We hired a carriage. My only question is whether it's related to my *Hidalgo*."

"Should it be?"

His smile didn't make it to his eyes. "No. But I've found it to be easier to stop a rumor in its cradle than one ripe and rampant."

Both captains turned away from each other.

"As I've only arrived myself," Detective Fisher said drily, "I won't have any answers for you. Possibly for days or weeks. Good thing you're here to stay a spell."

"Aye, but it will take only a moment." Captain Carroll stepped toward the body and an officer moved between them. "No need. I can read the net from here." He shook his head and turned back to Detective Fisher. "Not ours. The knots are Portuguese. Simple fisherman's net."

Mr. Paiva's face darkened, but Detective Fisher spoke first.

"We will take all things into consideration, Captain Carroll. Thank you for the information. I'll come around to see you once I begin my questioning. You may be of some help to us."

It was a dismissal, and Captain Carroll took it in stride. With a curt nod, he turned with his lackey and disappeared back into the milling fishmongers.

"And your observations?" Detective Fisher asked Captain Shorey.

"I saw the lady hook the net," he said, pointing at me. "She fished the body out. No one else knew it was down there."

This brought me from my seat. "I had no idea she was down there, either!"

"You took the pole," he said, with a languid shrug. "Your friend cried out, but you did not."

Detective Fisher waved a hand in the air. "I meant the net, captain."

They both turned to the body, leaving me alone with my indignation. Three shoppers pushed forward, eager to get their fish before the Misters Paiva were arrested, no doubt. A housewife began to haggle, and I tugged Becky up.

"We're done here," I said.

"But won't the police have questions for us?"

"No."

She dug in her heels. "I won't go to prison, Mrs. Kelly."

I sighed. "I've been. It isn't that bad. Come on. Detective Fisher knows we had nothing to do with it."

Her eyes were round as saucers. "But. How?"

"Becky, did you have anything to do with it?"

"No."

"Then why aren't we leaving?"

She was speechless. Truly a first.

"You don't actually think I'm involved with this, do you?" I nearly laughed. "Don't you believe me?"

"Smart girl." Officer Heyes kept a straight face, but his raised brows mocked me nonetheless. "Our dear Mrs. Kelly seems to always find herself in the strangest places."

"Your Mrs. Kelly?" Becky had placed a noticeable distance between us.

Heyes nodded while making continuous notes in the little book in his hands. "It's true she's been in jail, but I doubt there's any reason for her return. Unless?" He glanced up briefly.

"Insufferable," I muttered.

"How did you know the body was down there?" he asked.

"I didn't. I didn't do anything. I don't know anything. I'm going home."

"I'll write that down."

"And you can tell Detective Fisher I'm unavailable for questions, as I have no answers."

"Yes, indeed."

"Neither does Becky."

"Hm?"

"Rebecca." Becky's voice was weak with fear. "Miss Rebecca Ann Smith."

"Easily spelled." Heyes smiled. "And you still prefer Mrs. Kelly to your real name?" he asked. "That one's trickier."

"Your..." Becky gasped. "Real name?"

"Now you've done it, Officer Heyes." I threw my hands into the air, exasperated.

"What?" He turned away from us, all innocence, and joined the detective, his pencil never slowing.

Becky crossed her arms and narrowed her eyes. "What is he talking about?"

"I told you," I said. "I'm a widow. My husband died the

day I arrived in San Francisco."

"Yes, so you said. What didn't you tell me?"

The ferocious scowl I aimed at Detective Fisher's back didn't seem to make a dent.

"That Mr. Kelly was a crook and died for his sins. That we never consummated the marriage and his family had it annulled by the local priest." I blew out a breath. "Which leaves me in some kind of walking limbo. His name was the only thing he left me."

"And you wanted to stay here, so I offered to share my apartment over the shop." She appeared to be searching for holes in my story.

"Haven't I paid you a year in advance?" I asked. "Don't we get along famously?"

"Yes," she admitted.

"This city is no place for a single woman like yourself, Miss Smith. You have the luxury of safety in your shop that few women have. An older widow, such as myself, commands a certain level of respect and my derringer raises it yet higher. You cannot come and go without a companion, but I move about as I please."

To prove it, I pushed my way into the crowd around the body, leaving Becky alone with her worries. Heyes continued to scribble into his notebook. Captain Shorey was gone. Two officers wrapped the net carefully around the body as others approached with a litter.

Detective Fisher held the little Bible up to the morning sunshine. It was swollen and buckled, and the majority of pages appeared stuck together in one swampy mass. "Did this come with the body or did someone drop it in the confusion?" he asked without looking at me.

"Mr. Paiva held it up and everyone scattered," I said. "It was hers."

"There's no name on the inside or outside of the cover. No handwriting at all."

Why was he telling me this? "I suppose it could have come from any of the churches in town."

"Or the mission. Or the orphanages, asylums, or directly from the pocket of a missionary returning from Africa."

He hefted it. "This could be from anyone and anywhere. Useless."

Aunt Mary gasped.

"No cross hanging around her neck. No rosary in her pocket. Heyes, make a note," he said, and thrust it into my hands.

"Why would I want it?"

"You found religion yet?" He pursed his lips and walked away.

It was some minutes before either Becky or I could form words.

"Well," Becky said. "I never."

We started down the wharf toward shore and a sleek black bird dove from the planks in front of us. I could almost feel the cold water enveloping its feathers as it submerged.

"Do you suppose it was a terrible accident?" Becky asked, eager to divert us. "Perhaps the poor woman was on the docks before sunrise and caught her foot in a net. She tumbled into the Bay before anyone heard her cry out."

"It's possible. There were no floats on the net. If she tangled, she sank and drowned quickly."

"But. She was floating."

"Dead bodies float," I said, watching the black bird surface, shake his catch down his long, thin neck, and swallow. "Do you want to know how?"

"Oh stop," she said. "I'll have nightmares."

"I'm sorry. It's an awful thing to see on your day off." I drew her arm through mine and she didn't protest. "Let's find something to eat before we go back. My treat."

"How can you eat after what we just saw?"

"As long as it isn't eels. I won't eat snakes."

"Oh, Mrs. Kelly." Her grim smile chased some of the worry from her face.

"Or spiders." I shuddered. "Who in their right mind decided a crab was edible?"

"It's delicious," she declared. "Messy as anything to get at, but a lovely flavor."

I paused and considered the bird.

"What is it?" Becky watched it dive and counted ten before it bobbed up again, far from its original spot. Its black feathers had a nearly iridescent purple sheen to them.

"The cormorant," I said. "There's a tale from my childhood that says the spirits of those lost at sea come to visit their loved ones disguised as cormorants."

"It's vanished again." She turned us toward the wagon. "You've obviously not visited the Farallon Islands yet. Such a colony of them! I reckon every sea haunt from here to Bombay is sitting there, trying to reach their family."

"More old fishwives' tales," I said.
I climbed into the wagon, deep in thought.

Chapter Three

"NOW YOU SEE." Becky was smug. "Eels are nothing. You want adventure? You dine in an Italian restaurant." She held up the little paper menu. "Frog legs. I rest my case."

"I can cook those."

"Calves brains," she challenged.

"Yes."

"Yes?"

But I was distracted. The waterlogged Bible on the table in front of me appeared a lost cause. It hadn't been wet long enough to detach the ruined leather cover, but the paper was thin as onionskins. A luster among the curled pages caught my eye. A bookmark, perhaps? As I gently teased the clump apart, I could decipher the print of several pages at a time.

"I grew up on a dairy, Becky. I know one hundred and one ways to cook a cow."

"But you make desserts for the Palace," she said, reading the menu again. "Fancy ones."

"And I intend to create a tiramisu that surpasses the one here, but don't breathe a word of it to Mama Rosa."

The tiny restaurant was at the eastern-most end of

Broadway, a crossroads of sorts where most of the Bay traffic turned inland to work, play, or live. We sat at a tiny table on the ground floor next to a window with a view of the water. The kitchen was in the back and opened into an alley. The rooms upstairs were for the owners, Angelo and Mama Rosa Fiori, and the top floor housed what I very much suspected was a bordello.

It wouldn't do to mention it to Becky.

I'd dined here twice before and found their menu items incredibly fresh and cooked to perfection. The heavenly scents coming from the kitchen were impossible to miss from the street.

Becky feasted her eyes on the selection.

"Wasn't Captain Shorey…" Her tone and the return of some pink in her cheeks finished the thought for her.

"He tried to implicate me, Becky."

"He only wanted justice for the poor woman," she replied, avoiding my eyes.

"I was more concerned with that other captain. Carroll? He was deferential enough with Detective Fisher, but I imagine him to be a tyrant at sea. He's a man who gets what he wants."

"Speaking of getting what you want," she said, setting down the menu. "I'd like a helping of honesty, if you don't mind."

I pressed my lips together, then commented, "You'll forgive me if I noticed your loyalty flailed a bit on the dock."

"Well, now." She cleared her throat. "I've known you but two months and trusted you implicitly. Maybe it was a mistake." She left space for my reply.

"Karine Halvorsdatter Torkelson Langland from Water-
ford Township, Minnesota, is a mouthful, wouldn't you
agree? There are enough syllables in this world. Mrs. Kelly
gets right to the point."

"Oh." She glanced out the window. "And Detective
Fisher?"

"What about him?"

"He had no questions for us. Actually, seemed to avoid
us. If I were the curious type, I'd say he didn't like you." She
folded her hands on the menu. "Or he does. One or the
other."

"You and I aren't suspects in a murder case." A page tore
at the corner. "That should be good enough for you."

"Murder? What makes you think she was murdered?"

I was saved from answering by the arrival of a tiny fire-
ball of an Italian woman. Mama Rosa's husband did most of
the cooking and she insisted on serving each diner herself
with the local gossip and a basket of fried anchovies. She
placed the greasy paper-lined basket in front of us and said,
"Mrs. Kelly! You are good to come back!"

"*Ciao*, Mama Rosa! You see, I remembered!"

She nodded approval. "You want the *vino, signora*? Best
in house."

"No, *grazie*. Your Zuppa Toscana. Two. And the recipe
for it."

Her laugh was predictable and contagious. "Is only thing
keeps us from being paupers!"

"I'll trade," I said, pressing my palms together. "I can

give you a recipe for a cheesecake that will have your diners in tears."

Her smile was generous. "Can already slice onions." She picked up the Bible and examined it. "What is this you put on my table?"

"A woman was found dead this morning," I said. "Tangled in a net beneath the wharf. This was hers."

Mama Rosa dropped the Bible and crossed herself.

"The police are trying to figure out what happened," Becky said morosely, "but Mrs. Kelly thinks she was murdered."

"May she rest in peace."

I turned the Bible over. "What I can't decide is why a woman would go to the Bay with her Bible, but not anything else. They didn't find a bag or anything in her pockets. No hat, although that may have washed away."

"Her hair was down," Becky offered. "But again, the waves would have—"

Mama Rosa stared at the Bible with suspicion. "She jump, maybe?"

"You mean," Becky whispered, "she took her own life?"

Even I knew that was a cardinal sin, and Mama Rosa crossed herself again before asking, "You see a ship across the way? Far end of Black Point?"

"On the dune side?" I asked. I hadn't noticed. "Up past the swimming beach, where the seawall is going in?"

Her voice lowered. "A prison. For insane. They keep them on the boat. But if one jumps in…"

"Oh, no!" Becky leaned back in her chair.

"The *Euphemia*."

"The what?" I asked.

"Old ship. Not good for sea but still good for people."

"Mama," Angelo called from the kitchen.

She turned at the summons. "Is good she took Bible to her grave. God will have mercy."

"How tragic." Becky covered her mouth at the horrid thought.

"It didn't happen," I said.

"How do you know?"

"Did she wrap the net around her like a shroud before she walked the plank? Or did she aim for one on the way down?"

"Oh, Mrs. Kelly." She leaned over the table and gave my sleeve a tap.

With a sigh, I ran my thumb over the paper edges, trying to fan them. "What do we know about her? She's married. That much from the gold band on her finger."

"Then, somewhere, we have a husband searching for the woman. She would have been reported missing to the police, right?"

"Unless she was a widow."

"Was she wearing black? What color was her dress?"

We both tried to recall. "I believe it was brown," I finally said. "The water darkened it considerably."

Becky nodded. "She's devout."

"Only if this was hers." I continued to pick at the pages and Deuteronomy worked free.

"You think her murderer was devout?" She grinned as

Mama Rosa appeared with two steaming bowls of thick soup.

"It is an inspiration to eat at your table, Mama Rosa." I shook out my napkin and set it over the gloves in my lap.

"You won't get." She shook her head and wiped her hands on her apron. "Not for sale."

"But you are an artist," I said, holding my arms out wide. "Teach me."

With a chuckle, she went back to the kitchen.

Becky inhaled deeply before applying her spoon to the bowl. "Oh, this looks lovely, Mrs. Kelly."

"She'll make me beg for the recipe before it's all said and done, but I've already figured out most of the ingredients." I sipped my water. "It's how they do the sausage that might go to the grave with her."

Becky's reply was something between a muffled agreement and a moan as she swallowed more soup.

The edge of a thin card appeared to be tucked into the center of the book. Gently, I worked it free, but parts of the illustrated border had bonded with the pages and ripped away parts of scripture with it.

It was another three spoonsful of soup before Becky looked up.

"Oh!" Her spoon clattered to the table.

The tintype image was black and white but had a faded, waterlogged red and gold border. A woman perched on a high, narrow stool, laughing at the camera. Her dark hair flowed down her back and covered one breast in front, leaving the other exposed. Instead of a strategically placed drape, she wore a high stomacher with a narrow skirt apparatus that enclosed her legs in a fish tail that reached the floor. Bracelets crowded her wrists. Pearls formed a delicate net around her head.

"Madonna mia!" Mama Rosa dropped the plate of bread with a clatter, her face a study in shock.

"It was in the Bible," I said, heat rising in my face. "I just found it."

"Is that…" Mama Rosa stammered, "the dead woman?"

"No."

Becky stared determinedly out the window. "Put that away," she commanded.

I flipped it over. "You know what this is?" I asked Mama Rosa.

A brief conflict played in her eyes, and they sobered before she nodded. "Not mine," she muttered.

Becky kept her gaze out the window.

"Whose?" Everyone knew what happened when ships docked in San Francisco. Whether the men were from China or the frozen Arctic Circle, they took their year's pay in their pocket and flooded down Broadway, looking for the brothels. It was a deplorable fact that most of San Francisco society chose to ignore.

I had firsthand knowledge that San Francisco's society itself chose well-heeled establishments like my own Palace Hotel for such shenanigans, but you could find gentlemen's entertainment from Pacific to California Street for every budget, ethnicity, or taste.

Not that I traveled those neighborhoods. And I'd never

seen a mermaid. Not one who lived in a Bible in a dead woman's hands.

"Don't know," Mama Rosa said. "You throw away. Not for good girls like you." She fussed with the tablecloth and added, "Eat."

With a sideways glance at the overturned card, Becky straightened in her seat and obeyed. "It's delicious," she said, eager to change the subject.

Mama Rosa nodded approval. "I bring you cannoli. Best in city."

"I'm not leaving without your secrets," I warned her, and lifted my spoon as a sign of cooperation and goodwill.

She crossed her arms and stared me down. After a moment, she asked, "You know the woolen mill?"

"The abandoned factory down past the wharves?"

Her half-smile was coy, and I wondered who she normally reserved it for. It dropped ten years from her face.

"You add wool to your soup?" I asked.

It was preposterous to think she referred to any upstairs business, but the back of my neck crawled with the possibility. There were secrets and then there were secrets.

"Chocolate."

I waited.

"Dominico. Ghirardelli. He makes best chocolate. He moves his business there. Bought the mill."

Becky kept eating, but I waited Mama Rosa out.

"He makes my cocoa." She nodded. "Now you know. Tell him Mama Rosa send you." With that, she returned to the kitchen and shut the door behind her with a firm hand.

I dove into my soup and didn't resurface until the bowl was half empty. Then I slowed enough to take a bite of lighter-than-air bread.

"You know what this means." I sighed and tapped a finger on the card.

"Nothing good," Becky said.

"I have to show this to Detective Fisher."

"Oh, no you don't. You take me home first."

"This is a professional card," I said between swallows. "Like calling cards. I wonder whether they are given out to favorite customers or used as advertising to strangers?"

"It can't be too personal," Becky said, reaching for more bread. "It isn't signed."

"You noticed. Also, they aren't something I would expect a decent woman to have in a Bible."

"Maybe she was indecent."

"Her clothes were too nice." Although I wouldn't put it past her to have been a madame. "Her shoes might have told us the truth. Fancy means money and cheap will tell. No matter how nice the clothing is, shoes don't lie."

Becky shrugged and swallowed. "Maybe the Bible isn't hers at all. Maybe it belongs to a man."

"I think you pointed out earlier that a killer isn't likely to be carrying a Bible as he goes about his business."

"Can I add that a man of the cloth isn't likely to use that as a bookmark?"

My bowl was empty and the bread nearly gone. I crunched on an anchovy, savoring the salty snack.

"I suppose we'll let Detective Fisher worry about it." I

cleaned my hands on the napkin, then slowly put my gloves back on. "I'll drop you off with the fish first, and try to get to the jail and back before dark."

Becky rose with me, and I took two dimes from my reticule and placed them on the table.

"I think you're awfully brave, marching back to that detective's office with something like this," Becky said "He practically threw it away. He'll feel pretty silly when you tell him he handed over a clue like that."

"Or he'll think I'm reading something into it that isn't there. It wouldn't be the first time."

"It might help the police find the woman's killer."

I slipped the card back into the Bible as Mama Rosa materialized next to us.

"Or maybe help the police stop her livelihood," she muttered, pocketing her money and clearing the table.

It was possible, but not likely. When I considered what I knew of Detective Fisher, though, he was a fair man. Many of the police and politicians in this town weren't. And while any or all of them might frequent a brothel at some point, none would care to admit or discuss it in polite company. There was no getting around the fact that this trade was a huge part of the city's income and most of them paid regular, hefty sums to the authorities.

"I have to let the police decide what to do about it." I shrugged. "Probably nothing. As you know."

I let the words hang between us.

"Thank you for lunch, Mama Rosa. *Ciao*."

She stood, arms full of dishes, and regarded the Bible.

"How did the woman die?"

Becky and I looked at each other.

"I assume she drowned," I said. "She was in the water. There was no blood and her clothes and face seemed intact."

Becky had nothing to add, and Mama Rosa moved away with her arms full.

It was a safe assumption, and that was what bothered me now. There had been no floats on the net, but neither had there been any weights.

Becky followed me out into the afternoon sunshine.

I knew better than to judge the dead woman's occupation from her clothing. If she had, according to Mama Rosa's vague hunch, been a prostitute or had anything to do with the darker side of the city, then there were other ways to die.

She might have been poisoned or chloroformed before she dropped into the water. She could have been abused internally. Or she might have died of an illness and this had truly been someone's idea of a peaceful burial at sea.

There would be no answers until the police got to the bottom of it.

The sooner I got rid of the evidence, the better.

Chapter Four

I WAS NEARLY through my list of possible scenarios for the dead woman when Fisher dragged his fingers through his wild hair and said, "Stop, for heaven's sake. She was strangled, all right?"

The man kept himself well. Polished shoes. Straight tie. But he'd run a hand through his neatly combed hair so many times, there was danger of him pulling a fair bit of it clean out.

He rose from his chair behind the desk and stalked to one of the tall, narrow windows that let fretful light into the cramped office. "The net had been wrapped tightly around the woman, so we didn't realize it at first. Damn good try at disguising it, but there's no substituting rope marks for fingers."

"Oh." I slumped in my chair and let the wind out of my sails.

I'd taken the offense from the moment I entered the building, but after twenty minutes of vigorous explanations and, as he'd just cursed in front of a lady, it was time to let the man take a turn.

He did not apologize.

The Bible sat between us with the provocative card, discreetly turned over, on top.

Heyes entered, holding a cup in both hands, staring at the liquid inside with fierce concentration. He audibly released his breath once it landed safely on the desk.

"Thank you, Heyes." Detective Fisher remained with his back to the room and Heyes flashed me a quick grin before he left and closed the door.

The county jail stood two stories tall on a solid stone basement, presiding over the gradual downhill neighborhoods of Chinatown with its back against Telegraph Hill. Broadway cut east and west, but thanks to San Francisco's undulating landscape, its route from the inland Bay stopped far short of the Pacific Ocean, and most of the seedier population with it. This quadrant of town received the brunt of all incomers and the law was prepared to welcome them.

Chinatown was Fisher's specialty and though he couldn't see down Dupont Street directly from his window, it was an easy five-minute walk from the front door.

I lifted the cup and cleared my throat. "I was surprised to see you on the wharf yesterday," I ventured. "Wouldn't Sergeant Ross be first on a murder scene?"

It took a moment for him to turn around, and I remained primly seated before his desk, eyes demurely on my coffee as I took a sip, then forced myself to swallow the bitter brew.

"It wasn't reported as a murder case," he said. "Anyone can tangle in a net and fall into the Bay."

"I see."

Sergeant Ross kept his placard on the desk but seldom used it. By default, this was Detective Fisher's work space, and I felt the underlying current of rejection before the next words left his mouth.

"It's unfortunate you were present to witness it, but—as it has nothing at all to do with you, now the book and the card are returned as evidence—I don't expect to see you again."

"I imagine not."

"Don't misunderstand me," he said, retaking his seat. "I'm very grateful you returned it to us."

"It's the least I could do."

His eyes narrowed.

"I would also like to add," I said after another brave sip, "that a woman with a Bible would have few enemies. Who do you suspect?"

"No."

"I beg your pardon?" The coffee was burnt and luke-warm, but I forced myself to savor it slowly, like a cat with cream.

"No. You are not involved. You are not the police. You are not a suspect. You, Mrs. Kelly, have nothing whatever to do with this case, and I will not be discussing it with you."

"It's a simple conversation over coffee, Detective Fisher, nothing more. Be civilized."

He folded his arms and leaned back in his chair.

"I would expect someone to come around looking for her," I continued. "A husband or an adult child, perhaps. Did someone report her missing?"

Silence.

"It would go a long way to helping, wouldn't it? As the body didn't come with a name. You've likely put Sam on that task. A catalogue of missing persons would take some time poring over. And if she's not local, then the search could extend to other counties in all directions." I gave him a gracious smile. "Unless our mermaid is local. Rather points to a boat, does it not?"

"Are you quite finished?" he asked.

"Sadly, yes." I put the empty cup on his desk.

"You can't help yourself," he said, more to himself than to me. "But it will benefit me in the end."

"What can you mean, detective?"

"Ross put me on this case because I asked. Anything that involves you, I'm going to personally handle, Chinatown or no."

I didn't like the sound of that. "Why?"

His smile was pleasant. "Someday, you're going to lead me straight to the tong leaders. And then I'll be chief."

"Never going to happen."

"As long as you're in my town, it's only a matter of time."

"I swore an oath. I trust them. They trust me." I rose. "But you don't trust me, do you?"

He came to his feet. "The word of a criminal is useless, Mrs. Kelly."

"And what of the word of the police? For example, if I asked you not to follow me so that I could inquire in China-town about the woman, would you?"

His smile curled at the corners. "I would swear it, then send Heyes behind you."

"I thought as much." I straightened my hat and reached for my little bag.

"Tell me again why you were at the Italy Harbor this morning," he said.

"You know I was there on behalf of the Palace Hotel. You saw the wagon. I'm much too busy cooking to pay any mind to dead people."

"Cooking."

"You needn't sneer. It's unattractive. I'm a culinary wizard in their kitchen. Pearl said so only last week. I'd bring you a sample, but you appear far too busy chasing criminals to host tea parties," I said, gathering what was left of my wharf-trampled skirts. "I'll leave you to it."

"Why do you think I gave you the Bible?" he asked quietly.

I paused with my hand on the doorknob. "Blatant unprofessionalism."

"Nothing quite that fancy. It's because you turned up at the wrong place at the wrong time. Again. And if there is something that makes absolutely no sense at the crime scene, you seem to be able to connect it. I thought I'd use you like a divining rod."

"A what?" I looked over my shoulder, but my hand remained on the door.

"When science fails, God provides."

"Are you calling me an act of God? Aunt Mary just turned in her grave."

"Who?"

"Never mind. Use the correct term, detective. Water witch. I know how they work."

"Don't get testy, Mrs. Kelly. If you can be a culinary wizard, you can be a water witch."

"Do you have a point?"

"Yes. I know how *you* work." He waved a hand over the desk. "We appreciate that you are both efficient and meticulous."

"You used me?"

"And now your part in this is done. Thank you."

It was a minute before I could collect myself. I pushed through the door. "I can see myself out, thank you."

He followed me down the narrow staircase.

The entry office was small and efficient, containing a long bench down one side for incoming officers and offenders, and a large desk on the other to process the outgoing.

A gray wisp of a man sat at the desk in a rumpled, nondescript suit, pushing his spectacles absent-mindedly higher on his long nose as he bent over paperwork. A desk lamp cast more light on his task than the glass in the front double doors did.

"Good evening, Sam."

He blinked and rose with a nod. "Mrs. Kelly. Good to see you."

"Those the missing person's reports?"

He glanced down. "How did you—?"

"A lucky guess. I'm a baker now, and I want an opinion on my latest recipe. A cookie so tender it will make you swoon, Sam, and it smells like Christmas. *Snipp.* I'll bring it around in a day or two."

"You certainly will not," Detective Fisher said behind me. "You won't put your foot anywhere between here and Market Street."

I rolled my eyes at the ceiling. "The Palace is *on* Market Street."

"The district attorney has better things to do with his time."

"Indeed, he does," I said, turning on my heel. "We'll leave him to it, shall we? Good night, Detective Fisher."

I pushed through the door onto the landing and went down the side of the building on its wide wooden staircase to the walkway. Unlike the two stories above, the basement had no windows. Neither the morgue nor the jail cells had use for curtains, but the rest of the offices were without excuse.

If the police insisted on keeping the place in a state of utter bleakness, then good riddance. Once in a while, criminals escaped from rusted out cells through dilapidated and outdated doors. According to Sam, they struggled to hold a prisoner long enough to carry out an execution.

No one seemed to mind.

Gas lamps flickered up and down Broadway and I un-hitched the horse. A faint scent of rain had me glance up to assess the evening sky. The first stars winked back and the only clouds were on the western horizon.

The last days of September, I'd been told, heralded the wet season in San Francisco. Summers were characterized by a regular stream of overnight and morning fog that snaked around buildings so thick on occasion that it was a challenge to sort one roof from another. The fog rolled back to sea by the afternoon and gave the city its best and breeziest hours of the day.

Autumn turned the fog into proper clouds overhead, forming a permanently gray sky. Dreary days would be marked with drizzle and the patter of gentle raindrops as opposed to thunderstorms. It would grow chilly in the evenings but never turn to sleet and snow.

And occasionally, during the transition, we had a week of perfect sunshine. Today appeared to herald one. The crisp blue sky had been delightful for a day off, but I reminded myself to trade out my parasol for an umbrella soon. I turned the little borrowed buggy for home, looking for telltale fog and satisfied to find none.

With a little shudder, I passed Pacific Street and Detective Fisher's words echoed in my mind. I shoved back at them. Why should he ruin what had turned out to be a most exciting day? Scents followed me down Montgomery Street and I played my usual game, trying to decipher them.

Base notes of manure in the street and the tang of the Bay mingled with tobacco from the cigar stalls. Cooked fish, garlic, and ginger. Oyster sauce. Ground coffee. Baking bread.

Lights came on in windows as I drove past tall, narrow homes so crowded together the residents could lean out of a window and shake hands with the neighbor in theirs. Men pulled up on horseback or with empty wagons, done with the day's work and eager for supper. I passed Chinese,

Spanish, French, Italian, and faces with no frame of reference for me to label them.

When the weather turned just cool enough, it would be altogether wonderful for business. I'd arrived in town with a lifetime of old recipes in my head that were taking on new life beneath my hands in the giant, gleaming hotel kitchen. Instead of feeding my eight brothers on the farm, I now created pastries and desserts for San Francisco's finest diners.

It gave me a thrill every time I discovered a fresh and tantalizing scent or flavor in my wanderings. These informed the recipes I created for the Palace Hotel that couldn't be found anywhere else in the city.

Pearl, a fellow kitchen employee, always told me that like stuck with like. You would never find a Chinese herb used in an Italian dish, but this was why my skills were rising quickly to the top.

I was greedy for collaborative cuisines. I wanted them all.

Greed was something the fast-approaching building understood. Taking up an entire city block on Market Street, the Palace Hotel greeted me with open arms. She was opulent and saucy, and knew her worth. Her skirts took up space unapologetically and the glass crown on her head was a huge window that invited natural sunshine into the heart of the building, lighting up the Grand Court and seven layers of balconies within.

With a wink at Lotta's Fountain in the far intersection, I pulled along Market, passing the bottom floor of rented spaces. Some were offices, others were shops like the one Becky worked in. The dominant corner offices were taken up by the Overland Railroad Ticket Office. Each space had small apartments built above them, used for inventory or living space if they could afford to double the rent.

Becky and I shared the tiny rooms above her glove shop.

Turning down narrow Annie Street, I drove the buggy to the underground entry. The hotel basement held stables for guest vehicles and horses, walk-in pantries full of hotel detritus from forks to pillowcases, and the mechanical bowels that ran the elevators, boilers, sewers, electric cables, and water lines.

The underground labyrinth was lit with bare electric bulbs that cast shadows twenty-four hours a day and the human, beast, and machine cacophony never faded.

A uniformed man with skin the color of fine caviar stepped forward and took my horse by the halter.

"Hello, Mr. James," I said, climbing down from the buggy. "Thank you."

"You set the police straight, Mrs. Kelly?" he asked.

I handed the reins to him. "That man makes me so angry!"

"What man would that be?" He smiled.

"Detective Fisher. He doesn't listen to reason, that's all. I made some perfectly logical assumptions, and he told me in no uncertain terms to keep my nose out of his business."

"Well," Mr. James said, giving the horse a pat, "they do get almighty fired up about their territory. Dead folks is what they do, and they want the living to stand back apiece."

"I have no intention of doing his job for him."

"No, indeed. You won't be going back anytime soon, then?"

"No. I wash my hands of it."

"Yes, ma'am. That may be the answer after all." He led the horse away.

"Good night, Mr. James."

Moving slowly through the corridors, I found the door that opened into the glove shop stairwell and slipped the key into the lock, thinking about Lotta's Fountain. It was a pretty piece of functional art in the middle of the street, and it sat directly across from the bustling Detmer Woolen wholesale house on the far side of the Palace.

My mind went immediately to what Mama Rosa had revealed. And what she had not.

Chapter Five

I SQUEEZED MY eyes shut. "Do be quick about it, Pearl."

"I told you it'll hurt," she said. "Just keep your hands there for another minute. I'm almost ready."

A brief peek revealed the woman's back, still in uniform, bent over the occasional table, pouring boiling water into a teacup that I knew for a fact had no tea in it. Pearl was my kitchen companion, a coffee-colored woman with a heart of gold. Becky was downstairs minding her shop and Pearl and I had just gone off our shift for the day.

Pearl had worked in the Palace Hotel for several years and, though I was thirty years old and she was younger than I, in many ways, she was my superior. She'd come with me to my little apartment instead of going to her own home across town.

Her enthusiasm seemed overblown.

"I don't want to watch," I said.

"Then don't." She turned and smiled. "I've never known you to be afraid of anything, Mrs. Kelly. A little ol' needle is nothing compared to a harpoon."

Both eyes opened. "It wasn't a harpoon. It was a long pole with a big hook on the end."

"Got the job done, didn't it?" She lifted a little box and opened it. "So fancy." She held up a perfect drop earring. "The blue will make your eyes shine. What is it?"

"A sapphire, I think. With a diamond chip. They were a gift."

"Secret admirer?" She set the earrings back on the table.

"In a way." Aunt Mary had wrapped them under the Christmas tree for me right before her death.

"They're nice and heavy," Pearl said with approval. "They'll keep the holes pulled open while they heal."

My eyes snapped shut again. "Oh, get it over with, will you?"

"You can give me the ice now."

"I think it all melted down my sleeves." We'd chipped a bit from the hotel icebox as we left. I let go of my ears and held out my hands. A handkerchief dropped into them.

"For your tears," Pearl said cheerfully.

"Very funny."

I twisted the fabric in my lap and settled deeper into the chair. We only had room for two chairs and the table. A tiny kitchen area was within arm's reach, with only a couple of cupboards and a hot plate. A door led in each direction to the bedrooms and besides that, the open stairwell in the corner took one back down to either the shop below or the basement and shared lavatories.

The walls were painted, not papered. A coat tree in the corner, a clock on the mantle, a fern in the window, and a framed landscape on the wall completed the domestic simplicity.

I faced the window, but even the view of busy Market Street wasn't enough of a distraction from Pearl's service. My eyes stayed closed.

"What are you waiting for?" I asked, sitting ramrod straight in stoic expectation.

"I just needed to cut the apple. We've been at work since four in the morning, you know. You might be kinder to the lady about to skewer you."

I felt her fingers on my right ear and froze. "I'm sorry. Please don't kill me."

"Tip up a little."

The apple was cold on the back of my earlobe and the needle, scalded and swift, plunged through both.

She ignored my involuntary yelp. My eyes flew open in time to catch the spot of blood on the apple she laid down.

"Now for the beautiful ear bobs," she said.

I forced myself to watch the lovely blue jewelry as it came closer. It would all be over soon. It was worth a little pinch.

My eyes closed on an actual whimper as the post slid through my ear.

"We'll be done in two ticks," Pearl said. "Why don't you tell me what you put into that tiramisu today? I licked the spoon when you weren't looking. I nearly moaned myself. It's so rich and creamy."

Releasing my lower lip from between my teeth, I said, "I saw you do it and had to get a fresh spoon. Pearl, I've asked you not to do that before. The cream has to be extremely fresh, that makes a difference. And then there's the *Savoiardi*. You can't soak them too long or you lose the texture."

"Do you know you hum when you cook?"

"So I've been told."

"And you get this look on your face like you're going into battle."

I opened one eye. "I do not." Pearl picked up the apple, and I closed my eye again. "But my recipe isn't perfect yet. I've been working Mama Rosa over for her secrets."

"The Italian restaurant?" She gently tugged on my left ear, and I obediently tipped it toward her.

"Yes." I almost nodded, but caught myself. "She told me where she gets her cocoa powder."

"That's fantastic!" Her words were punctuated with a puncture to my ear and I spent the next couple of moments holding my breath while she finished.

"I tricked her," I said, "but if I'm lucky, I can still get her soup recipe, too."

I focused on breathing as she bustled around the room.

"I think Ida is so happy with your desserts that she'd double your wages for a new soup."

"It's one more item she could add to the afternoon tea menu. As it is, the ladies in our dining room are regularly sending compliments back to the kitchen. I'm quite delighted."

"Open your eyes."

Pearl held up my small mirror and deep blue stones winked at me from my ears.

"There's your smile," Pearl said with satisfaction.

"Thank you, Pearl." I took the mirror and peered from all angles. My hair turned up in a proper twist and left my neck exposed with only a lace collar around it. The earrings decorated the space between. "It feels a bit like hanging chandeliers," I said with a laugh.

Each sway of the dangling stones tugged at the ongoing pain in my ears, but Pearl had assured me they would heal in a few days.

"I don't think anyone in the kitchen will object," Pearl said, gathering her coat and hat. "We have a new dress policy, but it's only for the serving men. White jackets and black pants for all waiters and turned-down collars. They have to have black ties for the breakfast shift, but white ties for lunch and dinner."

She shook her head and struggled into her coat. I rose to help her.

"And everyone is to be perfectly clean shaven," she finished. "No beards or mustaches. Can you imagine? They say it's the new European way and we have to keep up."

"We do get guests from Europe," I reminded her. "They would know."

"Speaking of Europe. It's raining."

I finally looked out the window in earnest. "Ah me, I wondered if it might. I'm sorry you have to go home in it."

"Not at all, Mrs. Kelly. It was fun watching you squirm."

"I'm sure it was." I handed her handkerchief back. "Thank you. I feel so fancy."

"You'll spend the rest of the day tucked up nice and warm?" she asked. "No more fish deliveries?"

I crossed my heart with a finger. "None. Your Mr. James was kind enough to lend me a buggy last night, and I'm going to beg it again today."

"Where are you going in the wet? I thought you told Detective Fisher you would stay home and knit."

"If I knew how to knit, the nets we looked at would've made more sense to me." I frowned in thought. "Captain Carroll could tell at a glance whether the woman was wrapped in one of his nets or not."

"It don't matter whose net it was," Pearl said. "If she wasn't a passenger on a particular boat, then whoever did her in grabbed one at random."

"Given the fact that it wasn't the water that killed her, I have to agree. She could have died anywhere."

"Where is it you're going then, Mrs. Kelly?" Pearl pursed her lips, and a brow raised.

"So suspicious." I pulled a sturdy umbrella from the coat tree base and offered it to her. "I'm going to a chocolate factory. Can you imagine? If I want an Italian dessert to ring true, it needs Italian chocolate. Not the Dutch nonsense up in the kitchen."

She held up a hand and shook her head. "Don't you let Ida hear you talk that way. She pays a lot for her ingredients."

"She'll pay for this, too. I want to know what kind of bargain they make with hotels. It's a big account."

"They likely already make it for half the city." She put a hand on the stair rail. "But if I know you, you'll have us famous for it in no time."

I gave her a sly smile. "You'll say good day to Mr. James on your way home?"

"He's a gentleman through and through." Her eyes sparkled. "I'll let him know to watch for you. See you in the morning, Mrs. Kelly."

"Goodbye, Pearl."

Her steps pattered softly down the steep stairwell and she took herself out the door at the bottom.

I drifted back to the window. Ladies with parasols scurried down the sidewalks, caught in the drizzle. It must have just begun, and it was nearly noon. Hopefully, they would scurry into the Palace for tea.

The sidewalks gradually took on a shine and several people ran to catch a passing cable car. Most ducked into the glass-windowed area, but some were content with the open seats. Horses continued through the streets, but I knew it was only a matter of time before the muck built up on their fetlocks and most deliveries would not be able to access the higher hills in the city. Some streets were so steep, it was a wonder they attempted them even in dry weather.

Cable cars were a modern miracle.

With a sigh, I passed over my adorable new hat with the blue ribbons and reached for a plain, wider-brimmed straw and my everyday gray coat. The earrings would have to be enough.

The tiny, circular stairwell was industrial iron and echoed with each step. You could hear anyone coming or going from the apartment or the shop, so it wasn't surprising to find Becky waiting for me when I pushed open the door at the bottom.

"Let me see!" she squealed.

I turned obediently so she could properly admire my little vanities.

"And did it hurt too much?" she asked.

"Never felt a thing," I said.

My ears stung like the dickens, but I was afraid to touch them in case the bleeding started again. Pearl's command was to leave them in for at least two straight weeks. How I was supposed to sleep with them was another thing altogether.

"You really are one of the bravest ladies I know," Becky said, heading back to her shop counter. "I'll stick to brooches and my watch fob. I can't abide the sight of blood, especially my own."

She had an array of gloves fanned out in front of her and reached beneath the counter for a glove box.

"Dr. Park never showed up today." The box held two pairs of pink gloves and she added another from her assortment. "He always drops by the morning after my day off to bring the till and see that the ledgers match the cash box."

"He doesn't think you're pilfering?"

"Oh, no. He's just very meticulous. And punctual. I can't imagine why he isn't here yet."

I glanced at the door. The glass etching read, PARK'S GLOVES AND GAITERS in gold letters within a stylized glove, and beyond it, the gray day was busy turning the gray walkways, streets, and buildings grayer yet. Narrow glass cases lined both sides of the door from ceiling to floor. Lit by rows of tiny bulbs, a variety of gloves were displayed against pale green-striped flocked paper.

Men's gloves for driving or riding and heavier lined

gloves for work took only a small amount of space. The rest was a glorious riot of gloves for women and girls. Delicate pinks and eggshell blues, whites and creams and ecru. Some were elaborately embroidered and others bore lace cuffs or pearl buttons. If a shopper wished to attend the opera or be presented to the Queen, Becky was prepared.

The concrete columns that formed the arched door alcove, an integral part of the outside building facade, continued a motif of acorns and vines and set off the extensive collection.

"I'm afraid this weather has turned away your shoppers," I said. "Perhaps Dr. Park stopped for a warm meal on his way over."

She made a noncommittal grunt and said, "I've got to pull out our inventory of spats and men's cashmere mufflers. It always takes a week or two of rain before everyone takes it seriously."

"I miss my new hat already," I said.

"There are mittens and muffs in the boxes behind the curtain," she continued. "But I'll wait to see when Dr. Park thinks they should come out."

The shop carpet was thick and meant to keep dainty high-buttoned boots clean and dry. Crystal fixtures gleamed from the walls and the curtain she referred to slid silently in front of a veritable mountain of narrow boxes, all arranged by size, color, and material. Becky's professional competency and her impressive collection was such that I'd already purchased several pairs. At least during the summer, she did a brisk business.

"But I may as well pack up these lace mitts." She held up the pair in question. "They always make me think of picnics on the beach."

"Do they?"

Her cheeks pinked, but she busied herself with the rest of the gloves for another minute.

"I haven't been to the ocean yet," I said, "but it will keep."

She eyed my coat and umbrella. "Where are you off to?"

"The chocolate factory Mama Rosa told us about yesterday."

"So fast?"

"The early bird gets the worm, you know."

She tipped her head. "You aren't going back to the wharf, are you?"

I leaned back on my heels. "Why should I?"

"I've been thinking," she said, and went back to boxing the gloves. "The woman was so close. Right under our feet. And no one saw her. Now, maybe the fog hid her body as it drifted there. And maybe there was nobody walking on the wharf at night. There wouldn't be." She shook her head without a pause. "Since that's when the fishermen are all out working. But how did she float around in the Bay and no one notice her?"

"What do you mean, Becky?"

"It's just that the ocean is a safer bet." She stacked her boxes. "The ocean could've pulled her out to sea. And if not, she would have drifted sideways and been discovered maybe miles away from where she went in."

"I didn't know that."

"Well." She gathered her boxes in her arms. "Someday, we'll take a picnic and go see for ourselves."

Chapter Six

M Y DRIVE NORTH was swifter than the day before. The buggy was lighter and the streets in a midday traffic lull. After another twenty minutes of rain, the fickle clouds rearranged themselves and the unpaved roads, while damp, were not as muddy as they could have been. The air freshened as I drove along the Bay and I breathed it in. I passed the busy wharfs at a good trot and tried to keep my equally paced thoughts on recipes instead of murder.

The fast-approaching Pioneer Woolen Mill loomed ahead. Or what was left of it. A cluster of dilapidated buildings tucked into the gentle curve of the cove, with wharfs at the southern tip and Black Point on its northern side. The north shore road curved onto the dunes beyond, and the silhouette of a ship stood in stark relief against the pale sand.

I had no intention of going anywhere near the *Euphemia*. Insane people were clearly a job for the police. If the dead woman had been accosted and tossed overboard, I wanted no part in it. Had she been a visitor or an inmate? Either way, had one of the inhabitants lost control and killed her, then dumped her body in a panic?

I scanned the distant deck for signs of life and found

none. My gloomy thoughts were interrupted when the horse, wandering along with my wandering mind, veered back onto the road of its own accord.

The road widened in front of the mill proper. To one side of the road, buildings lined the water's edge. On the other, scattered equipment, broken wagons, and the rusting remains of machinery were strewn about like the cast-off innards of an industry, left to decay. The largest structures appeared to be warehouses, between two and four stories tall, but no smoke rose from the chimneys. Smaller buildings might have been offices, but the place was eerily deserted.

I pulled the horse to a stop and listened. Nothing. The place appeared abandoned. I silently cursed Mama Rosa for sending me on a wild goose chase.

In the distance, a bell rang. I squinted, trying to see beyond the buildings, guessing the mill must have a dock for both receiving raw goods and shipping finished products. Hitching the buggy in the shade of a large cypress, I made my way through the maze of deserted buildings toward the cove.

It was a regular rabbit warren, but I managed to reach the other side and walked directly into a chain of men carrying sacks from a small boat on the dock into one of the buildings.

In all, there were half a dozen transporting the cargo, all wearing narrow-brimmed hats low over thick brows, swarthy faces capped with heavy, drooping mustaches. The closest man met my eyes and never broke his stride as he said, "No entry, ma'am. We're closed."

The scent of wet wool mingled with straw, hot burlap, and something that tickled my nose with familiarity yet remained tantalizingly beyond identification.

I wasn't about to lose the trail now. I scurried behind him into the bowels of the dim warehouse and identified the man in charge, not because he was supervising—every man was busy shoving the bags into place—but because, instead of a pair of braces holding up baggy pants, he wore a proper leather belt and trousers with a sharp crease in them.

"Excuse me!" I called. "Hello, there!"

The cavernous metal roof echoed my words, and the man turned in surprise.

"We're not open for business, madam," he called, hefting his load onto the growing pile with a grunt.

"There must be some misunderstanding," I replied as he turned back to the doorway. "Is this the chocolate factory?"

Ladders, pipes, and heavy machinery crawled throughout the space, punctuated with crates, tools, and copper tubs. The giant bags were stamped. Cacao Beans. Ecuador. Picking my way around pallets, I hurried after him.

"We're still preparing for operation," he said without looking back. "The fermenter, roasters. Grinders. You have to go to our shops in town if you want to buy anything."

"I see." I caught up with him and matched his stride. "I'm the head pastry chef at the Palace Hotel. We are interested in creating new recipes in our kitchen with your chocolate and I need to discuss quantity pricing."

He stopped abruptly, and I caught myself before I bumped into a passing burlap sack. "You'll have to talk to the boss." He dug a scrap of paper from his pants pocket and presented me with a card. "Address is on there." With a nod, he went back to work.

"Another question, if you please!"

He paused again at the dock, this time with a frown.

"Are you here every day?" I asked. "Working?"

"Setting up the factory." He seemed confused.

I pointed toward Black Point. So long as we were standing here, it didn't hurt to ask. "The ship there. The *Euphemia*. Do you know anything about it? Seen anything unusual?"

He put his hands to his hips as the next large sack passed by. "It doesn't sail anymore. Nothing strange about a beached ship."

"And it's an asylum? You've seen people on board? Or maybe off board?"

A passing laborer grunted and said, "Yes! Ghosts!" Chuckles came from men along the line.

"It's not part of our business," the man said and turned for the dock.

I blocked him. "To put it bluntly, has anyone fallen overboard? That is, a woman was found dead beneath the wharf, tangled in a net. I only wondered if she may have come from that ship."

Although I had his full attention, I wasn't comfortable with it. He considered my question and said, "No. Used to be for prisoners, but now they all go to the jailhouse. No women."

"She wasn't a prisoner. Maybe a visitor."

The laborer came through again and hissed, "Ghosts! Only haunts on a haunted ship."

A harsh look from his boss kept him moving back to the boat.

"We never see anyone on deck," the man said. "Sorry. We have work to do." With quick, determined steps, he fled and put two men between us.

One of the men hissed again, and I gathered my dignity and the little card and left them to their task.

I drove south at a good clip before my curiosity could get the better of me and make me do something I was already regretting. Detective Fisher wanted me to stay out of it.

"A wise woman runs from folly," Aunt Mary said with approval.

"It is the honor of kings to search out a matter," I quipped back.

I happened to have searched out a matter. With a huff, I decided that made me nobility. Not a water witch. The man could very well interview ghosts himself.

I'd nearly turned the horse around three times before we finally pulled up to the wharf, and the horse stopped in his tracks, offended by my indecisiveness. The sky echoed my shifting, heavy, gray mood.

It didn't feel very noble to withhold information from the police.

Reins in my lap, I let my eyes wander. The morning crowds were long gone and only a handful of women remained, working among the drying nets. A small cluster of men gathered at the edge of the planks.

Speak of the devil. I knew that suit.

I'd hitched the buggy and crept within ten feet of the huddle before one of the men looked up and noticed me.

Captain Shorey's mild look of surprise was immediately quashed by a left hook from the man in front of him. He retaliated with a swift punch that made everyone, from suits to uniforms, leap into the scuffle.

I took an uncertain step back, and someone called my name.

The Paiva brothers sat, each in a small boat tied up close to the brawl. They appeared as dispirited as the orange-brown sails drooping, unfurled, to the decks.

"Mrs. Kelly! Careful!" Hiram Paiva called, coming to his feet and holding out a hand.

The melee came my direction, and I gathered my thick skirts in one hand, took his hand with my other, and leapt aboard. If not for his improper grip around my waist, the momentum would have carried me right off the other side into the water. The choice was between clinging to him or dropping to my haunches. I found myself plopping down onto the rocking boat, skirts billowing from edge to edge, staring wildly at the bobbing horizon.

"Careful!" my savior repeated, holding up his hands as if to keep the boat from capsizing with sheer willpower. His brother watched, amused.

"What in the world?" I gasped. "Why does it move so much? Are we sinking?"

The brothers shared a befuddled smile. I settled more firmly on my bottom and turned the slightest bit to face the wharf. One of the uniforms nearly fell into the boat after me, and I cowered, waiting for the impact.

"Enough!" Detective Fisher's voice cut through the curses and grunts of the fighting men. He collared a man who came up swinging, and Officer Heyes pinned his arms. Their struggle continued while Captain Shorey went nose to nose with Captain Carroll, both screaming inarticulately.

Officer Wilson's shrill whistle sounded the alarm and though the women along the wharf looked up, no one appeared from the city side.

"You don't have far to look if it's a killer you want," Captain Carroll said, breaking away from the group and smoothing at his vest. "Look it up, officers. The man has a past."

"You barge-swilling bilge rat," Captain Shorey said, fists raised. "Both a coward and a cheat."

"Gentlemen!" Detective Fisher held up a hand in front of both. "I'll haul you both in! You'll keep a civil tongue in your heads and answer my questions. Then I want you both back with your ships and stay there."

"You check into his records, detective," Captain Shorey growled. "There's a reason he's docked ahead of me and I can tell you why."

"And you're too late for the Oil Works, Shorey," Captain Carroll replied in a much calmer voice. "You take second place like a sniveling school child. It's professional jealousy and you should be ashamed in front of any good businessman. No wonder they won't work with you."

"No matter." Captain Shorey backed a pace and dropped

his fists. "I know what you are. You stay away from my ship and my crew."

"And I'll caution you to do the same."

Detective Fisher used a word that made my ears grow hot. "If you say another word," he said, "we're going to hold this little meeting in a cell. Understood?"

Captain Carroll nodded and Captain Shorey squinted a look of pure malice at him. Heyes had pinned his captive's arms behind him, and the man looked ready to rip Captain Shorey apart. I recognized him as Captain Carroll's man and a large triangular pendant dangled from a cord around his neck as Heyes's grip nearly bent him double.

"I'm not here to investigate the whaling business," Detective Fisher continued. "I'm here on my own, and you'll show some respect for it. I'm going to repeat the question." He turned to Captain Carroll. "How did you know the net wasn't yours?"

"I was told you would come to me with questions," Captain Carroll said, "not summon me back here. Be that as it may, the nets used on whalers are vastly different from those used in fishing boats. For one thing, we aren't after the little fish." Here, he sent the Paiva brothers a withering look. "We hunt leviathan. What few nets we employ are made of rope. Fishermen use cord. You can't catch a whale with a butterfly net, detective. Some of our ropes are thick as my arm."

Detective Fisher raised an eyebrow at Captain Shorey, who nodded and elaborated.

"We don't use nets to catch whales." He sneered at Captain Carroll. "We use harpoons. Bombs. We sink lines into them and ride them until they tire. The body is winched alongside the ship for processing. With chain and pulleys. Not nets."

"You both saw the dead woman?" Detective Fisher asked. They nodded.

"Either of you know her? Maybe a wife or a whore?"

They shook their heads.

He pulled a card out of his jacket pocket and I knew what it was without looking.

"Either of you seen this girl?"

Captain Carroll whistled and leaned in. "Nice. You collecting, detective?"

"Watch your mouth," Wilson snapped.

Captain Shorey shook his head.

"What?" Detective Fisher stared at each of them in turn. "Neither of you frequent the whore houses? There something in particular I ought to know about whaling captains?"

I put a hand over my mouth as both captains raised fists to Detective Fisher and Wilson drew his gun.

"Now, boys," he said calmly, holding up the card, "I just need a name. Or a location. Girl like this seems unforgettable. Maybe a sailor's dream, hm?"

"I don't frequent the city's slime," Captain Shorey muttered grimly. "My men do as they please, but as you know, they are black as pitch. Like me. The whole crew. If we were caught carousing with a fish like that, we'd be gutted by morning and you know it."

Detective Fisher considered his answer, then nodded. "I imagine it keeps them a bit more on the straight and narrow."

"Easy to be blamed for things." Captain Shorey's fists

migrated toward Captain Carroll, who grinned. "Whether they've done them or not."

"Detective Fisher," Captain Carroll said, straightening his tie, "I would be the first to arrange introductions for you with a lovely creature like that if I were acquainted. Sadly, I am not, but not for lack of trying, I assure you. As we've only been here two weeks, please grant me a little time to get to know your fair city on a first name basis."

Heyes's captive snorted.

"I don't want to hear about any trouble from either of you." Detective Fisher slid the card back into his pocket. "You don't so much as spit in the wrong gutter this winter. You got me?"

Surly nods were as good as he got. Detective Fisher jerked his thumb over his shoulder, and Heyes released his man. The party split into two small groups, walking stiffly away from each other.

Heyes shook out his hands, then reached into his pocket, pulling out a small notebook. "I'll try to get that all down, Fisher," he said. "Give me a minute."

Wilson holstered his gun, watching the men leave. "Filthy pirates," he muttered. "We'll have more trouble, you'll see. They can't help it."

Detective Fisher straightened his hat and waited until both captains led their men in opposite directions. His eyes took in the wharf, pausing to watch the working women for a moment. Then he turned to the Paiva brothers and saw me. His face registered disbelief followed by anger, and if I weren't too mistaken, a swift bout of embarrassment.

"What in the actual hell?" he asked.

Chapter Seven

"PAIVAS," DETECTIVE FISHER said. "I want to see your sails."

"Sails, sir?"

After the initial stare down, the man was ignoring me. I was as invisible as the rigging. Heyes could not keep a smirk from his face, but his eyes remained on his notebook as Detective Fisher worked.

The Paiva brothers rose and flapped the sails that hung from the crossed beams that created an awkward triangle at the back of each boat. They briefly disappeared from my sight, but after a few paces left and right from the dock, Detective Fisher told them to furl the canvas back into place.

He watched them carefully. "Mr. Paiva, you are normally fishing at night and home during the day?"

They did not appear to be twins, yet the men moved and nodded as one.

"And this is your usual berth?"

"Yes." Hiram Paiva seemed the spokesperson for the team. His brother remained mute.

"It appears to be the most desirable place," Detective Fisher said, scanning the dozens of boats tied to the wharf.

"It is," Mr. Paiva replied. "We pay handsomely for it."

"There are other designs," Detective Fisher pointed out. "Other styles of boats. Especially down on the far corners."

"Those are not ours." He shrugged. "Chinese."

"And you own your boats?"

"Silenas," he corrected. "Yes."

"They are particularly Italian?"

The brothers shared another incredulous look. "Feluccas are Sicilian. Best fishing boats made."

"And can you show me how you fish? How do the nets work?" He frowned. "Your nets are all accounted for, I presume?"

"Yes, detective. You, see?" He gestured to the nets strung up behind Detective Fisher, who appeared to have been caught flat-footed.

"These are yours?" He glanced at them, but continued his questioning with the men. "Tell me about them, then."

"They are cleaned every morning. Hung out to dry, and the women clean them after the catch is put into barrels."

"That is what those women are doing over there?"

"Yes. And keep them barked. They clean so we can sleep." With this, he made a particularly woeful face. "Is hard work, fishing."

"Barked?"

"Boiled in tar. To keep them strong."

Detective Fisher had walked away and lifted the edge of a net in both hands. "They're heavy," he said. "Coarse. Hemp rope?"

"Yes. Factory made, that one. Looms make them lighter.

The handmade ones over there are heavier. Twice as clumsy."

"Is anyone else missing a net? We asked around, but no one reported one stolen."

"Everyone fished last night," he offered. "Nobody angry."

He dropped the net. "How do you catch fish with these?"

"They are put off the back and dragged. Three hours each net."

"And where do you two normally fish?"

This brought the conversation to an awkward stop. Mr. Paiva screwed up his face in thought and his brother scratched at his beard, scanning the horizon.

"I don't need the details," Detective Fisher said, irritated. "Just in general. Nearby? Across the Bay?"

"Best fishing near the mouths of the rivers. We go after the salmon and bass, get best prices. If the bigger boats get there first, they lay out the double-ended long nets across the shallow reaches and we have to move away."

"So, it's a race to get to the best places first? Does that competition get out of hand? Anyone out there in a feud right now?"

"Is quiet right now. The paranzella takes all the rockfish. Different nets for different fish."

"Paranzella?"

"Heavy linen rope, drags the bottom."

"The Bay is crowded at night." He mused. "How do you keep from running into each other or over someone else's nets?"

"We have lights." He pointed to the lanterns hung bow and stern. "We have habits. Right of ways. Smaller boats get out of the way of bigger boats. And when nets are full, we come home. Sales begin at dawn."

Detective Fisher thought through this information and my leg fell asleep. After witnessing the animosity between the whaling captains, it was hard to believe there weren't active feuds among the local fishermen.

I held perfectly still.

"All these nets," he said at last. "They're everywhere out there, but you tell me you can keep track of them all. In the dark. Underwater. For hours."

"Yes, sir."

"What other nets do you use around here?"

"Handlines. Gill nets." He held up a smaller net. "The crab nets are stacked there."

"The circles?"

"Yes. They sit on the bottom, baited, and we pull them up later." He shrugged. "Is not crab season yet."

Detective Fisher shook his head. "That's too many nets, gentlemen. I need the one wrapped around the woman yesterday."

More shrugs.

"Anyone else out there at night?" Detective Fisher's voice had a desperate edge to it. "Water taxis, maybe?"

"No, sir. No taxis, everyone uses the ferry."

"Why do you know everything except how a woman drifted across the Bay and under this wharf without anyone seeing her?" He clenched a fist. "Someone knows. Someone saw her. And you two were closest."

From my seat, the water lapped softly against the pilings that supported the wharf, and an orange creature with arms like a star clung to the one in front of me. There was a two-foot gap between the shaded water and the decking, and the idea of a dead body floating there sent a shiver up my spine.

Hiram Paiva rose, and our boat rocked. "We saw nothing. We fished." He gestured at the nets. "Maybe she's *fantasma*."

"Fantasma?"

"Ghost," his brother said. "Women are very bad luck."

Heyes's pencil stopped.

Detective Fisher's eyes narrowed. "Where do you live?"

Mr. Paiva pointed up at Telegraph Hill.

"Heyes," Detective Fisher said, "take down their address. We'll pay you a visit at home, hm? See what you might remember. Maybe we'll take your nets and your boats away until you do."

The Paiva brothers growled and moved toward the wharf. My boat wobbled alarmingly.

"That's the second time I've heard about ghosts today," I said.

All five men stared at me. My leg had gone numb, and it was almost impossible to sit still much longer.

"If you believe in such things," I said, giving my hem a tug into place, "there's a ghost ship across the Bay. The *Euphemia*. I've heard that it's haunted, but there are any number of reasons our woman might have met her demise there."

A muscle worked in Detective Fisher's jaw. Mr. Paiva yawned and rubbed his ear.

"She could have been visiting the inmates there," I said. "And met with a violent welcome."

Heyes pocketed his notebook.

"The *Euphemia* is empty," Detective Fisher said. He closed his eyes and took a deep breath in and out through his nose. "It hasn't sailed in over twenty years. The ship has been decommissioned and is scheduled to be destroyed."

"That is the definition of a ghost ship," I said. His attitude had my back up.

"They plan to tow her out to sea," he continued. "Sink her off shore where no other ships will drag over the wreckage. It's in the way of the new sea wall."

"You said it yourself, detective." My leg ached. "She was killed first. She was in the water after. Why not on a ghost ship?"

"Because it would have been noticed." He looked at the Paivas. "Anyone see any activity out there in the last week? Heard anything? A light or a splash? It's quiet out there at night. Sound travels a long way. A scream?"

They shook their heads.

"A murderer has the ship to himself," I said. How could he not see how perfect this was? "And a scream would only make the place seem better haunted. Everyone would stay away. No one would investigate."

"Including myself," he said. "Good day, Mrs. Kelly." He waved his officers behind him and stalked away.

Both of the Paivas appeared unsure about what to do

with me. I eased my aching leg out and pins and needles shot up its length. The brother clambered forward in his boat and up onto the wharf.

It looked so easy.

Hiram Paiva stood behind me and waited. I was in the way.

"He didn't take your address, did he?" I asked by way of distraction. The boat rocked gently as I eased my knees up under myself. It was two feet forward and two feet up, with only a rope securing the bow to the dock. "It's nothing like a horse, is it?"

They did not return my nervous smile.

"Thank you for helping me out of the way earlier," I said, gathering my skirts and rising up on one knee. While the deck was solid beneath my boot, the boat rocked further as I shifted my weight. I stared at the rope, begging it to hold the boat steady for me, and rose to both feet.

In one swift motion, the boat dipped beneath me, and Hiram Paiva came from behind while his brother reached down as my arms madly pinwheeled.

My shriek didn't stop my valiant rescuers, even when I grabbed Mr. Paiva and nearly threw him headfirst into the water. Between them, the Paiva brothers dragged me onto the wharf where I knelt until I caught my breath.

"More ropes," I panted. "You need at least a dozen to hold that beast still."

Laughter came from the women up and down the line of nets, but Detective Fisher was blessedly long gone.

"I nearly grabbed for the rope," I said, rising with trembling knees. "What if I'd yanked it and released the boat? We'd all be swimming."

Well, I thought, they would be. I'd be sinking like an anchor. The idea merged with the image of the dead woman and I felt faint.

"The knot cannot be undone with a tug," Hiram Paiva said. "It tightens if you pull."

"A trick knot, is it?" I huffed, putting my clothing to rights.

They were rapidly tidying their things, and I wondered how long Detective Fisher had kept them waiting while he argued with the whaling captains.

"Every man on the water knows hundreds of knots," he said as he worked, "and they're all for something different. Rigging. Cargo. Fishing. Some knots are meant to release quickly and others are tight." He put two hands on his net and tugged. "Fish-proof. Storm-proof."

I leaned forward and inspected his net. "It's really just rope, tied into a million little knots."

He grunted and draped it in place.

"It's all the same knot. And you can tie these?" I asked. "Yourself? If one is broken?"

Mr. Paiva shrugged. "Like they say. It can't catch whales." He looked askance at me and more titters erupted nearby.

It was in the back of my mind. Something odd about the net around the dead woman.

"Do they sink? Or float?" I asked. "Your nets, I mean?"

The brothers were no longer smiling and their broad

shoulders drooped. I sensed their cooperation waning.

"Floats hold them open at the top." His voice was weary.

"So. They will sink if left to their own devices." I tapped the net with my finger. "I imagine they are hard to replace if you lose one."

Each hefted a sack over his shoulder and Mr. Paiva said, "If a fisherman loses a net, he goes hungry. His family does not eat. We never lose a net, Mrs. Kelly. Goodbye. Maybe we sell you fish tomorrow, eh?"

I planted my feet in front of them. "There's a killer out there. Someone who kills women and leaves them to rot like fish."

They glanced at the planks beneath their feet.

"You two saw the card Detective Fisher pulled out of his coat?"

They looked away. "No."

"You did. But he never asked you if you knew her."

"We are married. We have *bambinos*. Babies."

"That doesn't mean you don't know things," I pressed.

"We are going home. To sleep." They pushed past me.

"If you want the detective to leave you alone," I pleaded, "you have to help."

An exhausted Mr. Paiva paused and looked back at me. "The whale."

"What?"

He turned his broad back and kept walking. "Look in the whale."

I stopped near my buggy and watched them for a few more minutes as they trudged away.

What whale? The captains had whales aboard their ships, or what was left of them. Were the Paivas trying to cast doubt in the other direction? But all parties questioned insisted they knew nothing about any of it. No one claimed the net or the woman. The ghost ship appealed, if only to prove Detective Fisher wrong. Anything was possible there.

Giving my patient horse a pat on the nose, I frowned in thought. If the killer strangled the woman, then she was dead in his hands. Why a net at all? Why did she have to go into the water? It was a great deal of trouble to go to when one could simply walk away from an anonymous corpse in any alley.

For that matter, why the Bible? I climbed up into the buggy, utterly distracted. The book was small, but not small enough to slip into a lady's pocket. She'd have carried it, assuming it belonged to her. Perhaps it was wrapped in her skirt unintentionally in the struggle.

But if it wasn't hers, then the killer was making a statement. It had been placed with her deliberately. A last-minute benediction? Religious token? Not with a harlot's card tucked inside.

"Was our lady a lady?" I asked the horse with a gentle slap of the reins. The woman on the card was not the woman in the net. But did they have a job in common?

I drove south and passed Broadway without looking west, but I felt Mama Rosa's restaurant watching me. My stomach rumbled, but I hadn't the strength to upbraid her about the chocolate factory today. I slipped a hand into my skirt pocket and fingered the address card. Was there time to track down the chocolate and make my deals for the hotel?

The sky was a smooth slate overhead and the afternoon breeze came in fits, but it was not cold. I stifled a yawn. It was hard enough to navigate the course of a day without the sun, but it was nearly impossible to stay awake in this weather.

It truly was still broad daylight. The buggy slowed. Harlots were thick along Pacific Street. The Barbary Coast, as it was called, ran smack between the police station on Broadway and all of Chinatown on the other side. I had powerful, if underground, friends in Chinatown. A jail full of police was a block away. So long as the horse moved at a steady pace, where was the harm in taking a quick look around?

"Pride goeth before a fall," Aunt Mary said in a rather frantic tone.

"Nothing ventured, nothing gained," I muttered.

Boldly, I turned the buggy onto Pacific Street. The water hadn't revealed any secrets.

Perhaps the land would confess.

Chapter Eight

THE GRADUAL UPHILL of Pacific Street was said to draw men from the ocean with a siren call. Sailors fresh off the boat swam in schools to the glittering bait of the Barbary Coast and were cheerfully welcomed in the open arms of brothels.

Opium, gold dust and silver coins, card tables, and dice filled the gaps.

I passed Montgomery with a small pang of guilt. I'd promised Detective Fisher to never approach the jail from any other direction than straight up Montgomery. Everything south of Broadway and west of Kearny was unpredictable, and no place for a lady. These three blocks along Pacific above Chinatown were the most dangerous in San Francisco and no one walked them alone.

My head swiveled, trying to take in both sides of the street at once. It was hard to know whether the foot traffic was more or less than normal for a Tuesday evening, but there was plenty of it. There were tourist sailors wandering the walkways. Chinese locals with shaved foreheads and long braids down the back of silk shirts. Other men wore working clothes, boots, and suspenders, and while I could imagine them as miners, they'd more likely come from a factory or mill.

But most of the men were in everyday suits and bowler hats, in groups of twos and threes, chatting or puffing cigars as they perused the various billboards and windows. A man in coveralls pasted a repeated poster along the front of a building advertising THREE LIVELY FLEAS. The illustration was a woman in her petticoats and stockings on a swing, and what fleas had to do with it was beyond me.

Gentlemen came and went through various pub doors and most of them appeared quite steady on their feet. So far. The dusky atmosphere was tantalizing, but even with two women calling down from a window at passersby, the street felt well insulated from the evil I knew watched me going by in my buggy.

Full of clanging and chatter, a cable car passed by, but none got on or off. It was suppertime for families, and this area was not residential. Not for working families, at any rate. No delivery wagons or ice trucks drove by. Street sweepers were long gone.

I passed a tattoo parlor that claimed to cater particularly to ladies. Lively piano music came from two open doors, and I identified it as a saloon by the accompanying fumes.

Tightly wedged doors without signage or windows appeared to lead between buildings. Every recess along the city blocks held a loiterer in ragged clothing. Narrow alleys that would never see the light of day yawned black at the street, yet men were entering without a backward glance. If ever there were a place for thieves and ruffians, this was it. Some carried themselves hunched with heavy thoughts and others moved with desperate furtiveness.

Hard eyes followed my progress down the street and I took another broad survey to see whether any of these men were police. Finding none, I straightened in my seat and turned briskly around the next corner.

Dupont Street, while somewhat familiar, was already deep in mottled shadow. What time was it?

Voices here came from above and below, with women leaning from windows and suggesting a drink or worse, and open doors disappeared into basements while scents of the vilest sort drifted across the street.

Claustrophobia settled over me, and I tried to shake it off. I was only a block from Montgomery. I could drive away any time I pleased. I focused on the horse, sending it around the next corner and the sinking in the pit of my stomach made me clench the reins.

Laughter and cheers meant nothing good here. Men pushed each other out of the way good-naturedly, as they attempted to peer through a window. The plate glass had been blacked out except for a narrow strip at eye level.

I passed a sign for the Hippodrome. Spider Kelly. The So Different. The Bear. An awning in front of yet another bar room declared it to be the Gay and Frisky, advertising burlesque girls. Dance halls? I'd waltzed at a benefit ball at the Palace Hotel once. This was obviously a different style altogether.

Aunt Mary muttered to herself.

Two men dashed in front of the horse and I jerked on

the reins, coming to a sudden stop at the curb. An argument erupted from the bowels of the establishment across the street. Men came running from all directions and surged inside, only to be thrust backward again onto the pavement. Raised voices and raised fists appeared and a man shoved his way through the crowd, his nose spouting blood.

A single gunshot, and he fell into the gutter. Several hands picked him up and dragged him back inside. I sat, frozen in place.

Above the surging rioters, a deeply carved wooden sign hung from an iron arm.

The Whale? The Paiva brothers had referred to a house of ill repute.

There was no mistaking the sign over the door or the appalling level of crime it openly flaunted. What had I hoped to accomplish, driving through the Barbary Coast? In retrospect, boarding a ghostly ship full of insane people seemed the more reasonable venue of inquiry.

With a jerk, my seat rocked sideways, and I turned with the buggy whip raised in my hand. A woman bumped up against me, her skirts flapping wildly.

"Praise God!" she cried, wild eyes pleading, "Please help me!"

Her skirt and jacket were every bit as respectable as my own, though her hat was never meant for poor weather. Two short feathers nearly flew from her head as she attempted to crawl into my lap.

"Here now, sweetheart," a man on the walkway said, "I meant no harm!" He had his large, rough hands on the buggy and leered at her through bloodshot eyes. His clothing smelled as if he'd slept in them for days.

"Leave me alone!" she cried.

I wrestled my arm from her frantic grip and flourished the whip.

His eyes darted up at it as he took a fistful of her skirt and tugged. "You're the one as asked me first, darlin'. Come down and show me the error of my ways."

The horse snorted and tossed his head.

Laughter came from below, and I turned to see another ragged man at my elbow. "Do you fancy a revival, miss? I'll buy you a drink any day."

The man on the far side received the first sting of my whip. With a cry, he stepped back with his hands to his face. The horse lunged forward and the second blow fell short of the other ruffian as I braced my feet. His swift hands missed my arm by an inch as we careened down the street, nearly running over another pedestrian.

By the time I brought the horse back to a walk and looked around, we'd barreled down Powell Street and were in the midst of Union Square. All the shops were closed, but the streets breathed a comforting air of respectability.

"I'm so ashamed of myself," the women next to me said. She released the buggy and dabbed a gloved finger to her eye. "I just don't know what I'd have done if you hadn't happened to be sitting there."

Her deep velvet brown eyes were the dominant feature in an otherwise plain face.

"What was your business up there?" she asked. "You

seemed as out of place as I was." Her face turned red, and she leaned back in the seat. "Oh, I hope you weren't waiting for someone. It all happened so fast."

"No." Had I really been sitting in the direct line of a bullet? I took another minute to get my bearings and pull myself together.

"If I hurry, I can catch Roberta before she leaves to collect me," she continued. "I strayed. But I won't ask you to take me back."

"I'm sorry." Deliberately, I returned the whip into its holder and sent my horse an apologetic noise or two. "I was only passing through when the gunshot startled me. I'm thankful I was there to help."

"You were so courageous!"

"He deserved what he got. Why was he after you? Or don't men need a reason in that part of town?"

"I'm afraid I was quite naïve to be there in the first place," she said, and I cringed inside. "It's the vilest place I've ever seen. Makes South Dakota look like paradise."

"South Dakota?"

"Yes. I've only been here a week, if you can believe it. Come to stay with my aunt and help the missionaries."

"At the mission? Are you Catholic?"

She covered her mouth. "Goodness, no. We're mostly Baptist with a few hearty Methodists who join from their church across the street. We cover more ground that way." She extended her hand and said, "Miss Esme Walker."

I shook it. "Mrs. Kelly. And what business had you on the Barbary Coast, Miss Walker?"

"Distributing handbills." She held up a stack of papers. "Nearly lost them in the tussle."

"You were there deliberately? Alone?"

I absolutely ignored Aunt Mary's raised brow.

She lowered her eyes. "I wasn't supposed to go anywhere that far. Can you let me off here? I can walk down Geary Street. It's the one street I know."

"Where are you going? How far is it?"

"Just past Van Ness. On Franklin." She straightened. "Don't worry about me. I'm tougher than I look."

After what I'd witnessed, I had my doubts. "I'll drive you. It isn't far."

"But I'm keeping you from your own appointments."

"Nonsense. It's nearly dark." I urged the horse into a trot. "What kind of church sends innocent young women into the lion's den?"

"Oh, please don't think it's anything like that! If you'd kindly not mention it to the sisters, I would be most grateful. No harm done, thanks to you. You were my guardian angel today."

My silence did not reassure her.

"I was supposed to have a partner, but I convinced Sister Roberta to let me try a corner on my own." She anxiously scanned the road ahead of us. "We go out two by two. Like Christ's disciples. To educate the population on the modern perils and diseases of prostitution. The broken and depraved must be given the opportunity to escape their allotted place in hell."

My, but those words rolled right out into the light of

day. I glanced at her handbills. No illustrations so far as I could see. I hoped the depraved could read. In English.

"A city desperately in need of Christ," she continued, as if a speech or two had been memorized. "As Nehemiah says, the God of heaven will give us success. Sister Roberta told me Pastor Kincaid told her that pastors would rather be called to Africa or China before they'd set foot in San Francisco. She says he calls this city one of the darkest places on earth."

I pursed my lips, recalling that even the dark places had their codes of honor. "And do you plan to convert the whole city or just the prostitutes?"

"Oh, it's not so alluring in the light of honest day. That's when we have a chance. I watched a woman empty a chamber pot into the street from a third-floor window. This city deserves better. We plan to petition the mayor."

"To end prostitution?"

Her eyes were round. "Of course! They have no dignity. No future. They die young with none to pity them."

"What do you do with them once you've caught one?"

"We work with the San Francisco Ladies' Protection and Relief Society. Their place on Sandy Hill, Hospitality House, is both a home and a school."

My next question was aborted as she cried out, "There she is! Oh, Mrs. Weston! I'm here!"

The oncoming buggy had nearly passed us before pulling up short. A stout woman in a heavy shawl backed her horse until we were next to each other.

Miss Walker said, "Such perfect timing! Mrs. Weston,

meet Mrs. Kelly. She was kind enough to give me a ride and save you a few minutes. I can hop over into your buggy in one shake."

As Miss Walker took herself out of my buggy, Mrs. Weston looked me over.

"The Lord bless you," Mrs. Weston said. "It's very Christian of you."

"It was no bother," I said. "Miss Walker was telling me about your work on the streets."

"Yes." Her chin lifted another inch. "We turn neither to the right nor the left, but walk the straight and narrow road to salvation."

"I would hope your ladies don't actually walk them. Those alleys lead to anywhere but salvation, if you don't mind me saying so."

"Miss Walker? Were you anywhere near an alley today? I gave you strict instructions to remain on Montgomery Street."

"No," Miss Walker's quiet voice said from the road. "Of course not."

Mrs. Weston gave me a firm nod. "Our faithful ladies have marched on the streets since our congregation was founded and our Lord protects them."

"Murder happens, Mrs. Weston." I decided to let it drop. Miss Walker had a good scare, and it would do her more good than any sermon she might hear later. "But I am curious. Do your ladies carry a Bible with them?"

"The senior ladies do. Our work cannot be accomplished without divine intervention."

I perked up. "So not all. Senior ladies?"

"A few who can recite scripture from memory." She paused as Miss Walker clambered into her buggy. "Truly pillars in the church. They lead the cause."

"You wouldn't happen to know whether one of them is missing?" It was a long shot, and I took it.

"Missing?"

The ladies were ready to leave. If I told them about the dead woman, would it lead to fits of righteous indignation or a solemn vigil right here in the street?

"I did wonder," I said, changing course, "whether you'd actually met any of the prostitutes on Pacific Street."

"Heavens, no. We would never send our ladies there."

"Then I suppose you wouldn't keep records of the girls you've helped? Take the cards or photographs, perhaps? Of the depraved?"

She snorted in a very unladylike way. "Whatever for? When your former sins are washed away, there is no use in recalling them. Those cards should be gathered and burned."

"Do you? Gather them and burn them?"

"What congregation do you attend, Mrs. Kelly?" Her voice was sharp.

"I was raised Lutheran. Back home."

"And where do you call home, Mrs. Kelly?"

"Minnesota."

She slapped the reins on her horse's rump and drove him slowly around to face the other direction. When she was once more beside me, she asked, "Do you attend services here, then?"

"Not yet."

"You ought not try the good Lord's patience. Good night, Mrs. Kelly." The horse began to move.

"Miss Walker," I called, "who was to be your partner today?"

She turned and gave me a wave. "Mrs. Alden. Good night, Mrs. Kelly!"

I waited until they'd gone a pace down Geary before turning myself around and heading to Market Street. How were they planning to convert prostitutes without speaking to them? Was Miss Walker sliding handbills under the door and running?

It was a thought, that the dead woman had worked with this organization. Or that the card came from the Barbary Coast. I wondered whether Detective Fisher had already followed up on either idea.

I yawned.

Church was a place you went to be confirmed as a saint or a sinner. No one ever fell somewhere in between.

"I'm sorry." Aunt Mary sighed.

Chapter Nine

THEY WERE PERFECT. Round, high, toasted but tender, the scones were flaky, buttery pedestals for the imagination. Dawn had come and gone in a blur, but there was more to do. Pearl inhaled as she passed by and murmured in appreciation.

"Apricot currant," I said, transferring the two dozen to a platter. "I've made an orange sauce to go over the sticky buns and make sure the *riskrem* stays on ice until the very last minute that it's served."

"The what?" She put a spoon into the deep pot of cardamom-spiked frying *smultring* and lifted a perfectly cooked treat from it.

She called them doughnuts. Our guests called them delicious.

"Rice pudding." I didn't care what any of my Scandinavian recipes were called, so long as I was given complete control over creating them. "Next week, I'll work on floating island."

"Ida said she wanted more of your cone cookies," she said, dropping fresh heavy rings of dough into the sizzling pot. "Made in the waffle irons."

I sighed. "*Krumkake* takes too long. And half of them are broken by clumsy kitchen boys before they can be served."

"I'll find a safer spot for them." Pearl dusted the hot rings with powdered sugar. "They're so pretty filled with cream and fruit."

We'd begun in the kitchen well before dawn, working next to the baker, and usually finished our first offerings by the time the rest of the kitchen and dining room staff arrived to prepare the breakfast menu. They filled it with sweet breads and nuts, quail and trout, eggs and oysters, delicate jams and jellies, and a fruit selection.

Opened an hour ago, the dining room was filling nicely, and I had to wonder if the weather was to thank. It was another brisk, windy day that blew the clouds into tattered ribbons in a steel gray sky.

I wiped my hands on my apron. "I'm getting some coffee."

"Right behind you, honey. And can I say your ears are simply sparkling this morning?"

I gave her a quick smile. "They hurt like the devil."

Her soft chuckle followed me across the sumptuous Palace Hotel kitchen. It gleamed white from the deep sinks to the gas ranges to the immaculate walk-in refrigerator. The baker rolled past with huge racks of fresh bread as the chefs chopped fresh herbs and assistants squeezed oranges into carafes. The coffee percolator held five gallons of fresh coffee, and I served myself in a fancy white cup with gold trim.

I carried the elegant Palace serving ware through to the pantry walkway and helped myself to sugar.

"Mrs. Kelly!" Becky appeared out of nowhere and a sheen of sweat glistened on her forehead.

"Becky, are you ill?"

"I need you now! In the shop!" She grabbed my arm and coffee dripped onto my apron.

"Becky, you're scaring me. Calm down. Did you close the shop?"

Her hands trembled. "It's him, Mrs. Kelly, he's come to the shop, and I won't speak to him—I won't!—unless you're with me."

"Should we get the police?" Pearl marched up to join us.

"Who? Is it a customer?" I set the cup on a shelf and reached behind me to untie the apron. "Or is Dr. Park angry about something?"

"You should fetch the doorman," Pearl said. "He can deal with rough customers."

"I need you, Mrs. Kelly." And with that, she burst into tears, sending an incoming busboy quickly out the other door.

Pearl and I shared a concerned look, and she said, "Jumping Jehoshaphat. I'll cover for you. I don't know when you became more powerful than the police, but I'll send a dishwasher to fetch the doorman, too."

"Thank you." I handed my apron to Becky, and she mopped her face with it. "Becky? You've never mentioned it, but is it a … do you have a beau?"

But Becky was beyond words. Taking her by the shoulders, I steered her out of the pantry and down the metal servant's stairs to the basement. We moved through the corridors to our back door and she tried twice to use her key before surrendering it to me.

Pausing in the stairwell, I debated going up first for some sort of weapon. But I was willing to guess that whatever upset Becky had emotional roots, not criminal ones, or we would not be on our way in. This was something for a woman to deal with.

Honestly, I thought, pushing through into the shop ahead of Becky, how much bother could one make over a pair of gloves? Assuming my sternest look, I prepared to banish whoever had dared to ruin a perfectly good morning.

I nearly ran face-first into the man's broad back.

"I beg your pardon, sir," I said, going by, my firm elbow bumping into his, "but we will discuss your business at the counter."

Detective Fisher turned and followed my progress, and I kept my back to him long enough to subdue the heat in my face and the surprise in my eyes.

"Mrs. Kelly." Detective Fisher kept his hat on. "It's been too long."

I continued sedately around the counter, and Becky kept up close to me.

He did not move from his position in front of Becky's inventory. He'd pushed the curtain aside and Heyes was scribbling away in his notebook. Both were grim. Wilson stood by the door, admiring the display.

"Miss Smith informed me in no uncertain terms that she would speak with us only if you were present." He gave her a hard look. "I had no idea you were a lawyer."

"Does she need one?" Whatever they were here for, I only had a few minutes to deal with it. Why would Becky come running for me, unless she thought somehow, I could protect her? From what?

"Now." Detective Fisher placed himself directly in front of Becky and ignored me. He was getting good at it. "I've got as far as your name and address. And you are the proprietor of the shop?"

Becky swiped one last time at her face and put my apron on the counter. Fists on hips, I kept a stern gaze on the detective.

"Dr. Park owns the shop," Becky replied, taking her courage from me. "I run the shop every day but Monday."

"And how often is Dr. Park on hand?"

"He's here daily at closing time. To collect the day's income."

"When did you see him last?"

"Sunday evening. The shop is closed on Mondays and he normally comes next on Tuesday morning."

"He arrives mornings on Tuesdays? Why that day?"

"Yes. To bring in the till, you see. We don't leave any money in the shop when it's closed."

"And you don't close on Sundays?"

"Dr. Park is not a religious man. And we do get some customers on the weekends."

He nodded. What was he driving at?

"Indeed. Did Dr. Park not come yesterday?"

"No. I watched for him, but he didn't come." Her worried face turned to the door, as if willing Dr. Park to appear.

"Not in the morning or at closing time?"

"No." She glanced at me and wrung her hands. "He never brought the till, and I waited all day."

"Did it worry you at all that he never showed up?"

"I don't understand it. He hasn't come this morning, either, and he is as regular and punctual as a clock."

"What did you think prevented him?"

She swiped at her face again. "I just can't imagine."

"Do you have a way of finding him or communicating with him when things go wrong?"

"No, sir. He comes to me. No telephone or messengers. I have no idea where he lives."

By this time, I understood the gravity of the situation and wondered that Becky hadn't been more worried yesterday. She hadn't mentioned it.

"Seems that the gentleman you're after is not here," I said, and crossed my arms. "We have work to do."

Detective Fisher ran a finger along the counter.

"Are you on good terms with your employer, Miss Smith? Are you content with your wages?"

"Yes. We work very well together."

His eyes narrowed. "He allows you use of the upstairs apartment, correct? Does he ever pay a visit?"

"That's enough." I slapped a hand on the counter and he removed his. "What are you insinuating, detective? Because I share the upstairs rooms with her, as you well know. Of course we don't have gentlemen callers. Not employers, acquaintances, or family."

He tipped his hat at me. "I see. And do you, Miss Smith?

Have family in town?"

Her lips trembled, and she pinched them together before saying, "No. I grew up in an orphanage. They trained me for domestic service, but I had a knack for numbers. Dr. Park hired me from there and my salary and the apartment are generous compensation enough. I would never argue with him over details like that. He is a very fair man."

Detective Fisher took in the snap in her words and wandered to the glove display.

"Tell me about these gloves, Miss Smith."

"What, um, do you want to know? We carry a large variety from several vendors. Mr. Leaks is right down Market Street, so we carry only a few of his." She took in a breath. "Calfskin, sheep, horse, goat, dog, pig. The most popular are the Sierra Buck Gloves. They're hunted, and I think men feel a sense of power wearing them."

He faced her. "Power?"

She blushed. "We have silk for the opera with pearl buttons, too. Or lace."

"What, no baseball gloves?"

Wilson released a soft snort and Heyes kept his red face aimed at his notebook.

Becky did not smile. "Absolutely not, sir."

"Boxing gloves?"

"I'm sorry, no. And no returns. Once a glove has been worn, it is shaped to the wearer's hand, like a fine shoe molds to one's foot."

Detective Fisher nodded. "You've spent some time here, then. And you can hold your own with an angry customer, perhaps? Anyone angry in here lately? Demanding to see the owner, maybe?"

She bit her lip, and he nodded thoughtfully.

"Does Dr. Park gamble? Have debts? If you run his money, you'd know."

"I would not, sir!"

He ran a hand along his hat brim. "Good with numbers, Miss Smith? Have your cash drawers ever come up short?"

That was enough. "Are you implying she steals?" I asked. "Of all the insolent…"

He walked around the counter on Becky's side. "Anyone else touch his books besides you? I'll have to see them before we leave."

"I'm honest as the day, sir! Why, I'd never get another job on the west coast if I stooped to that nonsense."

I placed a gentle hand on Becky's trembling shoulder.

"You may go at any time, Mrs. Kelly. My business was never with you as I've told you repeatedly. This shop is closing and Miss Smith is coming with us."

My grip tightened, and his eyes narrowed.

"Dr. Park was discovered dead last night in unusual circumstances," he said to Becky. "We are rounding up everyone who had anything to do with him, personally or professionally." He took a deep breath. "It isn't much. We have yet to discover any next of kin and we need all the help we can get."

"You can't do this! I've done nothing! We need the sales to pay for the rent." She turned wild eyes on me.

"There must be some other way!" I said.

"Hand me your ledgers and collect your coat, Miss Smith."

Wilson flipped the little sign in the window to closed. He nearly lost his arm when a man burst through and collided with him.

"Hands up!" the man cried, and brandished a fireplace poker. "Step away from the women!"

Wilson had been caught between the open door and the display case, but Detective Fisher aimed his gun at shoulder level and said, "Police! Stand down!"

The intruder pulled up short, long enough for Wilson to wrest the poker from him. He looked around frantically and asked, "But where are the thieves?"

Becky and I untangled ourselves from each other. I'd never heard that tone from Detective Fisher, not even when he'd accosted the sea captains. The gun had appeared from nowhere.

Detective Fisher looked the man up and down and hol-stered his weapon somewhere inside his jacket. "You're the doorman? From this hotel?"

The man brushed down his valet jacket and nodded. "Yes, sir. I was told to run down here and defend the lady in the glove shop. Told the police weren't coming." His confused gaze bounced between everyone in the room.

God bless Pearl, I thought. That was the way to enter a room.

"Admirable." The detective paused. "Saves me a walk. I need to know whether you or your men noticed anything unusual outside this shop in the past couple of days. Anyone loitering where they shouldn't be. Someone testing locked doors. Odd noises at night."

The doorman stood tall and looked down his nose. "No, sir. We don't tolerate no shenanigans around this here hotel. Keep the sidewalks clear and clean. We have a reputation, sir."

"We face Market Street," he said. "That's a lot of bustle to keep track of."

"Yes, sir. But we keep eyes out. Nothing particular reported along the shops. No break-ins or riffraff."

"You'd know the difference between riffraff, as you call them, and legitimate shoppers, I presume. What about across the street? Do your eyes travel that far?"

He shrugged. "Can't stop everyone from admiring the Palace, can we? Couple of fellows sat across the street a spell over the weekend, but they's allowed."

"Watching this place?"

Heyes's pencil began to move again.

The doorman rolled a shoulder and clasped his hands behind his back. "Hard to know, sir. I've plenty of other responsibilities to tend."

"Could you give a description or recognize these fellows if you had to?"

"No, sir. Sorry, sir. All's I can recall is a brown derby, and a bottle passed between them."

Detective Fisher shook his head. "No call boxes in the shops. No guards. Your guest rooms have electric call buttons for ordering up maid service and employees can use telegraph communication connecting every floor, but these shops appear to be completely independent of the building proper."

"Yes, sir. They are rented space."

"And if there's an emergency?"

The doorman quietly held out his hand and collected his poker from Wilson. "I believe we summon the police. Sir."

The detective and Wilson shared a look. Heyes put his notes away and Detective Fisher said, "Thank you. That will be all. Back to work, everyone. Miss Smith, if you'd please collect your things and come with us, we'll be on our way."

"Mrs. Kelly," Becky said, clinging to my arm. "You must come with me. I feel faint."

"You stay right here," I said. "Give the detective the books. I'm going up for your coat and mine." My words for the detective were icy. "Don't you ruffle a hair on her head or I'll see you're held accountable."

With a huff, I took myself out the back door.

Chapter Ten

T HE RIDE TO the jailhouse in the policeman's covered
wagon was uncomfortably brisk, but sitting on a hard
bench in the building's basement morgue was cold in several
additional ways. The deep chill seeping through my coat
could only fend off the stale, sour scent of decay for so long
before forcing burial. The thick and suffocating scent of
death surrounded us.

I had a few questions for Detective Fisher, but I needed
to hear his first. Becky and I watched him move silently
around the coroner, Mr. Lees, and Sam, who'd followed us
down the narrow stone steps. There were two bodies laid out
beneath sheets on tables set in the center of the room and a
handful of others, wrapped in sheets, in an undignified pile
against the far wall.

"You up and left right in the middle of baking," Becky
whispered. "What will they say?"

I felt reckless in my anger and didn't lower my voice. "It
doesn't matter. We might both be out of a job, Becky, but I
won't have you abused by that man's egotistical ways."

A single electric lightbulb hummed faintly overhead and
cast a dim light over the pallor of Becky's face. "Bless you,

Mrs. Kelly, but we have to pay for a roof above our heads and the tea in our cups. I can't afford to be without my job." She sighed. "But I'm terribly glad you're here."

The terrible feeling in the pit of my stomach told me losing her job was the least of Becky's problems. I'd only seen Dr. Park in passing from the window of our apartment. Becky had nothing but good things to say about him and I'd never given him much thought.

But if the police—no, Detective Fisher, I corrected— thought they would pin his death on an innocent shop girl, they had me to go through.

"I have the authority to make you leave, you know." The man himself stood over us. "She's in no danger."

"I'll leave with her, then. Is she under arrest or not?" I bristled.

He turned away from me and said, "Miss Smith, I'm going to ask you to identify the gentleman here." He pointed to one of the tables.

Becky tried twice before rising stiffly. My head raced with insults. Had he no one else to ask?

Mr. Lees tugged the sheet down. A dead man in his late middle years, judging by the liver spots on his scalp and the lines in his face. Bulbous nose, receding chin, and something about the veins in his forehead unaccountably impressed me with a man who liked his whiskey.

"That's him." Becky sat again with a thud.

"Thank you, Miss Smith."

Mr. Lees pulled the sheet back into place. Sam observed from a corner of the room.

"I'll try to be brief," Detective Fisher said. "Dr. Park appears to have been stabbed repeatedly and left for dead on Sunday night. His wallet was still in his trouser pocket and it contained a business card with your glove shop on it. The only reason we brought you in, Miss Smith, was to learn as much as we can about him, and have your word on his identity."

He saw my mouth open and added, "It is our understanding that Dr. Park has no family in San Francisco and possibly no friends at all. He was doing the free lunch circuit with an acquaintance who saw the attack but had no useful information for us."

"Free lunch circuit?" Becky asked.

"There's nothing wrong with it. Most of San Francisco's taverns offer a free lunch, and men from every walk of life partake. He had a drinking buddy who accompanied him on the Cocktail Route, but had no other doings with him."

"Wrong with it?" I scoffed. "That route is known in my kitchen, uttered in low and derogatory tones. You're referring to Barbary Coast. Every saloon and bar on the street offers free food with a paid drink. The idea is to sell more drinks. Enough to loosen purse strings for further debauchery."

"I won't believe it," Becky said. "Dr. Park wasn't religious, but he wasn't a drunk or a ... not with his head for business."

"As I was saying," Detective Fisher continued, "he seems to have no family, no friends, and so far, as we can tell, no enemies. His landlady never interacted with him. He left the rent under her door once a month and made business deposits in the bank."

"The bank would know more," I pushed.

"So it did. Dr. Park owned five other businesses besides the glove shop. Each with minimal contact. He bought all of them three years ago, paid his taxes on time, and was a model citizen."

The room hung heavy with silence. If he watched Becky for some sort of reaction, he was disappointed.

I stood and settled my coat around my shoulders. "Then why," I asked, "does such an anonymous person have your interest? People die in drifts in this town." I pointed to the bodies and Sam winced. "And don't merit this amount of attention. What's so special about Dr. Park?"

I'd hit a nerve. I could see his brain working out how to answer.

"That's confidential. But we won't be opening the glove shop again until our investigation is complete."

Becky gasped.

"Unacceptable," I said. "When do you plan to have it complete?"

"We are fairly busy just now." He pointed at the other sheeted body.

"Is that the woman from under the wharf?"

Mr. Lees had joined Sam in the corner and their expressions were a mix of foreboding and anticipation as tension built in the room.

"You haven't found her killer yet?" I asked, hands on hips.

"No." He folded his arms across his chest and squared off with me.

"Where's the net?"

This question threw him a moment, but he rallied. "We tossed it in the trash heap. It wasn't the murder weapon."

"It was useful."

"It wasn't even a clever disguise. Our killer is a fool."

I was silent. Brooding. Something Detective Fisher could not abide.

"What?" he finally growled.

"There was something nagging me about the net. I had a lovely visit with the Paiva brothers and they told me all about nets."

"Yes. You heard most of it thanks to my interrogations."

"No. That is, there was more to it. The net wrapped around this woman was white. Or at least pale, wasn't it?"

All the men stared at me and waited.

"Wet and sea-logged," I said, "but not the molasses brown of the working nets on the wharf. The killer used a new, unbarked net. It didn't have floats on it because no one was using it. Yet, at any rate."

Detective Fisher turned on his heel without a word and went upstairs.

Mr. Lees and Sam looked at each other, then advanced slowly.

"The woman was strangled," Mr. Lees said. "I verified it."

I nodded. "And not with a rope, but hands. My point is that the murderer doesn't have to have anything to do with fishing. He strangled this woman and wanted a way to dispose of her. He didn't want to leave her body, as our Dr. Park appears to have been, for someone to stumble across. A new net was handy, so he took it and her to the wharf and dumped her into the water."

Both men followed my narrative, so I continued. "Maybe he thought the net was a perfect disguise for the strangling. After all, had she decomposed enough, you might not know the difference."

"True. Decomposition takes time, though," Mr. Less said. "Unless marine life is involved. Or birds." He paused and glanced at Becky, who was more green than white.

She jumped when the door upstairs crashed open. An irritated and rumpled Detective Fisher returned, dragging the net with him. He dumped it unceremoniously on the floor. The room filled with the additional scents of garbage.

Even stained with accumulated filth, the net was clearly untreated.

I bent over and lifted part of the net, admiring the uniform knots. "We need to find a place where nets are manufactured or sold. I don't think this was the work of a fisherman. Certainly not homemade."

Detective Fisher balled his fists at his side and remained silent. Sam had the beginnings of a smile on his face that he was hesitant to show and Mr. Lees had gone to examine the woman's neck, as if to confirm what he'd already confirmed.

"Mr. Lees," I said from the ground, "was the woman attached to the net?"

"What do you mean, Mrs. Kelly?" he replied.

"Was she wrapped in it? Tangled up, like? Or was the net physically tied to her body?"

Everyone looked at him.

"There are no other marks on her body," he said. "Only at the throat. I understand the net was wrapped quite securely around her before the fishermen cut it, but there are no chafing marks."

I ran a length of the net along its edge, through my hands. "There are other ropes. Here. And here." I examined the perimeter. "Same material. Hemp, did they call it?"

Detective Fisher knelt beside me and grasped at the questionable netting. Four lengths of rope tied into the edge of the net, but weren't part of it.

"Why the loose ends?" Sam wondered.

"It's just part of the net," Detective Fisher muttered. "Why wouldn't it be?"

"The knots." I stood and took the pressure off my knees, and held the rope in my hand toward the lightbulb. "It's tied with a very different knot from the rest of the net. The Paiva brothers were very clear on knots. Each tied for a specific purpose." I tugged on it, hard. "This knot is never coming undone without hard work."

"Which is the entire point of a fishing net." Detective Fisher's patience had worn thin and it showed.

"What did the other end of this rope tie to?" I asked and dropped it.

"The boat."

"It was new," I reminded him. "No one used it for anything. What did the killer tie her to?" I screwed up my face and thought. I pictured myself sitting, frozen, on Hiram Paiva's boat, staring beneath the wharf.

"Pilings." I smiled at Sam. "She wasn't dropped at sea or from a boat in the Bay. She never drifted, which is why no one saw her. The killer took her to that exact spot on the wharf and tied her up beneath it. The net actually prevented her from drifting."

Sam returned my smile, and it did something pleasant to his spectacled face. "That explains it. She is much too fresh for our first theory. It takes at least three or four days before a body will float."

"The net didn't float either," I confirmed.

"Directly in front of the Paiva brothers' boat slips?" Detective Fisher jerked the conversation back.

"It had to be done at night," I said. "While everyone was out fishing. Maybe the killer had no idea who docked where."

"Why didn't the Paiva brothers notice the body when they docked in daylight?" I didn't like his tone.

"It must have been below the waterline. Doesn't the tide go in and out?"

He didn't like my answer.

"You realized you just killed your own theory?" he smirked. "Our killer knows his knots. Has to be a fisherman."

I smirked back. He'd said *our*.

"I'm only grateful I don't have to pay a visit to an insane asylum on a ghost ship," I said.

"I told you, it's empty."

I shook my head and changed the subject. "I shared with you," I said primly. "Now it's your turn. Why is Dr. Park getting special attention?"

Sam chortled, and Mr. Lees studiously remained on the far side of the examining tables.

Detective Fisher sighed. He was a beaten man, and he knew it.

"He isn't a doctor. He signed everything as Dr. Jasper Park, but there are no records whatsoever for him before his business dealings, when he opened the bank account and rented his room."

"And? There are very few people in San Francisco you could call truly local."

He glanced at Mr. Lees. "And he was killed with a lance bomb."

Those two words didn't belong together in any context. "A what?"

A quick glance at Dr. Park told me nothing. His face had been intact. The rest of the body appeared nebulous beneath the sheet.

"Lance bombs are used in whaling," he said. "It's a long, hollow metal tube filled with dynamite. They light it, fire it like an arrow, and it blows up inside the whale."

I slowly lowered onto the bench beside Becky.

"In this case," he continued, "the lance was not filled with dynamite."

"You said he was stabbed. Repeatedly."

"You weren't supposed to know anything. About any of this."

He paused, daring me with his eyes to pursue the details. Becky slid her hand into mine.

I swallowed bile and asked, "You say the glove shop card was in his pocket? That's what led you to Becky. Why not follow up on the other businesses he owns?"

"Because the other businesses are brothels, Mrs. Kelly. They tend to refuse to identify clients, owners, employees, and anything else that involves questions from the police."

Becky squeezed my hand.

"And that was where you found him?"

"Yes. Apparently, there was a shooting there yesterday, but we don't know if it's related."

"The Whale?"

I could have bitten my tongue off. Never were two little words more damning. My mind churned with finding more words to cover them up, but nothing else bubbled to the top. I was caught.

Detective Fisher blew. "What in hell were you doing on the Coast?"

"Nothing! Just driving through on my way to ... to ..."

Oh, Lord.

"They shanghai people there!"

I had to give it to him.

He paced like an angry bear. "They kidnap in broad daylight and drug people and slit their throats at night. Jayhawkers and greenhorns from back East and men just released from the state prison. Answer me thoroughly, Mrs. Kelly. What were you doing in front of The Whale when a man was shot dead in the street?"

"I saved a woman," I said, and I could have sworn Sam was rooting for me. "Two rough men were after her and I drove her away. I lashed them with my buggy whip." I took a calming breath. "Not that I have to explain myself to you. This is the United States of America and I can do as I well please."

He stopped in front of us. "I am damn well going to find this woman and get her version of it. If she exists at all, which I seriously doubt."

"She does." I tossed my chin. "Her name is Miss Esme Walker, and she volunteers with her church for the Hospitality House on Geary Street."

Becky lifted my hand. "Oh, Mrs. Kelly! I know them! It's where I was raised. Well," she said with a glance at Detective Fisher, "the orphanage, but you're speaking of the Ladies' Protection and Relief Society. You see, detective, we are only telling you the truth."

I turned to her and smiled. "Thank you, Becky. In which case, you can answer another question. For me, this time."

She nodded. "Anything for you."

"Do you know a Mrs. Alden? She's been a crusader for the cause for years, I understand. An older woman with a zeal for the Lord."

She blinked. Her smile faded. Slowly, she turned to look at the tables.

"Detective Fisher," I said. "We've found your victim."

Chapter Eleven

B ECKY SWAYED ON the bench beside me and I stood, taking both of her hands. "You need to get some air," I said. "Mr. Merrill, could you find her some tea, please?"

"Of course." Sam stepped forward and held out a hand. "Allow me, Miss Smith. Officer Heyes knows how to boil water but I'd be ever so grateful if you'd show him how to wield the tea leaves."

Mr. Samuel Merrill was as mild a man as any I'd ever known. With a drooping mustache, weak jawline, and wire spectacles, it was hard to imagine the thin man as the current district attorney. He'd hired Mr. Isaiah Lees as coroner after Lees lost his bid for reelection as chief of police to Crowley. Lees had fired dozens of officers for misconduct and bribery, but it had been a drop in a bucket full of holes that Chief Crowley had no current interest in plugging.

Mr. Lees had taken his fight for justice into the morgue, a quiet, observant man with thick curling hair receding nearly to the top of his head and a beard trimmed to a harsh point at his clavicle. He was thorough, eloquent in social settings, and had expectations when it came to police doing their job.

I imagined he led Detective Fisher a merry time of it in general.

Both men had my respect, but I was still pleasantly surprised to hear Sam murmur, "Oh, well done, Mrs. Kelly." He tipped his head, briefly showing a small bald spot on top, then straightened and pushed his spectacles back on his nose. He helped Becky to her feet and tucked her hand into his arm. Slowly, they climbed the steps.

Mr. Lees placed himself on the far side of the tables and put his hands behind his back, waiting.

Detective Fisher and I took a moment.

Despite myself, I was drawn to the dead woman. If she was, indeed, the person Miss Walker had referred to, she had been a force to be reckoned with. I hoped she had gone down swinging.

Detective Fisher cleared his throat and ran a finger around his collar. "Who is Mrs. Alden?"

"I believe she belongs to the Baptist Church. A crusader of sorts against prostitution. Miss Walker said that Mrs. Alden was her partner. But hadn't shown up. That's why I found her alone in the wrong place."

He glanced at the body. "Very well. You may go now and take Miss Smith home."

It wouldn't be her home much longer. I did not regret our verbal jousting, but the dirty facts left a pall in the air that I wished Becky hadn't overheard.

At least we had the truth about Dr. Park.

I blinked. "So, he wasn't a doctor of anything?"

"His rented rooms were bare." His words were weary.

"No licenses among his paperwork or degrees on the wall. No bags or equipment or medicines. I need to get back to work, Mrs. Kelly."

I paused, thinking perhaps he would offer a modicum of respect for my efforts. He kept his back to me, staring at the bodies, and Mr. Lees raised an eyebrow at me over his head. That was enough. I gathered my skirt in a fist and made two steps up before the door opened.

The person filled the open doorway with his bulk and, backlit as he was, it was a moment before I recognized Captain Carroll.

"Twice in two days, sir! What the devil!" He squinted fiercely from a swollen purple eye.

Detective Fisher looked beyond the captain to the second man in the doorway. "Thank you, Wilson."

Officer Wilson gave him a brisk nod and closed the door, although he remained on our side of it. I wondered why, but wasn't about to bring attention to myself by forcing my way up and out at this juncture.

"A man can't be in two places at once," Captain Carroll said. "I won't dock in your blasted city again. You can count on it, profit or no."

He hauled himself down the stairs, and I retreated until I'd nearly stepped on a sheeted bundle on the floor. I needn't have worried about being caught in the middle. Captain Carroll had locked onto Detective Fisher.

Detective Fisher remained deadpan. "Exactly when were you in San Francisco last, Captain Carroll?"

Captain Carroll bellowed before he'd made it all the way

down. "Three years and I regret it bitterly. It's a cursed dock." He pulled his watch from his vest and nearly tripped over the net on the floor. He let loose with several colorful oaths. When he finally turned to the tables, he said, "The body again? I've told you all I know, and it's all you'll get. Nobody knows the woman."

"So, they all say." Detective Fisher remained as cool as the room. "However. This is a different conversation. Another body."

The captain snorted. "Can't keep 'em straight, eh?"

"A man this time," Detective Fisher continued, nonplussed. "And I think you'll have somewhat more to contribute." He motioned to Mr. Lees, who stepped to the foot of Dr. Park's body and gathered the sheet up to the bare ankles.

I looked away. Whatever damage had been done to him, I didn't want the picture of it in my mind.

The detective and the captain went over and took a long look at Dr. Park's feet.

"Well now," the captain said. "Whose is it, then?"

Detective Fisher nodded and Mr. Lees pulled the sheet at the other end and exposed the face.

Captain Carroll grunted. I turned away again.

"You know him?"

"Did. Was my first mate till the bilge rat deserted last time we docked here. Thought he ran off and died in some hole looking for gold." He sneered. "Would've been too good for him."

"You did not part on good terms?"

"The man nearly pulled a mutiny on me, so no. As I never caught him red-handed, I couldn't throw him in the brig, but that wouldn't have stopped me catching up to him on land. He disappeared, and he did it fast."

"Mutiny is punishable by death, captain." Detective Fisher's voice was soft.

"It is. There were two others found in places they weren't supposed to be and they got their fair flogging, but they all, to a man, pointed their finger at this bastard." He paused and shook his head grimly at Dr. Park. "Couldn't prove it, though."

"Thank you, captain. You've been very helpful. Does this man have a name?"

"Parker."

"First name?"

"Only name. Said he liked to park himself on the poop deck and read the wind."

"And how long did he sail with you?"

"Upwards of twelve years in all."

"Why would he mutiny after all that time?"

His face flushed. "Disagreed on location."

"And that was worth dying for?"

"He had omens about San Francisco and that was enough. When a man feels how small he is in the face of the sea, it does things to him. He starts talking to himself and making rash vows that nothing less than a sign from the gods can answer."

"Superstitions?"

Captain Carroll's fists clenched at his sides. "Call it what you must. We know it's real."

"Was he out of his mind, then?"

"No. Just adamant about my decision."

"Where did he want to dock?"

"We've always docked in Seattle."

"What changed your mind this time?"

"Money. We got here first and we're getting the highest prices for the season."

The two men stared at each other for a moment.

Detective Fisher nodded. "Then, perhaps you can help me with one other item." He nodded to Mr. Lees, who reached down behind the table and brought up a short metal rod. I stared openly as he held it aloft, balanced across both palms. It was more like an arrow than anything, with a pointed tip at one end. The flat end was capped and had three featherlike shafts around it. The thing was dirty, and I shrank back at the thought of its history.

"You recognize it?" Mr. Lees asked.

"You've got a bomb lance there," Captain Carroll said. "What for?"

"It weighs over twenty pounds," Detective Fisher said, taking the weapon from Mr. Lees. "Normally shot from a shoulder gun. You kill whales with it, correct?"

"Yes." Captain Carroll was frowning again.

"What about people? You mentioned execution earlier."

The captain took a step back, speechless.

"Your Parker was killed Sunday night with this." He hefted it a couple of times. "Someone came up behind him and ran it through. Left it in him. No bomb, but the job was done all the same." With that, he yanked the sheet from Dr. Park's body and I spun on my heel to face the wall.

"Good God, man, cover that up!" Captain Carroll muttered.

"What I want to know, Captain Carroll, is whether you found him and did it. A simple yes or no will work."

"No!"

The sheet rustled, but I held my ground.

"Do you have a bomb lance missing from your ship?"

"I don't take the inventory."

"No, but your first mate does, and the report would pass over your desk."

"We're in the middle of selling cargo right now. If you want to count crates, help yourself. We won't be clearing the decks for winter refittings until the sales are made and the boys are paid."

"Not just anyone could wield something like this." Detective Fisher's voice hardened. "It was someone strong and fast. Someone with a violent grudge. Someone with a statement to make. It didn't come out of a gun; it was done with his bare hands."

"I told you, detective. If I had required his death, I would have carried it out aboard my own ship where I have the full authority to do so."

"You do not, however, have that authority on land or in my city."

"I didn't do it."

"I'm holding everyone in your crew, from the mate to the cooper, accountable until I find the killer."

"We aren't the only whaler in port!" The bellowing was back, and I turned just enough to keep an eye on him. "Will you be doing the same for Shorey and his mob? A tub of snakes, every one of them. Don't see you hauling him down here for the third degree!"

"Captain Shorey and his men are black. Our only witness had enough wits about him to at least tell me the killer was a white man."

"The weapon could belong to either ship." Captain Carroll hauled himself up, and he was a head higher than Detective Fisher. To his credit, the detective did not shrink back. "I demand you search his, too. And you'll find more than you bargained for if you do, mark my words."

"Such as?"

"Go looking for a missing bomb lance and see if you don't find some hidden smuggler's holes in the process. The man is known for stopping in exotic ports and getting paid on the side for transport."

"That's a serious charge. Do you have any proof?"

"Only what my eyes see when they docked. Not just baleen coming off his ship." He nodded. "You take a look around."

"Just what do you two captains have against each other?"

"You've never hunted whales in the Arctic, sir. When there's two ships and one whale, the first man as gets his harpoon in claims the beast. Not all's interested in following the rules on the high seas, though. I lost two whaleboats to his arrogant rivalry, not to mention the money from that kill. It's not the first time we've clashed out there. He's a ruthless pirate."

The men had slowly worked their way to the bottom of the staircase and neither had once noticed me. I leaned back and tried to become one with the shadows.

"Where are your men today?" Detective Fisher asked. He still had the lance, and I kept my eyes away from it.

"Some on the ship, others in town, and some at the Arctic Oil Works."

"I'll start with the ship. Gather your men."

"We're in the middle of business!"

"Then tonight, once the offices close, tell your men they're going to skip the brothels and spend the night with the police instead."

"And Shorey?"

"I'll conduct this investigation my way, Carroll, and you'll be smart to help out. So far, you are the prime suspect in this murder by your own mouth."

"That was a foul trick, detective."

"Sometimes I get the fastest information with directness. I want every one of your men accounted for. I'll see you on board after six."

Captain Carroll barged up the stairs and Wilson hurriedly opened the door for him. His loud complaints carried through the corridors until they stopped with the slam of a door.

Detective Fisher turned and handed the bomb lance back to Mr. Lees and this time, I made it five steps up before he spoke.

"Mrs. Kelly."

I froze in front of Wilson and he opened the door a bit

wider. He tipped his head as if to encourage my flight, but I bit my lip and held still.

"This does not go beyond that door."

Not that I'd had any say about being here in the first place. I let myself out and went to the front office alone.

Becky and Sam were standing at his oversized desk, sharing a dingy teapot and two mismatched cups. Becky set hers down when she saw me.

"Mrs. Kelly. I can't believe they kept you down there with that awful sea captain. Are you all right?"

"I'm terribly sorry, Mrs. Kelly," Sam said, lowering his cup as well, "but it was all I could do to find two cups around here. Let me wash this one out for you."

"Don't bother, Sam," I said. "Please. We should go."

Becky adjusted her shawl and kept her eyes on the floor. "Thank you, Mr. Merrill. Amazing how a cup of tea can comfort a body."

"You had a shock, Miss Smith," he said, color creeping into his cheeks. "You needed the warmth."

Wilson joined us and said, "Did Heyes make that? And you swallowed it?"

Becky placed a gentle hand on the teapot. "He had a lesson today and was an attentive student."

"You'll have to come by and give him a quiz sometime," Sam suggested.

He met my eyes and retreated to the other side of his desk to rifle through some papers.

"I'm curious, Sam," I said.

His look had the feel of a hare caught in a trap.

"What was so peculiar about Dr. Park's feet?"

He released his breath in a *whoosh* and straightened. "You were down there. So, Fisher won't mind. Tattoos on his soles. They marked him for a sailor."

"Oh!" Becky laid a pale hand on the desk.

"How so?" I asked.

"A rooster on the bottom of one foot and a pig on the other. It's supposed to keep the sailor from drowning."

Becky and I shared a look. "Of all the crazy ideas," I said.

My earlobes still stung. I could not imagine holding still while being repeatedly poked with a needle. Fashion only went so far before it became folly.

"I'd have kicked the tattoo person to kingdom come if he touched my feet."

"Ticklish, Mrs. Kelly?"

Where had Detective Fisher come from?

I took Becky's elbow. "A begrudging *well done* might be nice," I said. "I suppose you meant to trap me down there with the blood and the bellowing?"

"That was not intended, and I meant what I said about walking away from these murders. I don't want you anywhere near a boat or a sailor or a ship or even the water. Leave it alone."

"Why, detective," I said with a sweet smile. "I thought you were inviting me to do your job for you?"

His jaw clenched.

"You needn't worry," I said blithely. "I am not doing your job for you. I am doing your job instead of you."

I ushered a very subdued Becky from the building.

Chapter Twelve

THE EVENING WAS brisk and the sun nearly down. Gas lights sputtered along Montgomery Street. A cable car passed, but we watched it go by dispiritedly. By unspoken agreement, we chose to walk slowly down toward Market and the Palace Hotel.

"He doesn't." Becky gave the words finality.

"Who doesn't what?"

"Like you. Detective Fisher. He's intolerably rude to you and I don't know why you allow it."

"I prefer to think of it as professional rivalry."

"You're a baker."

"I know that and you know that. But many times, a woman must be more than she is in order to get a job done. And Detective Fisher knows *that*. So, there we are."

We walked in silence.

"Thank you for staying with me today." Becky was pensive.

"I'm sorry you had to witness it. How could you know about Dr. Park's past?"

"It was not my place to inquire." She sighed. "He was kind, though, my Dr. Park. If mine was the only decent establishment he owned, then he'd done a deliberate kindness in hiring me and giving me a home. I choose to remember him for that."

But what was she forgetting?

"Was he ever forward with you, Becky? Forgive me, but if his former life was one of violence, I shudder to picture him in the shop with you."

"Never. If anything, he encouraged me to pursue the business and educate myself. He went over the books with me to be sure my mathematics were correct."

"And if you made a mistake, as I'm certain you might sometime?"

"Not pleased, certainly. The till might be over or under a few cents, but he would tell me it all came out in the wash, eventually."

"I don't think he made his real money from a glove shop," I said darkly.

"No." She patted my hand. "But he gave me a life, if only for these three years. I'm grateful. And I may be able to work in another shop, since I've got my skills."

"I am sure of it."

"But what about you, Mrs. Kelly? Where will you go?" She inhaled sharply. "You've paid me the year in advance. I … I don't have the money. I'm so sorry!"

Ten month's rent gone so quickly? Not that I had to have it back to survive. I had a healthy bank account.

"You're welcome," Aunt Mary muttered.

"I invested it," she said, her voice full of regret. "In fancy gloves and holiday items for the shop. I've not one spare dime."

A rather bold move for a shopgirl. I wondered whether she'd kept her side hustle from Dr. Park or if he'd encouraged it. Either way, the inventory would be sold at auction now, to pay the owed rent on both spaces.

"What's done is done," I said. "There is my job to consider. Perhaps a boarding house nearby." I patted her hand in return. "Although I am used to living in a large house with a rambunctious family. I don't like the idea of living alone."

"Oh, I hope you don't consider me rambunctious!" Her smile crept back.

"You are, and then some," I said.

"You never got your chocolate, did you?"

"No. The factory isn't running yet and they aren't selling there."

"The Palace loves you, anyway. Your job is secure, so I'm sure you'll find another home quickly."

"And you?" I hated to ask, but the girl needed a plan, and it was none too soon to make one. "You may find a shop to keep, but they don't all have living space."

She was quiet for a few paces.

"I won't go back to the orphanage," she said under her breath.

"It's a last resort, maybe, but they can't turn you away."

Her head snapped up. "I won't. I'll live on the street first."

I paused and tugged her to a stop. "Becky, what nonsense. What does that mean?"

"I won't step foot in the place ever again. I swore it when I left and I won't need to because I have a brain."

"You do indeed," I said, continuing our walk. "And you'll use it if nothing else surfaces. You'll go where you're protected."

"Brains are not attractive in a girl," she countered. "Neither is ambition. The ladies despaired of me for years before Dr. Park arrived, looking for just those things. The ladies couldn't pack me off fast enough."

I had to deliberately loosen my grip on her arm. The idea of Becky going off with a strange man who had actually been fresh from the sea and running from charges of mutiny made my skin crawl.

Sending their wards into domestic service had at least the assurance that a girl, surrounded by other staff, wouldn't be alone and defenseless.

"No laundry or housekeeping for you, then?" I'd thought about asking Pearl if she had an opening in the hotel.

Becky grinned. "Maybe there's an opening at the chocolate factory." She launched into several ways that the job could be turned to advantage, and I let her ramble, biting back the rest of the questions forming in my head.

Becky was a puzzle. I'd only known her a couple of months, but I held her in respect. A capable business woman and courteous roommate, she was kind and chatty and encouraged me to explore the city on our days off. I felt somewhat protective of the girl.

Once she was in Dr. Park's employ, had she lived alone the entire time? There were two rooms in the apartment. As far as I could recall, mine had been used to store gloves and shop remnants when I'd moved in. Dr. Park rented a room elsewhere and, as far as I could understand from Detective Fisher, lived a fairly bleak existence under an alias.

How did that fit with owning brothels and a former life on the sea?

I dragged my thoughts back to Becky. That she had come from an orphanage was neither here nor there. Most of San Francisco's residents had no roots to speak of. She had not identified Mrs. Alden immediately, but then, it had been a sudden and turbulent moment and neither of us had seen the dead woman's face up close. Somewhere in her past, the two had connected at Hospitality House, an orphan being taught her skills, and a Bible-thumping crusader.

What were the odds that Becky knew both of the dead people under Mr. Lees' care?

Two people killed in violent and, I had to believe, premeditated ways? Neither had been robbed. Dr. Park's wallet was in his trousers. Mrs. Alden's hand had a gold ring on it. They were connected by brothels. And Becky. But there, the trail ended.

It was safe to assume Dr. Park had not been accosted by a disgruntled customer over a pair of gloves. But what about a disgruntled customer from a brothel? Another two steps had me discarding the idea. His murder had taken place outside, not inside, where business was conducted. And how would a customer identify the elusive Dr. Park as the owner, regardless?

It wasn't a lover or an employee. I flexed my broad hand. I could do hard manual labor or peel enough potatoes for an army, but I doubted I could hurl a twenty-pound lance through a human. It could not be the work of a woman.

Detective Fisher, so far as I knew, only had Becky's books. Not nearly enough financial information to know whether Dr. Park had issues with gambling or owed enormous debts that were due. Had he been pursued by a vicious debt collector? If so, he'd hidden it well from Becky.

I glanced sideways at her. She couldn't abide the card in the Bible. But she had noticed it wasn't signed.

Was there any chance Becky had once crusaded before being hired by Dr. Park? And if Dr. Park had known about it … was that the reason he'd hired her?

Too many spinning parts were collecting into a pattern that was not at all comfortable.

"Then I suppose I'd weigh another twenty pounds!" Becky laughed, and I realized with a start that we were crossing Market Street in the wan gaslight of the Palace Hotel.

"It's serendipity," I said smoothly, "that I do not have a sweet tooth."

"Surrounded with delicious treats," she said, "and not a bite to eat?"

We paused at the glove shop door long enough for Becky to give it a firm tug and make sure it was locked. From there, we went to the corner and turned down Annie Street in silence.

It seemed cruel to question Becky any further today.

Other than the lights in many windows from the tall buildings on either side, the narrow street was unlit. Had we felt less at home, we might have paid more attention to the fast-falling footsteps coming up behind us.

A rough hand ripped my arm from Becky's and spun me around.

"You're sticking your nose where it don't belong," the man said.

His voice was deep and came out in a threatening growl. There was little about him that stood out other than the terrific strength in his grip and a long, raised welt across his face, from the top of his head to his chin. Hair stuck up in greasy clumps and the scent of liquor, sweat, and smoke rolled from his body.

He was Barbary Coast incarnate.

Becky grabbed for my free arm and cried, "Let her go! Police!"

The man raised a wicked-looking knife, and she screamed.

"Stay off Pacific Street unless you want to feed the sharks," he said, dragging me closer to his foul face. "I catch you there again, you'll find yourself trussed up like a fat hen in a shop window."

As the man brandished the knife at Becky's chest, she released my arm, backed away, and screamed again.

Windows crashed open, and shouts came from overhead. Boots echoed in the street from both directions. If the man had anything else to say, he left it behind with his threat, raced to the crates stacked against the far building and climbed them.

"Who's there?" a voice cried. "Stop!"

Our assailant hauled himself up onto the bottom of the

fire escape scaffolding and continued up through shadows.

"Mrs. Kelly!" Mr. James appeared beside us, panting. "Miss Smith, is it? Are you harmed?"

"No," I said, rubbing my arm, "but he's gone up there. Do you see him?"

Mr. James stared at the side of the building as another man joined us.

"Where is he?" Heyes brandished his revolver. "Which way, man?"

"There, officer." Mr. James pointed nearly at the rooftop. "You won't catch him now. Climbs like a monkey."

Heyes swore under his breath and holstered his gun. "You might have tried, Mr. ..."

"James, sir. No, sir." Mr. James put his hands behind his back and sent me an apologetic face. "I's told to watch the streets and the Palace. Can't go running after somebody else's problem. Who'd stay and do my job, sir?"

Heyes turned to us, clearly exasperated. "You aren't hurt?"

"He tried to take my arm off." I admitted. "But it's the first time I've been glad to report my sturdy frame held solid."

"He was going to kill us!" Becky stood in the street, shaking, with her arms wrapped around herself. "He nearly put a knife through us!"

"But he didn't." I pulled her into a fierce hug. "We are safe, thanks to these brave men." I met Heyes's eyes over her bent head. "Thank you for following us."

"I'll get fired for this," he said. "He told me to see you

two home safe. You weren't supposed to know."

"We are home," I said. "And safe. Your job is done."

"Ain't home yet," Mr. James pointed out. Several faces leaned from upstairs windows, watching the show.

I led Becky toward the arched underground entry. The men followed closely, taking in the surroundings as we went. Deliberately slowing my rapid breaths, I was forced to acknowledge that real danger circled us.

"Tell me what you know, Mrs. Kelly," Heyes said. "Maybe I can plea bargain."

"I know the man," I said, biting off each word. "This is my fault." I ignored the collective inhale around me and continued faster. "This man was on Pacific Street—Barbary Coast—and tried to accost the young lady who was in my buggy. I lashed him with the whip. He has a welt across his whole face and I put it there." I squeezed Becky. "Wish I'd struck him harder."

We entered the comforting noise and warmth of the basement compound. "Mr. James," Heyes said, "I want you to send men around the perimeter and make certain there are no other loiterers or broken windows or doors."

"Yes, sir."

"And I want to know if so much as a pin drops overnight. You keep a good watch."

"Yes, sir. So I was already told, sir. I came running before ever you got there. Sir."

"I appreciate that, Mr. James. I do. Thank you."

Muttering, Mr. James left us.

"And who told Mr. James to be watching us?" I asked.

"Not us," Heyes said. "You. And you already have the answer to that one." We all stopped at the door to our stairwell. "Let me search the place first," he said, holding out his hand.

I gave him the key and waited with Becky while his steps rang up and down the stairwell.

Detective Fisher's presence seemed to be everywhere, and I wasn't sure whether I was happy about it or not. I knew far more about two murders than anyone but the police ought. It was possible I knew more.

But the man with the whiplash could not possibly know that about me. As far as he knew, I was a woman who came between him and his prey. A woman who bested him and likely humiliated him in front of his rabble.

Heyes returned and gave the key back. "No one. Everything appears to be in place upstairs and down."

"What I don't understand," I said, "is how he found me. I can see why a man like that might want revenge. But I'm a stranger to him. I didn't leave an address."

"He must have recognized you on the walk home," he offered. "Maybe he was watching for you and followed you here."

"You followed me," I said. "And you didn't see him doing it."

"No," he admitted. "Fisher's going to kill me."

I gently pushed Becky through the open door and she dragged herself slowly up the stairs.

"He could have killed me," I said, voice lowered. "But he didn't. He warned me away from Barbary Coast. I have no problem complying. But this wasn't revenge, or I'd be cut across the face at the very least, or satisfyingly dead."

He cringed, but it was far past time to pussyfoot around the facts.

"He's taking orders from someone else. Someone powerful enough to hold his personal vendetta at bay," I said. "Tell Detective Fisher the answers are going to be inside The Whale. And the question is," I said, stepping through the doorway, "what exactly do I know that makes him so nervous?"

He was silent as the door closed.

"I bid you good night, Officer Heyes."

Chapter Thirteen

"YOU'RE HUMMING," BECKY said, her voice thick with congestion. I'd packed her to bed with a hot water bottle last night and hadn't seen her since. This morning's early rush of baking had taken my entire focus, and a full three dozen *Krumkake* now sat protected on a top shelf in the hotel kitchen.

Or what was left of them, I thought, shaking my head and bustling past Becky. Most had been ordered, exclaimed over, consumed, and complimented in the last hour before my workday had finished.

My other full day was just beginning.

"Keep that compress where I put it," I ordered.

With a grimace, Becky shifted the smelly bundle back into position, high on her chest beneath the quilt wrapped around her. She sat in her chair facing the din of Market Street, feet wrapped in three layers of flannels on a footstool. I wasn't the least surprised she was ill this morning.

"I'm not ill," she said with a sniff. "Just feeling sorry for myself."

"Either way, you shouldn't do anything but rest," I said. "You've endured one shock after another and you need it."

On the other side of the open doorway, I slipped my little derringer into a black beaded reticule.

"How can you hum at a time like this?" Her voice had shifted from petulant to anxious. "I know you're collecting your things in there." She stopped to cough. "Why aren't you staying here with me until the police arrest that horrible man?"

I stepped into the room wearing a coat and hat, my bag threaded onto my elbow. "For the simple reason that they aren't going to. Becky, the police have their hands full with the real criminals. Women are accosted on the street every night, and we had no business walking then. It was foolish of me, and I apologize for putting you in harm's way."

She sneezed into a sturdy handkerchief. "There are murderers out there."

"And I'm certain they don't connect me to either, whoever they are." I adjusted my hat. "No one will care that I'm doing a bit of marketing. I'm buying you some fresh ginger root and another lemon. Drink the tea I made you and sleep. It will do you good."

"I should be helping you," she said, slipping deeper into the quilt. "What are you humming, then?"

"It's the 'Battle Hymn of the Republic'."

She dabbed at her nose. "Off to war, are you? I thought so."

"Nonsense. I march everywhere. It's my natural gait. I had eight brothers to keep up with."

"I knew you had a big family, but that is impressive."

"All younger and faster than I." I paused and looked out

the window. The clouds could not make up their mind. "Not faster than war, though. We lost Halvor and Papa. And the twins came home much older than I. They refused to tell me anything except theirs was the best darn fighting regiment in the Civil War." I sighed and turned to her with a tight smile. "Fools."

"Do you miss them?"

"Every day."

"But you aren't going back?"

"Back to cooking and cleaning and milking for everyone else? No, thank you."

"But they can't protect you out here."

Wistful. That was how she sounded. I swallowed more words, trying not to pity her lack of family. Family was what you made it, not an accident of birth. Perhaps the way she lived, all alone in the world but head up and intentional, had attracted me to her in the first place.

"I've written home," I said, smoothing on my gloves. "They know I'm married and provided for. Quite happy in my new life in the big city."

"Why Mrs. Kelly, that's a lie!"

"Never you mind. I've done my duty by them and they will do theirs. I'm not in need, Becky."

Her face fell. "I've let you down."

"Only if you refuse to sleep." I gave her a bright smile and reached for my umbrella. "I'll be back before your tea cools."

I dropped down the stairs and hesitated with my hand on the doorknob. Pearl had scorched a tray of scones when I told her about last night's proceedings and flatly refused to ask Mr. James to turn a blind eye if I went out today. Between him and Detective Fisher's men, it would be a challenge leaving unnoticed.

Even if I went up into the hotel and tried leaving through the Grand Promenade front doors, the doorman would be sure to recognize me. I wasn't going after trouble, I told myself, turning the handle and slipping into the basement.

Just ginger root.

And the truth.

For Becky.

Taking my time, I worked my way to the basement exit. From dawn to midday, it was thick with grocery delivery wagons, laundry pickups, and business traffic. After noon, the commotion was replaced with sedate valet work, carriages, and buggies parked in the stables while their occupants dined or stayed in the Palace overhead.

There was no sign of Mr. James, but I hurried across the driving path and leaned up against a wagon filled nearly to the low ceiling with furniture. Bureaus with broken knobs and deep scratches over their top, chairs with three legs, and a huge mirror with a long crack in it. With a quick glance over my shoulder, I clambered into the back and wedged myself between a crate and a tarnished candelabra.

Standing room only.

A whip snapped, and the wagon lurched forward. I clung to the ropes that had been crisscrossed throughout the mass of debris, watching the basement recede with no sign of

DEATH AT THE WHARF

anyone's attention. We leveled out on Annie Street, and the sunshine crept between bed slats to land on my hat and a hint of breeze freshened my cheeks.

I rode the furniture wagon down Market Street until it stopped at a communal water trough at Union Square. Slipping down to the pavement, I shook my skirts into place and walked to catch the next passing cable car heading west. Listening carefully as the conductor called out the cross streets, I idly observed people coming and going while thinking through what I wanted to say to the Ladies' Protection and Relief Society.

If Detective Fisher had spent last night investigating Captain Carroll's ship and crew, then he might have continued on this morning with Captain Shorey's. If he'd been upset at all by our attack on Annie Street last night, he might be walking Pacific Street this morning instead.

I doubted he'd gone out of his way to track down Mrs. Alden's people yet. In which case, I was the bearer of bad news. How much would he mind if I told them? On the other hand, didn't her family have a right to know? To claim her body and plan a funeral? To mourn her loss?

To identify her killer?

I had so many questions, but they weren't necessarily going to answer them. The cable car line ended, and I completed my trek to the corner of Geary and Franklin Streets on foot. The streets became dirt on this side of Van Ness, and white dunes stretched ever westward, leading to the cemeteries and the sea beyond them.

Hospitality House sat atop a dune, a stately brick building rising four stories, the bottom clearly for workstations and the second welcoming visitors properly with a wide flight of stairs to an arched doorway beneath a columned awning. The top floor, tucked beneath the curving roof, sported a balanced number of chimneys and a central cupola with a small dome and, I very much hoped, a belfry.

Though the windows sparkled and fresh laundry snapped on a line behind the low wall marking the property, there was nothing to soften the picture. No trees or color or shouts of greeting or play. I climbed the front steps and paused on the top landing. Wind whipped around the sterile building, pulling at my skirts, and the empty stretch of dunes gave the place a desolate, almost forbidding air. It stood on the outskirts of town in the middle of nowhere. Two blocks away, Geary Street ended completely.

A shy young woman answered my knock. She wore a maid's uniform and bobbed her white cap when I asked for the president. I'd served on several committees back home and felt easily qualified to speak on equal terms with whatever matriarchy they'd established here. I knew their type.

"Yes, ma'am," she said, opening the door and ushering me into the foyer. "I'll see if she's available."

A whiff of lye and floor wax drifted in the foyer at the end of a narrow, empty corridor that shot a straight line down the dim center of the building. Doors along each side, all closed, the hall ended at a final, unadorned arched entry that was so shallow it could only be a back staircase.

The matching one on my left contained a stairwell, confirming my hunch. Beside it, on the wall, was an array of little plaques, each labeled with a number and spouting a hook with a key.

An arch to my right opened into a small and elegantly appointed drawing room.

Halfway down the corridor, a door opened and a moment later, a woman exited and came forward in purposeful strides. Her clothing and demeanor were all business, not a ruffle on her, and she fixed solemn and assessing eyes on me as she extended a soft hand.

"How do you do? I'm Mrs. Bugbee, the home's secretary. You've missed the shuttle, I see. The meeting is upstairs, third door on the right."

I shook her hand briefly. "How do you do? I'm not here for any meeting, although I must meet with the president, if you would kindly inform her. Mrs. Stowe."

"Do you have an appointment, Mrs. Stowe?" The disapproval on her face told me she already knew the answer.

"I'm afraid not. This is rather urgent."

"You aren't here for tomorrow night's march?" She looked me up and down. "You seem the sort to relish a rousing campaign."

"I've actually come for information. Or to give some, rather. Both, that is."

She raised an elegant eyebrow at my umbrella. "I see. We are delighted to welcome new patrons, of course, but I'm afraid Mrs. Gray's schedule is full for the week. We do encourage scheduling tours ahead of time."

Feminine voices echoed down the stairwell.

"You misunderstand," I said. "I'm here to discuss Mrs. Alden."

Her lips pinched together, and she glanced at the keys on the wall.

"You know her?" I asked. "She marches regularly, I believe, but hasn't shown up for her assignments lately?"

"Mrs. Gray, our president, is out," she said. "I'm acting as senior officer today. Perhaps you'd like to sit down?" She leaned into the stairwell and barked, "Cassie! Bring a tray!"

Ushering me into the little parlor, she said, "They are serving luncheon upstairs for the meeting. Coffee and sandwiches. Please." She gestured to the small horsehair settee, and I perched on the edge, pushing my toes against the threadbare carpet to prevent my slipping off.

Mrs. Bugbee sat in the single chintz armchair and regarded me soberly. "Mrs. Alden has been missing since Saturday last. It isn't like her." She folded her hands tightly in her lap. "Tell me what I must know."

"I'm terribly sorry to bear such news," I said. "But Mrs. Alden is dead."

Stiffening, the woman absorbed the information in silence.

"If you could direct me to her immediate family, or someone who can, such as the congregation she works with, I will tell them what they need to know."

She shook her head. "Impossible. Mrs. Alden lives here."

"Here?"

"Yes. She serves as matron to our older girls on the top floor." Nerves drove her to her feet. "Mrs. Alden has no relatives. She came to us alone in the world and has repaid our generosity a hundred times over." Mrs. Bugbee paced to the window. "She's gone missing a couple of times in the past, but only overnight. Nothing like this. I'm afraid I feared the worst. What happened?"

"I'm sorry. She was killed. The police are involved."

She turned to me. "Are you with the police?"

"No. But I was there when she was discovered and, as the police are notoriously slow in their proceedings, I thought it wise to come myself."

"I see."

It was as far as she got. The girl in the white cap appeared with a tray of sandwiches and two steaming cups. She left it on the side table and left without looking up.

"Do you mean that Mrs. Alden has no family?" I asked, as Mrs. Bugbee approached the tray.

"No one lives here if they do." She handed me a cup of strong black coffee. "She's the pillar of several committees and a true loss."

"Will you be arranging her funeral and burial, then?" I couldn't detect any actual sorrow in her voice.

"I'm afraid not. She'll have to have a pauper's burial like any of our orphans do. Age simply doesn't factor into it." She sat again, cup in hand.

"Shame," I said. "How many years was she here?"

"Nearly twenty?" She shrugged and glanced out the window.

"Are you certain she has no one? A husband, perhaps?"

She choked on her coffee, and I nearly leaned over to clap her on the back. When she rallied, she said, "Of course not. Heavens. We'd know. And she wouldn't live here, would she? What an idea."

I set my cup in the saucer. "She wore a gold ring."

She glanced into the hall and fiddled with a button on her jacket. "We keep meticulous records. Case files with births, deaths, burials, and diseases. A marriage certificate closes the file."

I decided to change tactics. "You say Mrs. Alden cared for the older girls? I've a friend who knew her. She was raised here. Rebecca Smith?"

"We have a great many girls go through our home."

"She's pale, independent, and can talk the ears off a mule. Preferred numbers to fluffing pillows. Left with a gentleman three years ago to tend a shop in town."

"Oh. Her. Had to spend inordinate amounts of time in isolation. Don't tell me she's dead, too?"

"What? No. She is ill, though."

She leaned forward. "Syphilis?"

I blinked and closed my mouth. "No. But her employer died and she may be homeless. Although I'm sure you'd take her in again if needs must."

"We most certainly would not. We are firm about the girls making their way in the world. Employment also closes a girl's file. We do our level best to place them. There are always new girls arriving to take their place."

"But you are supported by wealthy patrons."

Her eyes narrowed. "And nearly five thousand dollars in debt from adding another wing to the back of this building. It's a five-dollar yearly membership, Mrs. Stowe, and every penny goes to our five friendless women and one hundred seventy-eight children. Orphans, foundlings, divorced women. Hundreds of lost souls rely on us for housing, jobs, and meals, not to mention the ARK orphanage for babies and our home for the elderly."

I smiled. "And were I to donate a generous sum in the memory of Mrs. Alden, might I have access to the particulars of her life?"

She returned to her coffee, and her eyes took in every detail of my clothing. The umbrella screamed pedestrian. But my earrings hung heavy with possibility.

"I'm sure we could arrange things to our mutual benefit," she said.

"Indeed." I finished my cup. "For five thousand dollars, I must insist the new wing be named in her honor."

She rose. "I'll get the file."

"And the one for Rebecca Smith."

Chapter Fourteen

"MRS. ELEANOR ALDEN. Widowed. Lost her only child to cholera in infancy. Arrived San Francisco in 1864, alone and penniless." I looked up from the file in my lap. "She's been here ever since."

"Humble to a fault," Mrs. Bugbee said with fervor, "but what a crusader! Her specialty was marching against the brothels on Pacific Street. Why, I've known her to stand in front of the door and accost the men going in."

"That's dangerous."

"That's Mrs. Alden. Most of the orphans and foundlings we take in are a direct result of the debauchery in this city. The committee means to stop the evil where it begins."

"She would have made enemies."

"They will not intimidate us. Ten more will take her place." She glanced at a small clock on the side table. "As a matter of fact, the meeting upstairs should be ending at any moment. You can ask the women yourself."

I flipped quickly into Becky's file.

"Do you often send girls to shops? How do you know whether this man was trustworthy?"

"We can hardly question everyone willing to offer our

girls a home. But no, it's rare. We train our girls in the domestic arts. To work hard and keep their wits and morals about them. She was not forced to go with him. His information, such as he offered, is there."

No, I thought, I couldn't see Becky being forced to go anywhere. But Dr. Park had found her. How? Why?

The address of the shop was correct. Had Dr. Park done a deliberate kindness, as Becky had put it, in setting her up in a glove shop? Or was there something more to it?

On the other hand, had he known about her personal investment? She hadn't known anything about his other businesses. She didn't seem to know anything about him at all. Their relationship seemed stranger by the minute.

I handed the files back to her and rose.

"May I see her room before I leave?"

She stood, put her cup aside, and tucked the thin files under her arm. "You'll forgive me. You seem awfully interested in Mrs. Alden. Why?"

"I'm the one that found her. What remained of her." Mrs. Bugbee gasped. "An experience like that is very upsetting."

"I imagine so. What happened to her?" She leaned in and lowered her voice in a way that made my skin crawl.

She struck me as a woman who was more interested in the system than the people in it.

"I am not at liberty to say. The police will arrive at some point and perhaps have more details for you by then." I took up my umbrella. "I believe in her ideals. The woman perished in service to a noble cause. I could tell, even in death, that she was a worthy soul taken too soon. I should like to feel that I knew her … before."

"Where do you reside, Mrs. Stowe?"

I neatly avoided the snare. "My husband and I are staying at the Palace," I said casually. "We are accustomed to a certain standard of living and still looking at neighborhoods before we commit to purchasing a home."

She didn't miss a beat, this woman, but money talked and I wasn't quite done with my bluff.

"Your husband supports such a cause?"

I could see she doubted any man would publicly oppose brothels, and it was a fair point. My late husband had supported brothels of the first water, but she didn't need to know that.

"He supports me," I said with a smile. "And I ensure his philanthropic efforts are directed to the best local establishments. It would not be our name on the wing, after all, but Mrs. Alden's. Most of our donations are anonymous."

"Mrs. Gray will be delighted to make your acquaintance." She nearly minced. "Thank you, Mrs. Stowe."

I nodded and gave my earrings an extra swing. For my part, I was delighted that Detective Fisher would never know I was here.

"Shall I put you on her schedule for Monday afternoon? Two o'clock?"

"Perfect."

"And your card?" She held out a hand. Normally, I would have pulled out one of my elegant little embossed calling cards and left it for her. There were only two problems. I had a gun in my bag. And my real name on the card. I had my bag halfway off my arm, trying to decide what to do next when we were interrupted.

"Farewell, Mrs. Bugbee!" a woman called from the foyer. "A fine march tomorrow!"

"Thank you, Mrs. Bugbee!" Several voices filled the corridor as a group of women came down the stairwell.

I joined them, Mrs. Bugbee following, and offered my hand to each of them.

"Mrs. Stowe," I said. "And may I offer my wishes for a successful campaign?"

The ladies introduced themselves amidst the general hubbub and the girl, Cassie, appeared and opened the front door for them.

Mrs. Bugbee put a hand on Cassie's shoulder and said, "Take Mrs. Stowe up to see Mrs. Alden's room and then see her out." She straightened and gave me another smile. "You can leave it on the tray. I look forward to seeing you again next week, Mrs. Stowe."

She escorted the women outside, and I caught a glimpse of a waiting covered wagon in the drive.

Cassie took a key from the wall and said, "This way, ma'am." We moved down the corridor just as a familiar face appeared. Quickly, I turned away and nearly pushed the girl ahead of me.

Miss Walker and Mrs. Weston left the building, deep in conversation.

Cassie led me up the second stairwell at the end of the corridor and we climbed two flights before turning in to an open attic-style space full of tidily made beds. Clothing hung from hooks along the walls and sunlight poured in through closed, curtainless windows. The heat was intense.

She stopped at the far wall and slipped a key into the door there. "This is Mrs. Alden's room," she said quietly. "She isn't here right now." She shifted on her feet before pulling the door open. "We aren't allowed inside."

"Thank you." I wavered, then said, "Mrs. Alden is dead. That's why I'm here."

Her face crumpled, and she covered it with her hands.

Remorse filled me at once. "I am sorry to break such news like that."

She tried valiantly to stifle her sobs. "She isn't coming back?"

"No. I'm sorry." I reached for her, but she stepped away.

Leaving her to her tears, I went into the room.

I ran a quick hand beneath the mattress on the bed. It was draped in a colorful quilt and a rag rug in matching hues covered the hardwood floor. A flip of the rug told me it had nothing to hide. A bureau in the other corner had a hand mirror, hairbrush, and comb in a matched silver set. I lifted the billowing white curtain and peered through the open window at the city spread out below. The covered wagon disappeared down Geary Street.

Mrs. Alden had done well for herself.

I glanced over the empty porcelain pitcher and washbasin and pulled open the top drawer. Silk combinations weren't something I'd imagined when I thought of an austere religious widow, but what did I know? An embroidered corset with whalebone stays. Sheer stockings no one would ever know about except the wearer.

The second drawer held shawls and gloves and a deck of playing cards. My mind whirled. This woman was uniformly respected. She had earned a long-term reputation and lived here in a position of authority. Had she found a way to skim the donations and treat herself to what finer things she could get away with? Or had she been leading a secret life? One that involved a man?

The playing cards were generic and well used. With no particular trademark on the back, they could have come from anywhere. Mrs. Alden might have enjoyed an evening of solitaire before bed.

With a sigh, I closed the drawer and opened the bottom one. I shoved my hand into my mouth to stop the shriek, but it caught Cassie's attention, anyway. She put her head into the room and exclaimed.

"You've found it!" she cried, but could not bring herself to join me on the floor.

Gently, I lifted a fuzzy gray kitten from its petticoat nest. It opened a mouth full of tiny teeth, but nothing came out. It hadn't been asleep; it had been abandoned. Two paws waved at me with what little strength it had left.

Cassie's tears continued to flow, but she said, "She took it from Izzy. We thought it was dead."

I rose and made another scan of the room. There was nothing left to investigate. The umbrella joined my bag in the crook of my arm and I cradled the kitten in my hands, thankful my gloves protected me from the sharp ends of the tiny beast.

"Tell me what happened," I said, joining Cassie in the larger room.

"Pets aren't allowed." She locked the door. "Mrs. Alden was a tyrant. We all hated her." Wiping at her wet face, she turned to me. "I know it isn't Christian, but it's the truth."

"I see." The kitten's pink nose bumped against my fingers. "Why?"

"Such a pitiful little thing!" Cassie went to a bed in the center of the room. "Use my handkerchief." She wiped at her face with her sleeve and laughed. "Mrs. Alden won't ever know. But I'll tell Izzy. She cried for days." She took the kitten and bundled it up, tying a knot that left only its head free. "Come with me." Handing the kitten back to me, she led us down the stairs muttering, "*Ergi*".

"Did you just call me a coward?" I asked.

She turned with a blush. "Myself."

"You speak Norwegian? That is my ancestral language."

"*Ja.*" She led me past a girl in a pinafore scrubbing a window. "I came here when they put the two societies together. We used to have a separate Scandinavian one."

"Is that why they built the extra wing?"

We passed a door left open, and I had a glimpse of women silently sewing at long tables. No one looked up, but the door closed behind us as we descended to the main floor.

My stomach rumbled, and I mentally berated myself. We'd left sandwiches untouched on the tray, but I wasn't going back without a card. Cassie took my elbow and steered me out of the corridor and down the final flight of stairs.

When we entered the kitchen, several pairs of eyes turned

but not a sound was made. It was as if the girls had taken a vow of silence and, for all I knew, they had. German, Irish, Spanish. The youngest looked about five years old and the oldest matched my idea of Cassie's age, all of them hard at work.

Cassie never hesitated. She went to a table and gathered two sandwiches into a linen napkin. She gestured me to sit on the stool at the table and slid the napkin over. Then she took a sponge from the sink and a dipper from a bucket of water and carefully filled it from a crock on a shelf.

Every girl in the kitchen followed her movements as she dipped the sponge in cream and held it to the kitten's mouth. Though the kitten struggled in its bonds, it sucked eagerly. "Eat before cook comes down," Cassie whispered.

I took her word for it.

"The church wagon left," she continued, "but I'll send you out the side door. She won't see you."

I didn't have to ask to whom she referred.

"When did you last see Mrs. Alden?" I asked around a bite of ham and cheese.

"She left for the city on Saturday with the other ladies." She refilled the sponge. "And never came back."

"Didn't everyone worry? No one reported her missing to the police. She was practically family here."

She cringed, and someone dropped a pot. "Some of us have friends." She met eyes with a dark girl chopping carrots. "But none of us like the women who run this place. We work hard here and at least we're fed. But if they hire us out, they take our pay for the first year. We can't earn our freedom."

"What?"

"Nobody tells the police if we go missing," she said. "The police don't care. If they did, they would have fired those ladies and saved the little ones."

"Little ones?" I looked at the youngest girl, and she scrubbed her pot again with renewed interest. Who had taught her to stay silent and how? The children I knew made nonstop noise, whether they worked or played.

"The babies." Cassie ran a finger over the kitten's nose. "I worked the orphanage before I begged to come here." Had her tears ever truly stopped? "Babies left on the doorsteps for days before a nurse would pretend to find them. Diapers left so long they had sores and urine dripped from the mattresses to the floor." She stopped and wiped her nose on her shoulder. "I saw nurses feed them poison from dirty bottles. I saw them! Said the baby was going to die anyway, and it ended their suffering."

The girl across the table stopped cutting her vegetables and came around to put her arms around Cassie. I left the second sandwich untouched and took the sponge from the wet table where Cassie had dropped it. The kitten was asleep.

"Take it with you," Cassie said, sniffling on her friend's shoulder.

"I have sponges at home," I said, standing. "You saved this little one, Cassie. Thank you." I put a gentle hand on her trembling shoulder. "Mrs. Alden is never coming back. Perhaps you can take her place and make a difference here."

"You'll speak for me?" she asked. Her eyes cut into my heart.

"I'll do what I can." I tucked the kitten against my jacket and a collective sigh ran through the room. "Now I must go shopping." I tried for an encouraging tone. "We are out of ginger root."

I'd gone three paces toward the door when eager hands thrust a knob of ginger into my jacket pocket.

I grinned. "Well now! And do lemons also fall from the sky?" It triggered more scrambling as smiles bloomed in the kitchen.

Never was a lady more burdened than I as I walked away from the imposing building on the dune. Lumps in every pocket, umbrella and reticule dangling, a gun rendered useless by the sleeping kitten I cradled in both hands.

And the overwhelming weight of what went on behind closed doors in the Ladies' Protection and Relief Society.

I had a much better picture of the late Mrs. Alden. The woman had been harsh, direct, self-serving, and fearless.

My roommate was the bigger mystery. When I told Mrs. Bugbee Becky was ill, why was syphilis the first thing that occurred to her? And what was I to infer from her mention of isolation? Furthermore, if Becky's first year's wages had been redirected here, Becky had been completely at the mercy of Dr. Park.

What had happened between Becky, Dr. Park, and the Ladies' Protection and Relief Society?

Chapter Fifteen

B ECKY WAS SPEECHLESS. Or very nearly. The kitten consumed her attention as it curled in her lap after yet another feeding of cream. Although she'd claimed to have slept the whole time I was gone, her illness had progressed rapidly from congestion to laryngitis. Her words were few and strained and obviously brought her pain.

It left the conversation to me, and I wasn't in a hesitant mood. I talked for the both of us.

"I don't understand the need for pets," I said as I sliced ginger into a cup. "Animals on the farm have a use. They have a reason to be there. A cow is for milking and a dog is for herding. Cats," I turned to jab the knife in her general direction, "are for catching the mice that eat the grain that feed the horses."

The smile on Becky's face had me turn back to my task again. What was done was done, and done thoroughly.

"Cats are ten to a street corner," I muttered, pouring in the boiling water. "Why do we need one on ours?"

If I'd known Becky's passion for the tiny creature would surpass even Cassie's, I might have dropped it off with Mr. James and begged it a home in the stable where it could hold a respectable job. As it was, Becky had instantly tucked it away in her quilt with rapturous fuss and Mr. James had looked up at my arrival and thrown a proper fit.

"Mrs. Kelly!" he'd hollered from the basement depths, "where in tarnation you been? How'd you get out? What's that you got? Just get yo'self back inside this very minute!"

I'd let myself in without comment. After the long trek home, I was glad to unburden myself and fix a late lunch.

"It seemed such a place of decency," I continued. "Not a speck of sand inside. Quiet. Industrious."

After adding a dash of turmeric powder and a squeeze of lemon, I set Becky's tea at her elbow.

Her expression darkened as she looked up.

"Indeed." I made myself comfortable in my chair. "I have more questions than answers for you."

She attempted to clear her throat, grimaced, and reached for her cup.

"The woman I met with, a Mrs. Bugbee, was rather cavalier about her girls in general. There is a high demand for their services, I dare say, but to toss girls out into the world with relief instead of concern … and get their first year's wages behind closed doors … well, I can't make heads or tails of it."

I sipped my coffee, a cup of robust and lightly sweetened delight that reached all the way to my toes.

"Criminal," Becky croaked.

"I dare say. You must tell me more, Becky. I'm not the prying type, but we mustn't have secrets from one another if we are friends. If the information might in some way help find Mrs. Alden's murderer."

"Glad she's dead." Becky's whisper, while not entirely unanticipated, was still shocking.

"I can't think that keeping discipline among orphans and rules against pets carries the death penalty." Not that I didn't feel the woman deserved some consequence for her behavior, but I defended authority on principle and to keep Aunt Mary out of it.

"She was there when I showed up," Becky said, pulling at the words. "I was eight years old and so sick. Family all died from it on the ship." She sipped more tea. "Half the passengers were buried at sea."

"I hadn't thought about that," I said. "I assumed the orphans came from right here."

She shook her head. "Some of us are immigrants. Ten years with that Alden woman. She hated me. She hated everyone. Bitter."

"I see. Mrs. Bugbee mentioned something about isolation."

"Silence is golden," she said, and left me to infer what I would from it.

"Ah. In that case, why not tell me how you came to be employed by Dr. Park? That is the strangest thing of many strange things."

After another sip, she gave me a wry smile. "I learned her secret. Been thinking about it all day. How she punished me."

"Secret?"

"Married."

I nodded. "I understand that a marriage is grounds for dismissal from Hospitality Home. That explains the ring on her finger. If she hid that all these years, I have to believe her husband isn't here. Her file said widowed. Well," I considered it. "Abandoned more likely?"

Becky shrugged. "Alive, though."

"How did you find out?"

"She had his picture. I found it and she beat me."

"Beat you?"

"If I told anyone, she'd be sent away. So, she sent me away first."

"Are you sure he's alive? Gone all these years, why couldn't he be truly dead and she a widow?"

"Why did she beat me, then?"

I sipped, contemplating. "Did she always wear a wedding band?"

"Never."

"Then, if she was wearing it on one of those brothel crusades, she must've used it to prevent men's advances. The way I still wear mine."

Her eyes widened. "You were attacked there! Ring or not!"

"Yes. That's true." The rules of society were nothing more than fluid suggestions open for interpretation in this town. Coming West was both a promise and a trap. Nothing was ever as it seemed and while a person could reinvent herself, she couldn't count on the rest of the city to go along with it.

"Tell me the rest."

"Dr. Park came and took me away."

"Why?"

"He wanted me to keep the shop."

I gave her a stern look.

"Somehow, Mrs. Alden knew him and told him to take me. She must have." She ran a hand over her throat. "All day, I've thought about why. They got my first-year wages." She finished her tea. "They got rid of me. But. She hated me."

I held out my hand, and she gave me her empty cup. Her eyes filled.

"I think she assumed I was going to one of his brothels," she whispered.

"Oh, Becky." It was possible. No, I thought, probable. Why else would syphilis come to Mrs. Bugbee so quickly?

"I knew nothing of his brothels, but of course I was suspicious anyway!" she hissed. "I spent every night wondering if he was going to come into the apartment. He had keys. I was going to run to the docks and stow away on a ship. Go back to my grandparents in Ireland."

"But it never happened," I said.

She shook her head and leaned back in the chair, stroking the kitten's impossibly soft fur. "She was cruel enough to have considered it."

"Dr. Park couldn't do it," I mused. How did a man wanted for mutiny turn around and save an innocent girl like Becky? I looked at the kitten and sighed. You never knew about people.

Unless.

The thought was so fast and so dark that I rose to hide my face. "I'll make us another, and add honey for your throat," I said. "It must hurt even more now. I'm sorry."

And I was. Had Dr. Park been reserving Becky for something else? Five brothels and one glove shop seemed a silly setup for a man of the world.

"Dr. Park told me I could keep the shop so long as I made him a profit and I kept the deal," she croaked after me. "My wages went to Hospitality Home, but he housed me and made no further demands. I never paid rent. But he never paid me wages. I wanted you to move in so I could have my first ready cash ever. He didn't know you moved in ... I deceived you, Mrs. Kelly."

I stood in the doorway with my back to her.

"The only way out was to be successful, so that's what I did," she said, her words fading fast. "I kept my head down and worked around the clock. I was never going back to Mrs. Alden."

"That's enough for now," I said, moving to the kettle. "Rest your voice."

If what she'd said was true, Becky was still a maiden. And Parker was still a vicious sailor.

Who owned a brothel or five.

If he'd been holding her prisoner for a special customer ... or waiting for the highest bidder...

"Karine! For shame!" Aunt Mary had had enough.

I shook myself and drizzled honey into the cup. Three years made my theory weak. Nobody waited that long for an investment like this. "As a matter of fact," I told Aunt Mary,

159

"the younger, the better."

Aunt Mary vanished. She was likely petitioning the Almighty for my soul at this very moment, and I left her to it.

When I returned with Becky's cup, she blinked awake and reached for it.

"I am glad to be here, and that's the end of it," I said with a reassuring smile. "The details can wait."

In the hush that followed our synchronized sips, something crashed beneath our feet. Clutching my cup to prevent a spill, I said, "The shop!"

Becky sat frozen in place and muffled voices from below confirmed my guess. I left my cup on the table and hurried into my room.

"Open the window!" Becky cried. "Call for the police!"

I came back with the derringer in my hand.

Becky gave a squeak, one hand still holding her teacup and the other protecting the kitten.

"It will be too late," I hissed. "Stay quiet. I'll shoot if I must, but the scoundrels will run when they see me." I was already moving carefully down the stairs. "Lock yourself in your room if you hear otherwise."

I paused with my hand on the doorknob to the shop. They'd broken into a shop on Market Street in broad daylight. But if they had anything to do with the murders, I needed to know who they were. The police would never get here in time to find out.

Taking in a deep breath, I cocked the hammer and pushed the door open with my hip.

"Stop right there!" My voice roared with nerves, and I

held the gun in both hands, aimed directly at Detective Fisher's face.

An arm knocked into mine, sending my shot into the glass display case by the front door. The sound of shattered glass mingled with outraged oaths as the derringer left my hands and I found myself forced bodily to the carpet.

It was some time before the commotion subsided and, of the party, I was the first to gather my wits and brush myself off. I got to my feet without a single offer of assistance from the San Francisco Police Department.

"By God, Mrs. Kelly." It was Sam, and it was all he said.

Officers continued to scramble about, some with stacks of boxes, others picking through the glass and the gloves. Detective Fisher stood aside, hands on hips, and stared at me.

"I thought you were thieves," I said.

His eyes narrowed. "You were going to shoot me. And I would have had hours before I actually died to tell you exactly what I thought about it."

"But I didn't."

"I might anyway."

"Mrs. Kelly," Sam said, taking my elbow. "Please step aside so the men can finish."

I allowed him to lead me to one side of the counter.

"What's happening?" I asked.

"The place was burgled," he said. "We were called in. But nothing seems to be missing."

The officers were going through stacks of glove boxes, some behind the curtain, others on the floor. Every drawer behind the counter appeared to have been rifled and the display case, thanks to me, was beyond repair.

So were my hopes of sighting anyone related to the murders.

"Becky said Dr. Park hadn't returned with the till," I reminded him. "They broke in for nothing."

"Did you hear anything today?" Detective Fisher asked me from across the room. "They must have made noise. The door lock was broken."

"Well, now." I thought fast. "Becky is very ill today, what with all that's happened. She's been sleeping. And I ... I had cotton in my ears once I was home from work." I looked at Sam. "She snores something powerful."

Detective Fisher moved slowly toward me, and I stiffened.

"Mr. Merrill discovered something interesting today," he said. "He went over the books for this place. There appears to be a major discrepancy."

"Oh?" I glanced at Sam, but he wouldn't meet my eyes.

"An additional ten thousand dollars where it has no reason to be. Entered as a series of small deposits on the side, like."

I supposed I was gawking because a tight grin developed on his face.

"It doesn't match Dr. Park's bank account. Although anything can be laundered through a brothel. Any idea where Miss Smith might have acquired such a tidy sum?"

"No." But he caught the brief pause, prompting me to add, "I gave her a year's rent money up front. She told me she invested it in inventory."

"How much?"

He was right. "Not ten thousand. But that's a fortune! Where did it come from?"

"I was hoping you could tell me."

The men pushed broken shards of glass up against the wall with their boots while I tried to gather my own thoughts into anything that made sense. Becky was terrified of the police, and I'd labeled her with a shyness that now seemed ludicrous. And the morning on the wharf? She had seemed appalled that I'd been intimate enough with the police to have spent a night in jail.

"We pulled inventory sheets," Detective Fisher said. "The stacks of boxes against the wall tell a different story. Not all of them contain gloves. Many are empty. It looks like our Miss Smith was taking on the side. For years, I'd say."

"But. That can't be." Could I have been so deceived? She was a very skilled actress, if so.

"We have some questions for her," Sam said, his words hard.

"But she's sick," I said. "She can barely speak. And she's terrified of police stations."

Why did I feel the need to protect her? She'd already admitted to lying to me and working a side hustle behind her boss' back. She'd been happy to see Mrs. Alden dead, for heaven's sake.

"Are you going to arrest her for swindling a dead man?" I asked. "What's the point?"

Detective Fisher waited a beat, as if he wanted something

from me. A confession. But I had nothing.

"This," he said, reaching into his pocket. "This is the point, I believe."

He held a large, ornate coin in his palm. The dull gold was unmistakable.

"Miss Smith may not have wielded the weapon," he said, pocketing the coin again, "but with that kind of fortune, she could easily have arranged it."

"I don't understand," I murmured.

"Here's another, sir." Heyes held out a pale pink kidskin glove. Broken glass had etched an ugly scar along its palm.

Detective Fisher took the glove, held it by the fingertips, and shook. A gold coin landed in his hand.

"Let's go upstairs," Sam said.

I ran my eyes over the gloves still mounted on the wall. The glass door had been propped open and, as an officer stepped outside, I noticed the men across the street. Two ruffians, brown derbies pulled low over heavy brows. They turned and sauntered away, but not before one of them gave me a wink.

His face was a mess of scars and sweat, the livid red welt I left on him standing out like a brand.

Chapter Sixteen

I BANGED ON the door again. "Becky, come out. Everyone is all right and the police need to ask you some questions, is all."

Only Sam had come up with me. It was decent of Detective Fisher to make the concession, but he'd only given us a quarter hour to decide whether she would be hauled to his office for more.

They were still searching the glove shop and confiscating boxes.

My frustrated words betrayed my extreme inclination to shake both the truth out of Becky and the smile from Detective Fisher's face.

Our burglars had gotten what they had come for.

"Allow me, Mrs. Kelly. Please." Sam's soothing voice brought me to my senses. "Miss Smith? This is Mr. Merrill. I wonder if you wouldn't mind speaking with me for a minute or two?" He grinned my way and pushed his spectacles up. "I promise not to ruin the tea."

I backed away and took a few precious minutes to tidy the space, clearing away Becky's abandoned quilt and gathering two fresh teacups. I pointedly added some *Snipp* on a plate. Cookies were not considered bribes in a court of law.

Sam held out his hand and offered me the derringer. "Next time, put a foot back to brace yourself. It was too easy for me to knock you down."

"I'll keep that in mind," I said, accepting my gun.

The door to Becky's room cracked open, and she peered out at us. She'd dressed and smoothed her hair into a twist, but her eyes were swollen and her nose red.

"We have perhaps ten minutes before the detective decides what to do with you," Sam said quietly. "I'd like to inform him of your patient cooperation and assure him that you are eager to be of help."

"What … what's going on?" she whispered.

"Your shop was broken into," he said. "But we are taking care of it." He gave me a raised eyebrow and a subtle nod of his head that suggested I clear out.

"Right." I gathered my coat and hat again and pulled the umbrella from the stand. I wasn't going to be caught unprepared if we took another fast trek uptown to the police station. With each step down the stairwell, I grew angrier. I shoved the derringer back into my bag before I was tempted to try some more target practice.

Detective Fisher stood outside, and I joined him on the walkway. The shop had been ransacked. There was no other word for it. Becky's beautiful inventory sat in drifts in the back of the police wagon, guarded by two officers, while two more finished securing the room.

The afternoon sunshine was deceptive. I pulled at the

collar of my coat as the breeze tugged the ruffles on my hem.

Detective Fisher had dark shadows under his eyes and a rough stubble on his cheeks. He saw my coat and bag and drew his own conclusions.

"Abandoning Miss Smith so soon?"

"Leaving her here, as should you. She isn't going anywhere, and she didn't do anything."

"Or she's a stone-cold actress who's swindled a lot of people. Including you, I think."

I looked away. Had I been nothing but an easy mark to Becky? A well-to-do woman in need of a room with a companion? I hated to think so.

"We only found a few coins so far, but we haven't searched it all," he continued. "If there were ten thousand dollars' worth sold previously, she couldn't have stored them all in here. Any idea where they might have been piled over the course of three years?" His eyes wandered up to our windows.

"So far as I know, the room I rent was vacant. Used for storage." No point ignoring the facts any more.

"There you are."

"It's too convenient, you know."

"If I hadn't seen it with my own eyes, I would never have pegged this place as crooked. She almost pulled it off."

"What, exactly? How can you assume she did this? Why couldn't it be Dr. Park's nefarious work?"

"And she had no idea her gloves were filled with gold?"

"He's dead." The officers paused to listen, and I lowered my voice. "Why not let her keep what money is left after the debts are paid?"

"Who does this belong to?" He held the coin in my face. "Miss Smith? Dr. Park? Where did they get them? Who was buying them? We haven't seen a coin like this in thirty years. They made them during the rush in '49."

"Is this about last night?"

More heads turned.

He pocketed the coin. "The burglars were looking for this. Must have. How did they know it was here?"

"How can you be so naïve?" I asked. "They didn't know what they were looking for or they would've taken it. You stood in the shop and showed them what they missed. I saw them watching across the street."

Frowning, he looked from the shop entrance to where I pointed.

"It's the same man. The man with the welt across his face was watching this whole time. For whatever reason, he thinks I know something and his boss wants me to stay away from Pacific Street."

"That's a unanimous vote," he muttered.

"Regardless, I think there's something much bigger going on and Becky is caught in the middle of it. She should remain here for her safety."

"What if you let me do my job, Mrs. Kelly?"

"Admit it. You need my help."

"I most emphatically do not."

"You'll be heading to Pacific Street next, then?"

"I beg your pardon?"

"The Whale. It's concealing something."

"It sure is. Dr. Park's employees."

"He owns it?"

"And four others. We don't go into The Whale. Too many criminal elements in one place."

"So, there are others you are willing to enter?" I asked, watching him closely.

"We walk a regular circuit, watching for trouble in the street."

"From outside? What if there's trouble inside?"

"Most of these places are harmless, Mrs. Kelly. Only a few are as bad as The Whale."

He ignored my open mouth.

"Madame Bertha hosts Sunday music recitals."

"Honestly."

"They pay hefty fees and we leave them alone." He slouched. "As entrepreneurs, they bring money into the city from all over the world and keep it here. Madame Johanna personally mails invitations to her exhibitions to elite customers."

"I think you're distracting me. The lance bomb was premeditated hate. You can't saunter around with one in your pocket, not even in Ross Alley."

"And no one confessed to seeing it. No one in either whaling ship could swear they had one missing." He ran a hand through his hair. "Those two captains are docked off Potrero and would cheerfully fire cannon at each other if they thought they could get away with it."

"But it had to come from one of their ships," I said.

"Not necessarily. There's no way to identify it."

We were interrupted by Sam's arrival. He put on his hat and said, "Nothing, Fisher. May as well leave her here."

"Are you telling me she has no idea where these coins came from? Where did the money come from? She kept the books. She had to have seen the same figures you did."

"That's just it," Sam said. "She claims there were four books. I had five. Where'd the fifth come from, boss?"

"Don't call me boss. And somewhere in the shop."

We all turned to look into what was left of the place. The officers came out and Heyes began to secure the door.

"I'd say trace the coins if we can," Sam said. "Bound to find at least one in circulation." He rubbed a hand over his chin. "What I can't figure is, if this is Park's operation, why didn't he run coins through his brothels? Easier. Anonymous. Everyone knows this is his place." He jabbed a thumb at the sign on the door. "Nowhere to hide here."

"Knowing Park hid them I'm going with he shouldn't have had them in the first place."

Sam grunted. "Stolen."

"Knowing how Park died tells me it could be related."

Another grunt.

"His accomplice seems the likeliest suspect."

"No." My word snapped into their conversation.

Sam pursed his lips, then said, "If it isn't her, then we have to consider every sailor on those ships."

"You have to either way," I said, "because she's too weak to have committed the deed whether she paid for it or not. You find the killer and you find the mastermind behind the scheme."

"The brigs have only been docked for a week or two," Sam said, pushing his specs in place. "When would Miss Smith have had time to seek out and hire one of them to kill her employer?"

"Why does it have to be one of them?" Detective Fisher asked. "When was she hired?"

"Three years ago," I said, although she hadn't been paid, possibly ever.

"Same time he appeared and opened the shop and the brothels." He mused for a minute. "Not a coincidence. Perhaps he hired the one woman who could be trusted. Can't imagine anyone on Pacific Street able to launder gold coin without stealing it from the thief. Smart man."

"She didn't know." I couldn't tell him what I knew without admitting I'd been out this morning, but either way, it didn't look good for Becky. A woman alone in the world couldn't be blamed for fending for herself, and though I'd assumed our friendship included honesty, I was, instead, the one person she had to lie to.

"Somebody knows, Mrs. Kelly." He smiled. "I'm inclined to look into Miss Smith's past. If it is as invisible as Dr. Park's, I do believe we'll be on to something. My guess is that they've worked together for much longer than three years."

"She claims to be an orphan," Sam said. "Knew that Mrs. Alden woman, remember?"

God bless Sam. The *Snipp* worked.

"That's where I'm going next." Detective Fisher squinted at me. "Sam, make sure the wagon unloads safely at the station. Wilson, you're coming with me. May as well find Mrs. Alden's next of kin while I'm there. And you, Mrs. Kelly. Where do you think you're going?"

"I'm going out in the buggy. It comes with a whip."

"And you already have a shadow because of it."

"I certainly hope he follows me. If he gets close enough, it will be an easy shot." I gave my bag a pat.

This time, both hands ran over his hair. "Don't do anything rash, Mrs. Kelly. I don't have the manpower to rescue every crazy female waving a gun."

"No, because you'll be having tea with the Ladies' Society."

He cut me a look.

"You aren't going anywhere near Chinatown or the Barbary Coast. Not the station or the whaling ships, either. Swear it, Mrs. Kelly, or I'll have you in cuffs and load you into the wagon before you can blink."

"I swear." He actually glanced at my hands as if I were a child crossing my fingers. "I'm going to see a woman about a recipe. For work." I smoothed the buttons on my coat. "And if I hurry, I can get there and back before the sun goes down."

"Heyes, go for her buggy."

"Sir?"

"You've only been living here for the past twenty-four hours," he said gruffly. "Bring it around yourself. I'm not sending her down another alley alone."

I bit my lip. If Mr. James mentioned my morning truancy, I wouldn't let him forget it the rest of his life. We all waited until Heyes pulled up at the curb behind the police wagon. He handed me into the driver's seat without comment. Sam climbed into the wagon.

Detective Fisher never took his searing gaze from me and it seemed a real pity we couldn't work together like perfectly intelligent adults. "Heyes is staying here for Miss Smith, who is now under house arrest. If you don't come back, no one is going after you."

"It's only the chocolate shop," I said. "You'll thank me one day."

No rejoinder issued forth, so I turned the buggy and merged into the late afternoon traffic. Taking Market Street east felt safest. There was nothing suspicious about Union Square and there was an abundance of fine shops the length of Van Ness, but the moment I passed Lotta's Fountain, I drove around the block and trotted for Montgomery and the north shore.

So long as I could get ahead of Sam's wagon, no one would see me heading for Mama Rosa's restaurant.

Turning right at Broadway, I tried to look over my shoulder to see whether anyone was following me. I couldn't decide if my preference leaned toward the police or the criminals, but it seemed no one at all was interested in my journey. I hitched up in front of the restaurant, determined to get some answers.

My nose led me through the door and I looked for an empty table. The supper hour provided a good crowd of predominantly Italian bachelors on their way out to a full night's work who ignored me, even when Mama Rosa bustled in with four full plates of hot pasta in her arms.

"Mrs. Kelly!" she cried as she passed out dishes. "*Ciao, bella!*"

"*Ciao*, Mama Rosa," I said.

Now unburdened, she wiped her hands on her apron and nodded at an empty chair. "Sit! Sit!"

I shook my head. "I must speak with you. Alone."

Her hands flew out, a gesture taking in the whole room. "I have guests!"

"It's important," I urged. "One minute of your time!"

She frowned and leaned back on her heels. "I already give you enough secrets."

"You mean sending me to a factory that isn't open yet?"

A couple of spectators cheered, and she smiled.

"You smart girl," she said, wiping her temple on her sleeve. "Is work, these secrets."

"Where can I get the chocolate today?" I gave her my sternest tone.

She lifted a shoulder. "Other side of the hill. Powell Street."

"Telegraph Hill?" It was a fair drive around and would take me right past the police station.

She nodded. "Closed."

"It can't be yet!" A whistle from across the room seemed to be on my side and I smiled.

"Before you get there, it will be." Her words rang true and someone clapped.

"Mama!" The call came from the kitchen.

"Wait!" I called as she turned. "Where is the nearest net

factory? Where are fishermen's nets made?"

She waved a hand over her head as she went into the kitchen. "Ask them."

Every eye was on me, and though the chatter in the room had died down, the eating never slowed.

"Mrs. Kelly?" The voice in the corner belonged to none other than Hiram Paiva. "Why you want a net?"

"The dead woman," I said, and the room fell silent.

"Is a woman's business," a man across the room said darkly.

Mr. Paiva shrugged. "You need Sabine."

General chuckles in the room had me confused. When Mama Rosa came through again with another load of suppers, the man nearest me said, "Ask the witch. She saw the dead woman." He tapped a fat finger between his eyes and nodded.

"What?" Mama Rosa cried. "Nobody eats now? You think maybe you get better somewhere else?"

To a man, her guests attacked their plates and resumed talking amongst themselves.

"Witch?" I asked, stepping in front of her.

"DeMattia," she said. "Sits on the wharf until sundown."

"Thank you." I left the building.

"You come eat before you go home!" she called after me.

Chapter Seventeen

TELEGRAPH HILL WAS thrown into relief by the sunset behind it. All rocky crags and nearly sheer cliffs, it made vertical jumps interspersed with homes and in places seemed impossible that homes were built, not truly onto, but into its sides. It was common for horses to lose their footing on the steep road and go down in the harness to be dragged behind a heavy-laden runaway wagon.

Perched on high and overlooking the sparkling water, it was, so Mama Rosa told it, as close to living in Sicily as a homesick immigrant could get. Lemon trees and vineyards did not thrive as well in the damp of San Francisco, but our California earthquakes could rival any volcano's rumble.

At its pinnacle, Layman's Folly perched in stark relief, a two-story wooden octagon done up like a castle with tiny turrets and an abundance of lightning rods. It was a German brainchild meant to lure tourists to the top. I'd never taken the hike to see it firsthand, and I was thankful now that I wouldn't have to climb any part of Telegraph Hill to speak with a witch.

Resolutely, I approached the docks, looking in all directions for women. Scattered fishermen worked among the boats, preparing for the night's labor. Nets along the rail inched slowly toward their respective owners' boats, each carefully coiled or bundled into place. Gulls and cormorants swooped low, screeching among themselves, landing on pilings and rooftops or simply dropping to float on the water.

The women should have finished their work and been gone long ago. I stepped out onto the planks, moving quickly enough to avoid words with the men who glanced up at me. If I'd missed the witch, whoever that was, my trip had been for nothing. My only option left would be to ask any of these fishermen where they bought their nets.

And if the nets were made at the cordage factory, it meant a trip south all the way to Potrero Point. I'd never make it in time.

Mama Rosa owed me dinner.

I nearly reached the end before I looked twice at what appeared to be two piles of laundry at the edge of the dock. Only when one moved did I startle and stop in my tracks, not ten feet away. A thick wool shawl turned and a wizened face peered out at me from beneath it. Dark skin with deep wrinkles twisted into a grimace. The smile showed several missing teeth, and the eyes retreated until they were two black holes.

They could have been discarded sails, or the accumulated rags of sailors gone for a swim. Hotel linens going out in the laundry wagons were tidier. The second stack hadn't shifted, but I had to believe both were actually humans bundled up against the chill, enjoying an evening by the water.

The elderly woman, for so I judged her by the wild gray hair within the shawl, extended an arthritic hand and beckoned to me. Three steps closer, and the second turned, once again freezing me in place.

The second woman's hair curled jet-black beneath the gray shawl, but her face was firmly in mid-age, her tense, square jaw set off by fiercely snapping dark eyes.

I was not welcome, and I imagined the stream of foreign words pouring from her mouth said as much.

When she stopped, I said, "DeMattia?"

The old woman nodded with enthusiasm and muttered in the same language. Finding them was no use if I couldn't speak Italian.

"Mama Rosa sent me," I said. "Fiori." It was all I had.

The women looked at each other, and I had the strangest sensation I was speaking to the laundry again. They sat with their feet swinging over the water and the elderly woman had a few more things to say before concluding with another wave of her claw.

The dark woman looked up at me again and said, "Who are you?"

"Ah, English," I said, relieved. Slowly, I let myself down to the planks, sitting carefully in the center of the dock. But the opaque water grew dark ahead of the sky, and the gentle lapping beneath us did nothing to relieve the tension crawling along my back.

All I could think about was a dead woman bound beneath us, left to the mercy of the Bay.

"Mrs. Kelly," I said. "I was told you might know something about the dead woman they found under the dock."

Her eyes cut back to the elderly woman. "We don't know her."

"But you know about her?"

"No."

"Mama Rosa said—"

"Rosa believes the whispers of a mad woman."

The elderly woman turned, swinging one leg up so she could face us. Her clothing was a mirage, the layers blending and transforming into indistinct shapes. From deep within her bundle, she screeched at her companion.

"Not mad," the dark woman amended. "Sabine has the eye. She does not know, but she sees."

Was it a riddle? "What did she see?"

"You do not believe," she said.

"Were you two down here when a man brought a woman after dark and tied her under the dock?" I slapped a hand on the planks.

"Yes." The word tore from her reluctant mouth.

"Then you saw something."

"In the dark? From here?" She pointed back to the shore, and I spent a minute calculating. The dusk was deepening and though we easily could have seen everyone driving along the road from here, there were no lights there or on the dock. The moon was a waning crescent. With only starlight, could anyone from our seat have understood what they were watching?

Certainly, the killer would never have searched the dock or known he shared it with these two women.

"It must have taken some time," I said. "The woman was already dead, but clumsy. Heavy. Wrapped in a net."

The women were silent.

"The fishermen would have already left for the night," I said. "Why were you here?"

Sabine continued to smile at me, her elderly face bobbing a bit as if in agreement.

"We come every night. Mama wants to sit on the water. It reminds her of her childhood."

"All night?"

"Until she is tired of seeing."

We both looked at her.

"Sabine saw him coming before he arrived. She told me to be still and wait."

"What else did she see?" I asked.

She adjusted her position to face the old woman and asked in a low voice. Sabine replied in a long, uninterrupted string of words that sounded like a song. Or chanting. She rocked side to side and her dark companion watched, mesmerized. Eventually, as the sun set, her words faded away.

The dark woman took a deep breath and blew it out. Blinking, she said, "She saw you."

I swallowed and waited for the rest.

She turned to me. "I am Inez DeMattia. My mother's grandmother had the eye. It skips generations." She was no longer hostile, but her face remained solemn and her tone defensive. "I do not have it."

Despite myself, I looked across the water to the ship *Eu-*

phemia and rubbed my arms against the sudden chill.

"I am not superstitious," I said. "I don't believe in ghosts or visions or phantasms. But I respect your mother."

Whether it was enough or not didn't seem to matter. Sabine gave Inez a hard pinch on the arm and she continued with her translation.

"She says a man killed the woman and brought her here. It seems you already know this."

"Who is he? Who killed her?"

"He is only darkness. She describes him as darkness."

Hadn't everything been cloaked in darkness by then? I tried a different question. "Why did he bring her here? Why the water? Why the net?"

"He was in a hurry. He was angry. Late. He hated her." Here she looked at her mother with a frown. "But he was sorry?"

Fishermen swarmed the dock. Mooring lines were released and boats of every shape drifted away from us.

"You make it seem like an accident," I said. "You don't accidentally strangle someone."

She shook her head. "It's a vision. Or perhaps ... a feeling."

"Does he work here? Live here? Is he in one of these boats? Why here?"

"Nothing here. He knows no one. Alone. In a hurry. Always hurry."

I let that sit. We already knew the net hadn't been used. He wasn't a fisherman or a whaler. But he'd wrapped a woman in a net. One of Detective Fisher's theories we'd discussed came to mind.

"Was there another woman?" I asked. "Could a woman have hired this man? Told him to kill her?"

A hired killer might feel impersonal. Vague. If this was how her gift worked, then I would fish for feelings.

A woman scorned should make an emotional impact. Considering the items in Mrs. Alden's room, a love triangle wasn't a stretch. I stared at Sabine eagerly, but she continued to look out at the dark water.

"How did you know this?" Inez leaned back. "Do you also have visions?"

"No!" I was more rattled than I wanted to admit. "It's a guess."

Her words were hesitant. "She speaks of another woman. A young woman."

"She did? Who? What does she look like?" Even as the words left my mouth, their zeal brought me to my senses.

Did I truly think an old blind woman knew what she was talking about? I scolded myself for wasting time on gypsy brouhaha. I needed to get myself home before we were completely isolated out here in the dark.

"She was there," Inez said. "At the death. But her presence has no color. She is pale. Out of focus." She shook her head again. "How do you say it?"

I was suddenly at a loss for words.

"She says there is a broken family. And knots." This time she stared at her mother's back. "All of them in the net?" She turned back to me. "It does not always come through clearly."

I hefted myself up and my knees protested. "I must go." This was nonsense. There was nothing here that helped.

"There is more," she said.

"None of this can be proven," I replied, arranging my skirts. "All of it is guesswork and could apply to anyone."

"Mary."

That brought me up short. "Who?"

The darkness put us all into the shadow of Telegraph Hill, and I could no longer see her face.

"She says Mary loves you."

I leaned down at her. "Who are you to tell me something like that?" It was a common name. It meant nothing. But anger welled up behind my snapping words. "This isn't a game!"

"What does it mean?" Inez was completely unruffled. "Sabine says everything is white."

I turned to go and realized just how dark it was. Distant voices floated over the water and lights twinkled on the hill. The first stars were out. Just because the docks were quiet didn't mean we were alone.

I fought to bring myself under control. Aunt Mary was none of their business.

Feeling for the derringer in my bag, I said, "If you wish to walk back with me, I will drive you home."

"We are content." Inez turned back to stare into the water next to her mother.

Trying to shake the feeling of eyes following me, I rushed over the place I'd found Mrs. Alden. I didn't believe in haunts. Or witches. Or regrets. The DeMattias became blurs in the night and had disappeared entirely by the time I was back in my buggy.

I passed Mama Rosa's without stopping. Her place was busy with animated male voices and the laughter of women, but the clientele would no longer be honest, hardworking fishermen.

Part of me wanted the warmth of my bed and the reassurance of a locked door, and another part wanted to leave town and never return. I urged the horse to a trot through the quiet streets, paying no mind to the shadows we passed and forcing myself to address Sabine's miserably unwelcome words.

A pale young woman at the murder of Mrs. Alden.

Becky, glad that she was dead.

Becky, suggesting a trip to the wharf.

Becky, playing with the long pole.

"Oh!" The horse dropped into a walk, and I said, "No, not you! Get on!"

A frustrated tear ran down my cheek, and I dashed it away in irritation. This would never do.

How had I not seen it? The killer had wrapped the body and tied it to the pilings. When the tide came in, the body was submerged and unnoticed by the fishermen. Either way, after enough days, the body would have decomposed and been discovered, but the killer would have ample time to remove himself from the murder.

But suddenly, the whole arrangement felt very much staged. As if the killer had wanted the body found sooner.

And in that spot.

Because those four pieces of rope, the extra ones he used to tie the net to the pilings, had been fastened to the net with such secure knots they had still not come undone. But the other end of the ropes, every single one of them, had loosened from the pilings simultaneously and allowed the body to drift into sight.

While Becky and I were standing there.

It had certainly made us appear innocent.

Or had it? I sniffled. Appalled, I wiped my wet cheek on my shoulder.

Had Becky attempted to throw suspicion on me? How could she have known I had a past with the police department that left me with lifetime immunity from things like suspicion? She could not have seen me coming.

But Sabine DeMattia had.

Sabine had seen a pale woman at Mrs. Alden's death.

Becky running my rent money into inventory. An extra accounting book with numbers much higher than a glove shop would ever make. Three years with Dr. Park, gold coins, and no salary.

Had Becky finally become an independent woman? And had Mrs. Alden found out? Had Mrs. Alden threatened to turn the scheme in to the police or demand a cut?

Was murdering her the final piece of Becky's elaborate bid for freedom?

I inhaled sharply. If Dr. Park—a sailor at heart—had been an accomplice, or even the lead all along, he would have known. Maybe he was the killer we were after.

And if he was, then Becky knew. And maybe Becky had

decided her Dr. Park was in her way.

Maybe he'd demanded a bigger cut. Or all of it. Maybe she hadn't liked the idea that he held yet one more thing over her head and her life.

I turned the buggy onto Market Street, annoyed that I couldn't prove to myself that she'd been either in bed or at work during the times of the murders.

With my early-to-bed, early-to-rise schedule, we seldom crossed paths at home. I'd simply assumed.

The fact was that both were dead by the time Becky and I walked the wharf in search of fish. And if Becky needed a fast way to absolve herself, hiding in plain sight instead of running was a good choice. Especially if she could cast shade on the unsuspecting Mrs. Kelly.

I shook my head. "Does this make me a water witch, then?" I asked Market Street.

"You don't believe in such things," Aunt Mary said.

"Then what are you?" I asked.

"A memory."

I let the tears come. There was no one to see them.

Chapter Eighteen

"YOU SURE THE girl is well and truly ill?" Pearl asked, wrapping silver settings in linen napkins. "She's not pulling the wool over your eyes?"

I blew a strand of hair out of my face. "It's all she can do to keep the kitten fed, and as her fever comes and goes, put her teacup to her lips."

Although it meant delaying the strong conversation I intended to force her to have with Detective Fisher, at least her illness meant Becky was stuck in bed while I was out.

"Even in her stupor," I said, vigorously beating the egg yolks and sugar in my bowl, "Becky is adamant that she had nothing to do with anyone's murder, and we both were in tears when we went to bed last night."

Pearl tsked and said, "My, my. It's a hard thing to wrap my mind around, that girl being so wicked."

"I can't have her arrested. I can't even turn her out of the place." The bowl nearly whirled from my grip as I whipped the eggs. "There's no proof. Nothing but a rambling old woman who put the idea into my head."

Pearl's lips pursed, and she remained silent. If I didn't know any better, I'd think she didn't buy my theory.

"I have to find the partner. Miss Esme Walker." After combining my eggs with mascarpone, I reached for the cooled tray of *Savoiardi*. "She was the last person to see Mrs. Alden alive. The older woman may have said or done something before she disappeared. The only way I know how to reach her, though, is when she's on a street corner."

"You nearly got killed, or worse," Pearl said with some fire. "You aren't going back to that hellhole."

"I can handle myself," I said. After dipping each crisp cookie into a mug of espresso, I sliced the tips from them with a knife as big as my arm and layered them into footed crystal goblets.

"Why don't you go back to that house they run?" she asked, and I regretted confiding so much in Pearl, but a body needed company when there was baking to do. "They'll give you her address."

"No, and you won't mention it to anyone, either." I gave her a stern look, and she returned it with an impish one of her own.

Pearl had a deep and abiding respect for the police and had more than once ratted me out to Detective Fisher.

Resolving to keep my mouth shut for the rest of the morning, I went back to building my tiramisu. At this point, I didn't care if she did tell him. If the detective and I could find a truce, I didn't doubt for a minute that we'd get to the truth faster.

We could find the man who murdered Dr. Park. And that man would know everything.

"Miss Walker was at Hospitality House, though," I said.

"She and her keeper, that Mrs. Weston. They will be with a larger group tonight, marching. Something big is planned for Pacific Street."

"On a Friday night?" Pearl straightened and frowned. "It'll be chaos up there."

"I think that's the idea." Each goblet filled with creamy layers.

"Mark my words," she said, shaking her head, "nothin' good's gonna come of it."

"They seem to think so. There seems to be more than one church involved. I believe she's Baptist, but they all unite on behalf of Hospitality House."

My knife flew over a block of chocolate as dark as my thoughts.

Were all the women who marched along Pacific Street acquainted with the brothels the way Mrs. Alden seemed to have been? She must have known their business doings at the very least if what Becky claimed was true. How else would Mrs. Alden have known how to send Becky with Dr. Park in the first place?

If Miss Walker was any indication, I thought wryly, I had to say no. Esme's tracts had been in her own hands, not a harlot's.

Mrs. Alden had to have been one of a kind.

"But you know that wouldn't happen."

I snapped back into the kitchen and realized I'd missed Pearl's words.

"My girlfriend and I go regular, and it keeps my mama from worrying over my soul." She smiled. "Pastor Ketcham likes to flavor his sermons with brimstone."

"Pastor?" I tried to catch up.

"He's generally open to lost souls, but not to white people. Their Baptist church'll be on the other side of town."

"I can't look for her in every Baptist church by tonight, Pearl. I'm going to see if I can't find the group somewhere along Montgomery Street. I can't imagine them being there after dark. If I time it right, I won't be anywhere near Pacific."

She rolled her eyes. "Why don't you let that nice detective do his job, Mrs. Kelly?"

"He didn't talk to Becky. He doesn't know her real connection with Mrs. Alden and if he did, he would lock her up and throw away the key."

"And serve her right, if'n she did it." Pearl cocked her head at me.

It was grating, hearing my common sense come out of her mouth. She could sense my conflict and took even more confidence from it.

"You trust far too easily, Mrs. Kelly. You know better."

"She's been nothing but kind to me." I scowled at the powdered cocoa tin. "It doesn't make sense."

"It does. But you get to the bottom of it so's you can sleep at night, because that girl done lied, stole, and maybe hauled off and killed a man." She nodded to herself. "Or a woman. Or both."

"Pearl!"

"Ladies, if you please. The breakfast rush is on."

Our conversation ended promptly as Ida passed by with

a scowl, and we both hurried to finish our tasks. Each of my masterpieces went into the refrigerator to mature overnight. Tomorrow, I'd decorate them with mint and raspberries as they were served.

I went over and over the brief words Becky and I had exchanged before falling asleep, exhausted, in my room with a locked door and a headache.

It hadn't been my most subtle moment, but there was no denying I was emotionally involved. My late husband, Detective Fisher, and now Becky had used me for their own selfish reasons and I was bone weary of it.

Pearl watched me swallow down the leftover espresso, but kept her comments to herself.

I stomped my way down the kitchen stairs, untying my apron as I went.

Last night had been unbearable.

"It can't be done." Becky's pale face was red with splotches, either from temper or fever, it was hard to say. But her eyes glittered with injustice.

"What can't be done?" I demanded.

"Hiding a coin in a glove."

"I saw it with my own eyes. It was in one of the gloves in the wall display case."

"If you keep something in a glove for any length of time, the glove molds to it. Even if the coin is removed, the imprint of its shape remains. I would notice if I held the glove in my hands."

"Not in the display case?"

"You might not see it, mounted like that. But if I put it

in or took it out, I would. See it or feel it. And I put them all in." She closed her eyes. "Without any coins."

"What about the boxes? An empty box could hold several coins, no glove needed."

"I suppose so. But the box would weigh more than a pair of gloves."

I had to agree.

"We opened the shop with hundreds of pairs of gloves," she said. "That first year, your room was simply filled with boxes. We ordered from so many companies. Not only gloves, of course. We wanted the shop to be first rate."

There was that word again. We.

"You never met Dr. Park before he collected you at the home?"

She grew sullen. "You don't believe me."

"I'm just trying to understand how coins could go through your shop without you knowing about them."

"I'm sorry," she snapped. "I have no idea. Dr. Park helped himself to inventory. He had access to the display cases. Sometimes, he made sales in other places and hand delivered them."

"You told me he never went upstairs."

"He didn't. If he asked for certain items, I went up and fetched them. There were more than fit into the shop."

"Did you ever have customers come in that were less than respectable?"

"Mrs. Kelly," she cried, "it's clear you think I'm lying to your face. Please. I won't discuss it anymore."

She'd fled to her room and slammed the door.

Now, standing in front of the basement laundry bin, I toyed with the idea of simply running away from home.

"Don't do it." Pearl stood beside me, adjusting her hat. "He says you already put his job on the line yesterday."

Mr. James materialized and stopped short of reaching for Pearl. "How do, ladies?" His smile was for his sweetheart. "I expect you found work enjoyable this fine morning?"

When he turned to me, it disappeared. "Now, Mrs. Kelly, you're to go right on home and rest."

"Mr. James, I wouldn't for the world jeopardize your position here. I apologize for leaving yesterday. I needed some air."

"Well, now." He raised his chin and sniffed. "No harm done, I reckon."

I summoned a smile. "And thank you for not telling Officer Heyes."

He nodded.

"You need somewhere to stay, honey?" Pearl's gentle words reconciled us.

"I will see it through. Thank you, Pearl."

I left them knowing full well Pearl would tell him everything and if Heyes asked, Mr. James would pass it on.

Wearily, I let myself into the stairwell, determined to apologize to Becky too. It made no difference what either of us said. The faster I got to the bottom of things, the faster we could all go on with our lives. I would tell Detective Fisher everything I knew and everything else I suspected and let him get on with it.

In the meantime, I would keep the peace.

As I ascended into the apartment, there was nothing but peace and quiet in the place. The chairs were empty and the kettle, as I reached for it, cold. Empty teacups and a quilt tossed onto the table brought a fresh wave of guilt over me. All signs pointed to Becky, regardless of what the details turned out to be.

But what if the signs were wrong? My gut refused to go along with my head.

"Becky?" I called. "I'm home. Let me bring you some fresh tea. I'm sorry for last night, truly."

I put water into the kettle and set it to heat.

"Would you like me to take a turn feeding the kitten?" I listened for a reply. If she were asleep, all the better, but a roaming kitten could find mischief. "I'll take it for you," I called again.

When no reply came, I tiptoed to her door and gently turned the knob, cheered that she had at least not locked it.

The bed was rumpled. The room was empty.

"Becky?" Moving swiftly through her room, I opened her bureau drawers and looked under the bed. I searched every inch of the apartment before admitting to myself that she was gone.

Her things, most of them, were still in her room, but her watch fob, brooches, gloves, and little handbag were missing. There was no trace of the kitten. And no note left behind.

My legs gave way, and I fell into a chair.

Had she decided to flee after last night's accusations? Did that speak to her guilt or to her innocence? I'd been harsh. Pushed for answers and gotten the same ones over and over again. But where would she go?

Had she been escorted out against her will? I would swear on a Bible that she was terribly ill. Defenseless if someone had made their way inside. She had either been carried or dragged or stumbled out in a stagger. I wracked my brain, trying to think of anyone we'd missed. Anyone outside of our circle of suspicion.

The kettle's scream brought me to my feet. Putting it away again, I retraced my steps, locked the door behind me, and raced back through the basement to find Mr. James.

Several shouts brought two valets and a groom into the drive, but it was a few minutes later before Mr. James was located, coming in from Annie Street. One look at my face brought him running.

"Mrs. Kelly?"

"Have you seen Miss Smith? Sometime this morning? She's gone."

Mr. James balled his fists at his side, but kept his well-trained voice modulated. "No, ma'am. Haven't seen hide nor hair of Miss Smith. Only you, coming and going from work upstairs."

"Thought you said she went inside?" Heyes appeared out of nowhere and Mr. James's eyes widened. He panted softly, and I realized the two had likely been outside discussing me.

"I did." I pressed my lips together to keep them from trembling and told myself I was overreacting.

"Says Miss Smith is missing," Mr. James said. "I was watching for Mrs. Kelly, sir, like you told me. Miss Smith was supposed to be incapacitated." He looked completely put out.

I turned to Heyes. "You didn't see her leave?"

"I keep making circles around the building," he said. "I can't be everywhere at once. And I keep an extra watch on the glove shop in case someone decides to break in for another look."

"I don't know if leaving was her idea," I said. "She's very ill."

Heyes took my meaning. "Mr. James," he said, "please go to every groom and valet here and just make certain no one saw Miss Smith leave through here, either alone or with company."

"Yes, sir." Mr. James vanished.

"Do I need to search the apartment again?" Heyes asked.

"No. She isn't there."

"She isn't in the shop. I was just there, looking in from the front. The door is secure."

I stared bleakly after Mr. James.

"As no one seems to have heard screams," he said, "we will assume she left on her own accord. Any idea why?"

My face fell. "I might have been harsh with her last night. About the murders."

He waited.

"At the moment, I think Becky is more of a suspect than Detective Fisher does."

"You accused her of murder?"

"I just wanted to know what she did and why," I said, miserable to the core. "If she left because of me, so be it. But if something horrible's happened to her, I'll never forgive myself."

His face grew hard. "Mrs. Kelly. I respect you. And I think you're brave and even smart for a woman. But you aren't understanding criminals and that's why Fisher keeps you at arm's length, as it were."

"Pardon me?"

"She ditched, Mrs. Kelly. The girl is caught red-handed, and she cut and ran before we could slap cuffs on her."

There was no hope either way. Becky could be anywhere on God's green earth and we were likely to never see her again. His words hit home, and I stood firm, absorbing them.

I'd been lied to for the last time.

"There now, Mrs. Kelly!" Heyes nearly panicked at the sight of my imminent tears. "All's not lost!"

Drying my eyes through sheer willpower, I said, "I must go, Officer Heyes."

"Then I'm going with you and nothing you can say about it, so just don't say it."

I was already headed for a buggy, Heyes trotting behind. The man who was hired to kill Dr. Park and the woman who'd last seen Mrs. Alden alive and the fiend with a fresh scar across his face were all in the same place.

Barbary Coast.

And God help Becky if she were somewhere in the mix.

Chapter Nineteen

B Y THE TIME my boots stood squarely on Montgomery Street, my courage had returned. Heyes rode shotgun, graciously left the driving to me, and spent the brief ride trying to convince me to go all the way to the police station first.

Now he stood next to the buggy, looking in all directions. "I think you know more than you're telling, and I'm sticking by you to find out what." He patted his holster. "My gun is coming along too. But two guns are better than one."

"He refuses to work with me."

"Or it's you refusing to work with him. Must you be here? You can stay at the station while we search the area."

"I'm the only one who knows who we're looking for," I pointed out.

"Indeed." He paused to gape at the large group of women milling about on the next block up.

There were more than I'd expected, and though it was not yet dusk, the streets in every direction steadily filled with foot traffic. The variety of faces remained congruent, even in the confusion. Chinese men drifted in groups through alleys. Italian men laughed together in a doorway. The women remained in a skirted group. Businessmen. Sailors. Like all of San Francisco, communities stuck tight together, bumped up against each other, and rose and fell with the landscape like boats on waves, each trying to see over the other's head.

Or into each other's pockets.

"He's here," I said. "Must be."

"Fisher?"

"No. My shadow. The man with the new scar on his face." My eyes roamed, looking for places where other shadows might congregate.

"I don't like it, Mrs. Kelly."

"I have a gun. You have a gun. And I'm going to find Miss Walker in that group of women." I glanced at him. "Are you willing to make small talk with fifty females?"

"Have mercy, Mrs. Kelly."

"Then I'm going to ask you to head to the station and find Detective Fisher. It will make you feel better. I'll be right here for the next hour, speaking with these ladies. Just talking. Nothing's going to happen here."

"You find her first."

"Suit yourself." I walked boldly into the melee and Heyes, to his credit, remained firmly by my side.

Skirts parted around us, and some women, overcome by their solemn duty, ignored us, while others gave Heyes more than one look. The first in fear and the second in approval.

"Praise God," a woman cried. "I told you ladies that the law was on our side!" She stood on an overturned crate near the center of the group and pointed our way. "The city is full of hard men and women! We do not march before soft and repentant hearts, but bold and defiant ones! Take courage ladies! We have the support of both God and man!"

"Hello," another woman said, taking my arm. "Didn't I meet you yesterday at the house?"

She was vaguely familiar, but then most of the faces were. For all I could tell, the virtuous march appealed to a certain type of woman. One bestowed with an abundance of free time and a shortage of beauty.

In this place, it was an advantage. Possibly the only one they had.

"I may have," I said, gently reclaiming my arm.

"Which church are you from, dear?" she asked.

"I am looking for the Baptist persuasions. A Miss Walker? Or Mrs. Weston?"

She craned her head to search, and I wandered in the other direction as the rally cries grew louder.

"Savages from every compass of the sea! They bring their wicked ways and stolen girls and sell them to the highest bidder in these very streets!"

I cringed. An image of Mrs. Alden dragging Becky into something like that was inconceivable. Assuming, of course, that anything the girl ever said to me was true.

"Our daughters are not safe while Pacific Street and Chinatown teem with evil and debauchery. Our husbands are not safe from the lurid offers of dance and drink! Our sons are not safe from the opium dens and gambling halls! When will we put a stop to this blight on our fair city?"

If Becky had lied about it all, then she'd slandered the harsh but pious Mrs. Alden and Hospitality House. She'd been in on it with Dr. Park all along.

"Save these unfortunate souls! Girls who found themselves here through no fault of their own! Slaves to man's depravity! Build the foundation of Christian morals and civilized values onto every street corner!"

"Hear, hear!" cried the surrounding ladies. They surged forward, then back again for more.

"Hear, hear!" cried three passing men, then they hooted with laughter and turned a corner.

"Use your influence, virtuous women! March for the greater good and carry heaven's forbearing forgiveness to the lost souls among us! Teach them to flee their rank immorality! Heal them! Help them escape this fate worse than death!"

Heyes had his palm resting over his gun, and his mouth turned down.

"Lutheran sisters, let me hear your amen!"

"Amen!" The response came from my left.

"Methodists!"

"Amen!"

"Baptists!"

The answering cry helped me find my direction, and I pushed through to find Miss Walker and her fevered group. As I reached for her, the women around us surged again and my hand on her elbow kept her from going with them.

"The handbills!" she cried, giving me a tug. "Let's get ours!"

It was impossible to know whether she'd remembered me from our previous adventure, but I dug in my heels and she looked at me this time.

"Oh!" she said with a smile, "it's you!"

"Miss Walker," I said, "we need to talk."

"Isn't the rally glorious?" Her face beamed. "We never had so many at once back home." She turned a questioning look on Heyes.

"Fisher is just around the corner at the station," he said grimly. "Give me ten minutes."

I nodded, and he headed up the street for Broadway.

"He's leaving?" she asked.

"He's going for reinforcements." Although, I mused, for a cause entirely of their own.

"Lovely! I feel as safe as anything now. My aunt worries for nothing, but I can't talk her out of it."

We were bumped and shifted sideways to keep our feet, and a woman took Miss Walker by the arm. "Oh, where is Mrs. Alden? That is her pedestal, and no one makes a finer speech than she does!"

Before Miss Walker could answer, I asked, "Can we step away for a moment? I can hardly hear."

She glanced from me to the speaker and back, then nodded. In a flash, I steered her out of the group and planted us next to my buggy.

"There you are," she crooned, stroking the horse's nose. "Brave steed for a brave deed."

"In regards to that incident," I said, "is Mrs. Weston here as well? Will she miss you?"

She turned to face the cheering women. "Yes. Somewhere. Sister Roberta is making sure there are enough tracts to go around. The printer is a woman nearby but I haven't been to her shop yet. We may run out."

"You are very enthusiastic for a newcomer." I wondered if it waned once she was away from the influence of her sisters.

"I was a missionary in South Dakota for a month before my aunt wrote to me. She's elderly and needs a companion, but I can't not support the cause wherever I may live."

"I don't doubt it. And where is your pastor, Kincaid, tonight?"

She only hesitated a moment. "He is indisposed. Or he would have gladly participated. Gave us our blessing as we left."

I was sure he had.

"We have the petition here. The one we're collecting signatures on for the mayor. To make prostitution illegal in San Francisco. You must sign it before you go."

"I'm not going anywhere."

"You've come to march!"

"Apparently." Still no sign of the police and I wondered what was keeping them. Criminals, or the sheer mass of women?

"Will we catch one, do you think?" I asked. "A harlot?"

"Goodness, what a question! We aren't catching anyone. Just marching."

"Then why the handbills?"

"To show we're serious. I'll put one in every man's hand I pass. Beginning with you." Miss Walker thrust a handbill into a passing gentleman's hand.

He backed away quickly. "I beg your pardon, miss!" was

all he said before tossing it to the pavement and continuing his walk.

"These men are marching to their doom," she said gravely. "They cannot take a harlot to their bosom and not be burned."

It was my opinion the man was marching home to a wife and a hot meal, but it was none of my business.

"I'll be brief," I said, wondering how this was going to end. "It's about Mrs. Alden. Your partner."

"She's back?" I had her full attention.

"No. I'm afraid she was found dead on Monday morning. I'm sorry."

Her mouth opened, but nothing came out.

"If you're faint, you should sit down."

She blinked rapidly. "It can't be true!"

"But it is. I saw her with my own eyes."

"You did? And you didn't tell me?"

"I didn't know you were acquainted with each other, or I certainly would have. I'm sorry to tell you now and here, but I had no other way of locating you."

Her thoughts were far away as she dug into her sleeve and pulled out a handkerchief.

"Miss Walker, I think you might have been one of the last people to see her alive."

"Oh!" She wiped her eyes.

"If you can tell me what you were doing the last time you were together, it would be very helpful."

Her eyes narrowed. "For who?"

"The police. You saw the officer with me?" She nodded.

"He's gone to bring more."

"For me?" she squeaked. "What did I do?"

"Nothing!" I put a soft hand on her arm. "Only, you might be able to help them find out what happened to her."

"What? What happened to her? Oh, God have mercy!" With that, she sat down abruptly on the pavement.

This would have created a scene had Montgomery Street not already had plenty to choose from.

After a look at her, I decided my knees were getting too old and my budget too tight for hefting my bustled and ruffled skirts up and down in the dust. I offered her a hand, and she allowed me to lift and guide her into the buggy seat.

I gave her a minute to collect herself and said, "You must tell me everything you know from the last time you saw her. It was here, was it not?"

She nodded. "We were marching together, and she was teaching me how the ladies here work."

"Why did she partner with you?"

"I'm new and she's been around the longest. She trains all the new girls. She's the best. I was honored."

"I see."

"She was faithful." She sniffled into her hanky. "The ladies told me she never missed a march. Gave rousing speeches."

"That sounds like her."

Miss Walker never missed a beat. "I only went with her three times, but she had the respect of everyone we passed. Every man seemed to shake in his boots when she came by."

"But what happened on Saturday?"

"A truly fearless woman. She would've taken on the devil himself; I have no doubt."

We were in danger of holding a vigil, right here and now.

"Oh, wait until I tell the others!" she wailed.

"Miss Walker, collect yourself," I scolded. "You'll do her no favors by falling to pieces on the street."

She straightened in her seat. "No. No, you're right. She'd never stand for it. I apologize."

"The two of you walked up and down Montgomery on Saturday? Here?"

"Yes. She was telling me about each cross street as we passed it. What horrors lurked on them."

"How very cheerful. And was anything out of the ordinary? Either in the way she behaved or spoke?"

"Not that I would know."

"True. Let me try something easier. Did she wear a gold band on her finger? A wedding band?"

She scrunched her eyes in thought. "Her gloves were on, but I doubt it. She was against vanity and jewelry of any kind. In our line of work, it's asking to be robbed."

"There's a spot of logic. What was the last thing you two did before you were done?"

She looked down at her hands.

"Did you finish the route? The training?"

"Mrs. Weston was due to come for us," she said without looking up. "Mrs. Alden saw something and became distracted. I thought she'd gotten herself overly excited with her various speeches, but maybe she saw someone being abused or hurt. She didn't stand for it if someone did in her presence."

DEATH AT THE WHARF

"Do you know that firsthand or did someone tell you so?" Three days wasn't enough to know anyone and the girl had taken an awful lot at face value.

"For shame. She has a powerful virtuous reputation, Mrs. Kelly." She sniffled. "Had."

"What happened?"

"It isn't my place to say."

"Mrs. Alden was murdered."

It had the intended effect. Like a dose of smelling salts.

She startled and looked at me. "She was a noble woman and I won't tarnish her memory!"

"Do you recall the man who attacked us?" I asked. "Do you know he's been following me ever since? Threatened me?"

Her face was white. "You thrashed him with the whip. Across the face."

"And he isn't like to forget and forgive. I need to know if he's connected to the death of Mrs. Alden and you are the only one who can help me."

Her head swiveled as she looked around us in a panic. "He's here?"

"We can't help it if he is," I said. "So long as we stay with the group, we are safe."

She scrambled from the buggy. "I have to tell Mrs. Weston. The ladies will be crushed to hear they've lost their best crusader."

"Miss Walker." I placed a hand on her arm. "What did she do? What was the last thing Mrs. Alden did?"

"She left me." Her voice was a whisper. "She left me on

the corner alone and I told Mrs. Weston that she'd decided to go shopping and would get home on the cable car."

"You lied?"

She pinched her lips together and nodded.

"Why?"

"I was embarrassed for her. One minute she was extolling the virtues of abstinence and the next, she'd seen something so interesting that she dashed away and never looked back. She never even finished her sentence."

"You don't know what she saw? Think hard."

"No. I looked and looked, but nothing seemed out of place."

"And you didn't go after her?"

She swallowed and shook her head. "I stayed on Montgomery. Like a coward."

"And you didn't tell anyone?"

"I hoped she would show up. The day you found me. I was looking for her."

"Oh, dear."

"And she was killed! What if I'm to blame? What if I'd gone after her? Could I have saved her? I'm not that brave!"

"If you'd followed Mrs. Alden, I have no doubt you would also have been killed," I said tightly.

"You think the man you hit with the whip killed her?"

"Someone did."

Chapter Twenty

A s MISS WALKER and I rejoined the group, it transformed from a huddle into a long, undulating line of women, shoulder to shoulder, slowly making its way up Montgomery.

"Are you planning to enter Pacific Street?" I asked, as the front of the column turned inland. "I thought it was forbidden to you all."

Her face was tear-stained and forlorn. I could tell she was looking for her mentor, Mrs. Weston. For any familiar face of comfort. "It is. But today is our biggest march. We want the politicians to take notice. We are trying to make an impact before the holidays and bad weather."

"Convenient. Will we be stopping anywhere along the route?"

"I don't think it's in the plan." She watched the column of women funneling into the Barbary Coast. "That's where Mrs. Alden went. When she left me."

"Will you show me where?"

"Yes." She put a hand on my elbow.

"You remember which one?"

"Yes." Her grip tightened.

"We are safe," I reminded her. "So long as we march with these women, no one will touch us."

"Intoxicated barbarians!" cried the women passing by. "Save the family!"

Miss Walker looked around and nodded. What few men currently shared the street with us appeared decidedly unhappy with the group, but none of them offered their opinion. If the Chinamen heard or cared, they had good reason to ignore the women. These women didn't have the vote, but their word over any immigrant's voice was law. With a single insult to a female, a man could be hung.

It went both directions, I noted. These women knew who did their laundry and cleaned their homes. It would never do to offend the help.

I did some searching myself. Where was Heyes? He'd been gone much longer than his boasted ten minutes. It was impossible not to see our group of protestors and even less possible to hear them. I thought it over. Even he would admit that staying with the march was safer than staying with the buggy.

He'd catch up.

It seemed, without her own group handy, Miss Walker was at a loss how to proceed. The front of the march was already out of sight, and I had no intention of being the rearguard in a parade of insanity. We shoved our way into the line and took our place between women carrying signs.

All I had to do was hold out my hand and a stack of papers landed in it.

"Let's go." I gave her a tug and her hand never left my elbow.

Hopefully, the signs waving before and behind us would divert attention, and I could find out what I needed to know without the man with the scar spotting me. The ladies' enthusiasm kept the line moving right along. We'd be back around the block in no time.

Miss Walker took courage. "I will march in Mrs. Alden's honor," she said, lengthening her stride. "After all, she looks down on us and is cheering us forward. I can feel it."

Mrs. Alden wasn't the only thing looking down on us. The noise brought pedestrians to a halt and upstairs windows opened in every direction.

"Misery!"

"Poverty!"

"Disease!"

"Debauchery!"

I had to remind myself the attention was not on me personally, but on the group. I kept my eyes forward and my steps steady. There was only one thing that mattered. Discovering where Mrs. Alden had gone before she was murdered. Her killer was ahead of us.

We were marching right to him.

I peered into corners and alleyways for the man with the scar or anyone taking a particular interest in Miss Walker or me. The street was full of people and yet I felt safe, if only because I was with my kind.

The kind that had justice and truth flying from the mast, if a bit uncomfortable to hold.

"Insanity!"

"Indecency!"

"Pollution!"

"Profanity!"

We turned at Kearny Street onto Pacific Street and the awful realization that every door along both sides was disgorging its inhabitants. The women kept their chins up and their gaze forward, modeling good citizenship and sainthood to the confused and depraved.

Aunt Mary gave a nod of approval.

Most of the men on the walkways were dressed in suits and bowlers, with a random top hat that insinuated a higher class of patronage frequented by the establishments. Some were putting on their coats as they walked away and scowled at the women. Others scurried out with their hats in front of their faces and slunk down the nearest alley. Still, there was a man or two who exited a doorway, lined his toes with the gutter and raised a fist in return, shouting words I couldn't repeat.

Bartlett Alley on our left swarmed with Chinese men, shouting to each other and running from door to door. It was full, from one end to the other, of Chinese prostitute cribs and gambling houses. Its reputation alone had me shudder as we marched by and I wondered what those girls thought when they heard our cries.

Whether it mattered.

We passed Spider Kelly's and two men came out with a fiddle and flute, and men near them clapped along with whatever tune they'd set our march to. The women's faces set like flint.

Miss Walker nearly dragged me to a halt. "That's it!" she

hissed in my ear, looking in the opposite direction. "That's where Mrs. Alden went!"

As I'd feared, it was The Whale. The men pouring from that dark maw were considerably lower in class and higher in alcohol. Some staggered out of the way as others pushed them aside to stare at the intruders. It was not my imagination. All of them had guns at their side.

What had we gotten ourselves into?

Two doors down, I spotted him. The man was quickly lost among others lurking near the cross street, but I had clearly seen the line down his face. It was impossible to know whether he'd seen me, but I moved up close to the women in front of us just in case.

Mrs. Alden had seen something so important that she'd deserted a proselyte on the street corner. So important that she'd gone into the vilest saloon on Pacific Street. Alone.

And was never seen alive again.

I frowned as I continued to scan the area. Mrs. Alden had worked this place for nearly twenty years. She knew everyone, and they knew her. Including the brothels? She must have, I thought. How else could she have hooked Becky up with Dr. Park?

I paused, and this time, Miss Walker dragged me forward.

My theories depended on whether Becky's accusation was true or not. If Mrs. Alden had been chummy enough with the owner of a brothel, Dr. Park, to do business with him ... then the crusader had a side racket going. And a definite conflict of interest.

Otherwise, Dr. Park had asked for a secretary shop girl and Hospitality House had simply hired Becky out, and Mrs. Alden had nothing to do with it.

All in or all out?

I shook my head. Miss Walker's claim pushed Becky's further into the area of truth. Mrs. Alden had, of her own will, gone into The Whale. That smacked of something bigger than righteous indignation.

Another glance at the surrounding women had me going back over the rest. True, Hospitality House had files that could be easily tailored if someone chose to do so. That they had one on Becky and confirmed her growing up there was enough to prove that Becky and Dr. Park had only met when Mrs. Alden connected them.

And over the course of the last three years, the two had set up in an innocuous glove shop, selling thousands of hidden coins on the side.

It was a commerce triangle. It had to be.

That both Mrs. Alden and Dr. Park now lay in the morgue was intriguing.

That Becky's name kept landing right in the middle of every theory was horrifying.

Did she orchestrate the murders? Or was she a victim? Did it matter now?

Somewhere in the center was a missing link.

And a killer or two.

Dupont Street rolled down on our left, where all of Chinatown, it seemed, fought for a place to watch the show. Packing the street and leaning from every window, they smoked cigars and squinted, whether in curiosity or in restraint of something more evil. They regularly filled these streets on every Chinese festival, but I doubted they'd ever seen anything like this.

I caught another glimpse of our attacker. Closer now. Scrutinizing the group. Moving with us. Searching.

I hadn't meant to push forward, but the women in front of us waved their signs and raised their voices as the line slowed.

"Why are we stopping?"

"Keep going!"

"Go around them!"

But others had the same idea. The line became amorphous, filling the street, and tempers flared as a sense of fear added to urgency. No one wanted to halt on Pacific Street. Handbills were dropped and signs clutched in both hands.

Clouds parted here and there in the distance, filtering afternoon sunshine through a murk overhead, then a single sunbeam broke through long enough to illuminate the problem.

The police had formed a line across the street, forcing the women to turn up Stockton Street and away from Chinatown.

Sour men poured out of saloons and dark doorways, scowling with their hands on holsters.

The front of our column broke and swarmed the line of police and shouts could be heard the length of the street. I strained to see who was where. If Heyes and Detective Fisher were in the middle of this argument, it explained their earlier absence. The situation had become critical.

"We march for piety!"

"We march for purity!"

"We march for decency!"

"We march for reform!"

The women were going to get the city's attention, but not necessarily in the way they expected.

The police boomed back.

"You'll go back on Broadway! Stop in at the station if you want to complain. Chief Crowley will be happy to give you a cell for the night!"

The station was probably unstaffed by now, but the ladies wouldn't know it. There were telegraph connections in several places, and the police used the call boxes for emergencies.

I stood in the middle of the intersection as another dozen police officers gathered in Dupont Street. The Chinatown Squad came with them, brandishing long-handled axes and lengths of pipe. Forming a line, they blocked all access north. I turned as whistles blew from behind us at the end of the line. Officers from the docks swarmed in from Montgomery Street, pushing us relentlessly onward.

We were surrounded. Herded like cattle.

The women turned and made a stand.

"A blight on this city!"

"For shame!"

A stampede was imminent.

"Miss Walker, stay back," I cried as she tugged me forward. "We don't want to get in the middle of the fray."

"But that's why we've come! To get these men to listen to us! They're a captive audience."

The shadows grew longer.

"I think we might be the captives," I said, lowering my voice and leaning into her ear.

At once, she looked around. The man with the scar stood three feet away, staring at us. She bolted and ran headlong into the group, shrieking for Mrs. Weston.

With a frustrated cry, I whirled toward Dupont Street, securing my bag in the crook of my arm. I had the information I'd come to collect and I wanted out. Now.

I dodged between the men in my way, handbills scattered behind me. Rough hands reached for me and missed. Taunts and shocking offers and laughter spurred me toward the line of officers. They'd protect me on this shortcut to the police station. I'd wait for Detective Fisher there.

I reached the line as someone grabbed my hand and yanked me to a halt.

"Help!" I cried with a struggle. "Let me pass!"

"You go on to Stockton, ma'am! No skirts this way! Off with you quick now!"

Though I'd caught the squad's attention, none moved from their position. Two ruffians stepped in front of them, blocking their view as the man who'd grabbed my arm twisted it behind my back.

I came down hard on his foot with my heel and swung my bag into the face of his friend. It loosened the grip on my arm just enough to pull free.

"Oy!" shouted one of my would-be protectors, "Let 'er be!"

My captor threw his hands in the air in mock compliance as others pushed in around me, forcing me, step by step, away from Dupont.

Feminine laughter rained down on us.

"Come back, loves! You don't want that bitter stuff!"

The woman watched us from the third floor, hair loose to her waist, bosom spilling from her corset. Others joined her from various windows. "You're safe, gentlemen! The police are on our side tonight!"

"We have a redhead up here, gents!"

"How much in your pocket? She wants to know!"

Men whistled back from the street.

"Special tonight! French kisses less than a dollar!"

The men roared their appreciation back up at them.

"Come down, child, and be saved!" cried a lady behind me. She waved her sign at the windows.

"Yes, come down!" cried the drunk beside her. "I'll take ye to paradise!"

The woman whirled and hit him squarely with her sign. The harlot held out a porcelain pitcher and emptied its contents over both of them. After that, everything was a blur.

I wasted precious seconds fumbling at my bag for my gun before giving up and simply swinging it at every hand that reached for me.

There were no longer recognizable groups in the street, but sailor, beggar, factory worker, and every manner of ill-bred male carried a scent of liquor and opium, tobacco and sweat. The smiles were threats, their helpful hands lewd, and for the first time in my life, I felt the fear of a woman treated as a thing.

In that moment, I became feral.

The large hand that came down on my shoulder might have buckled the knees of a less hardy woman. Shocked by the strength in the fingers digging into me, I still attempted to wrestle away from them.

"Hold up, there!"

A second hand came around my waist and steered me forcefully onto the walkway.

"Make way!"

A dozen hands reached for my face and I writhed away from them in my captor's grip.

"Sharky, ye took hold of the wrong type there, lad!"

"Who's this then?"

"It's the woman as was in the jailhouse."

"She with the police?"

"We'll find out soon enough. Make way there, I say!"

"Carroll! Ye brought your own tonight?"

"Here now, he can't do that!"

"Cap, she's the one, I say!"

We entered a doorway, and the noise from the street receded. A shrill whistle pierced the thick, malodorous air.

"Makin' 'em handsome now? That there's a miracle, boys!"

The room exploded into laughter as the heavy hands dragged me into a dark corner and thrust me into a chair.

"Now. You'll sit and you'll squeal till I have what I want."

Three large men sat around the tiny table in front of me, effectively blocking any hope of running. Backlit in the dim light, they could have been anyone and, now my arms were free, I scrabbled into the bag tucked into my lap.

"Speak up, missy," growled the voice. "You're either looking for trouble or you *are* the trouble."

"Aye, which?"

"Toss 'er upstairs, Cap. She needs a might persuading."

I pulled up the derringer and aimed it directly into his face.

Chapter Twenty-One

O NCE AGAIN, THE room erupted in laughter.
        A hand reached for the gun and a man said, "No.
Let 'er give it a rip. Let's see what she does."

"Let me out of here," I said.

"It's a pop gun, Cap. Only stings till you pull out the bullet."

The ambient sound in the room dropped from shouting into conversations. The clink of glass, the bounce of dice, and the slap of playing cards receded as a tinny piano started a tune from across the room. My actions hadn't garnered any particular attention.

I took note of the door from the corner of my eye, and two or three high, narrow windows mostly covered with sacking and surrounded with mounted scrimshaw. Men gathered around us and blocked the rest of the room from view and I could have sworn one of them had a whip lash down the middle of his face.

The sun was going down, but the building held the heat of its occupants in a stifling grip. A bead of sweat worked its way down my back.

"You won't make the door alive," the large man observed.

"That'll be the both of us, then," I countered. My arms were steady and my finger slid onto the trigger.

He reached into his jacket, and I drew a deep breath. I held it as he withdrew a cigar and struck a match on the table. I slowly released my breath as he drew smoke deep into his foul lungs.

In the spark of light, I'd recognized the swollen, multicolored eye and bulbous nose of Captain Carroll.

"Detective Fisher is going to love this," I muttered.

"We aren't on the best terms as it stands," he said. "Who are you?"

"Mrs. Kelly."

"How is it every time I look, you're with the police, Mrs. Kelly?"

The man beside him snickered, and I spared him a glance. It was Captain Carroll's shorter and meaner shadow. Black muttonchop whiskers, a battered cap, and a cheek full of chewing tobacco.

"Last time I saw you," I said, "Officer Heyes had you in a headlock."

The man whipped out a hand and knocked the derringer from my grip. Instead of firing, the gun smashed into the wall and fell to the floor, out of sight.

Captain Carroll growled around his cigar, "Cut it out, Sharky." His eyes never left mine. "My first mate should be working, but try keeping sailors away from a parade of women." Chortles came from several tables. "Funny finding you here, though."

His first mate scowled. "It's her. Told you so, Cap." He

leaned back in his chair and fingered the large, triangular pendant hung from his neck.

The walls to either side of our corner held row upon row of bleached jaws full of teeth that looked just like it.

I kept my tingling hands below the table and rubbed some life back into them.

Captain Carroll blew a long stream of smoke at me. "You his wife?"

"No. I have no relationship with Detective Fisher." Then again, I had no easy answers for my presence, either.

He gave me a cool look. "You run the glove shop?"

"No."

"She does, Cap! We saw her!"

"I know the woman who does." Whatever Becky had done, I didn't want the blame for it.

The captain and his first mate shared a look. Sharky infinitesimally shook his head, and they turned back to me.

"I didn't peg you for a Bible-thumpin' do-gooder," Captain Carroll said. "Ain't much use for one of those."

"She's lying." The voice came from the group standing behind the chairs, and I wondered if Captain Carroll had his entire crew here for the evening.

"And you?" I countered. "What did you lie to Detective Fisher about?"

"That detective came nosing around this morning. Real obnoxious, that man. Has no idea what he's doing."

"On the house, Cap." A barman slammed a tall glass of beer in front of Captain Carroll. "For the show." He gave me a wink before walking back through the spectators.

"He has two dead bodies and there's a killer on the loose," I said. "Makes a man obnoxious."

"I'm not involved in his little problems," he said, reaching for his drink. "But the man is like a gull. Won't leave. Won't land. Just keeps circling."

"Ask her, Cap."

I squinted at Sharky. "Have you been spying on the glove shop? Broke in, maybe?"

He shrugged, and Captain Carroll observed him over his beer.

"What do you want with the glove shop?" I had my suspicions.

"Nothing," Captain Carroll said. He grew thoughtful, then added, "We wanted confirmation on Parker's whereabouts. After he went toes up, I had to be certain about all of his … shops."

His men leered at each other. Behind them, the bar grew louder. I could make out the backs of customer's heads as they lined up at it. A massive mirror ran behind the bar, flanked by enormous paintings of mermaids gathered around a shipwreck in a storm. Men staggered up the rickety staircase near our table and female laughter greeted them overhead.

"Dr. Park was murdered right outside this building," I said. "And I think you know something about it."

He scowled. "That detective's had every cooperation from me and my crew. He's been aboard the *Hidalgo* from stem to stern. He's not pinning a murder on us."

"Who else would use a bomb lance?"

"You were there. Yes." He grew thoughtful and blew a perfect smoke ring. "In the morgue." It hung over the table and I longed to slap it out of the air.

"I know you and Captain Shorey are enemies," I pushed. "Neither of you would shrink from pinning the murder on the other if you could."

Captain Carroll sat up straight and his men backed away from his chair.

"Sharky. Who's on duty?"

"Boggs, sir." He spit a stream of black juice onto the floor.

"I want two more of you bilge rats back at the brig. Now! Stand at the moorings and let none aboard."

"Aye, sir." Through some internal ranking system of their own, the spectators dissolved, some to other tables and others out the door. I was left with the captain, his first mate, and two others with forearms the size of hams.

Sharky growled. "They know us in Seattle."

"The money was here," Captain Carroll said. "You got us ahead of the bastard and that's all that matters."

"Aye, Cap. We've got more and we've got better."

"Damn right." He took a deep pull on his beer. "Shorey'd have blown us to smithereens if he could."

"We outran him." Sharky turned to his mates. "Nobody gets the upper hand on us, lads."

Captain Carroll squinted at me with his good eye. "That detective boarded the *Alexander*. Says he found nothing. Fool."

"Ask her, Cap." Sharky leaned over the table. "I tell ye, she knows."

"Detective thinks a whaler did in Parker. I say he's wrong. So, tell me this, Mrs. Kelly. Who did it? You?"

"No."

"Then what are ye doing here? What are ye doing any-where? Why are you with the police?"

"I'm looking for the man who killed Dr. Park. And if you aren't him, then we have no business here." I put my hands on the table. "I'll be going now."

"Our business concludes when I say it does. Why are ye caring about a dead sailor?"

Staring at the man, I could easily see him murdering Dr. Park. There was no reason why he wouldn't kill me, and I imagined the room would cheer him on. The women's march had to have finished by now. No light came in through the windows and the police would be on high alert for the rest of the night.

Nobody was coming to look for me.

"A friend is involved," I said.

"And who might that be?"

"That's my business."

"Need persuading?"

Aunt Mary had her hands to her heaving heavenly bos-om.

"How about a horse trade?" I asked. "I'll give you some information and you give me some. We appear to be on the same path."

He chuckled. "Only I don't care as much as you do."

"What do you care about?"

He cut his eyes at Sharky, then slipped a hand into his

vest pocket.

"What do you know about this?" He tossed a heavy gold coin onto the table.

"Nothing." The word came out a little too quickly.

He pursed his lips, then said, "It came to me in an envelope. No note. Just the address of a glove shop."

"Then you know more about it than I do."

"Curious. Why it came from there. Who sent it." He nodded at his first mate. "Sharky here says you ran the shop. He says you'd know."

"I don't." It felt exceptionally foolish to admit any knowledge of the coins, but there was no mistaking the look in either Sharky's eyes or the man in the back of the mob. They'd seen me discussing the coins with Detective Fisher. I had to give him something.

"I don't run the shop. My friend does. It was broken into. Things were stolen."

He picked up the coin. "Like this coin?"

"Detective Fisher found a coin like that in the shop."

"Only one?" He slid the coin back into his pocket. "Generous of Parker to give me one of a matched pair."

"I don't know how you got it," I said, "but Dr. Park is dead. And my friend is missing. Seems like an unlucky coin."

"Gotta be more, Cap," Sharky muttered.

Captain Carroll nodded and leaned forward. "Mrs. Kelly. Where is your little friend?"

"Missing. I have no idea."

"Convenient," he mused. "I'll have to insist you tell me where the coins are. How else can I find the source of my mysterious envelope?"

"I don't have them."

"Someone does." Sharky laid his hand on the table, holding a bone-handled knife with a double-edged twelve-inch blade in it.

The captain's smile was broad, and he relaxed back in his chair. "Now, Sharky. Give her a moment to think it over. Mrs. Kelly, this is an exchange, and I'm a man of my word. Have to be in my profession. I'm also beholden to my first mate, here, for general compliance. When I give orders, he makes sure they're carried out."

He clapped Sharky on the back and activated another stream of spittle onto the floor.

"You're the woman we want. The last one standing, it seems. I'd hate to see you go missing like that friend of yours."

"The police have it." My eyes never left the knife. "They took every last thread from the glove shop to the station. You'll have to ask Detective Fisher about it. I have nothing."

"That is regrettable." He leaned back in his chair and said, "Joe, come on over here a minute."

The barman joined us, wiping his greasy hands over his vest. "Yeah, Cap? Another beer?"

"The lady has questions." He squinted at me and waited.

"You know the owner here?" I asked. "Dr. Park?"

"Rumor says Park's dead." He directed it to Captain Carroll.

"He is," I said. "How did he get his hands on this place? How long ago?"

"Who offed him, Cap?"

"The lady, Joe."

The barman turned a wary eye on me. "Park bought the Typhoon fair and square. Outright with a bag of gold coins. Saw it m'self."

Captain Carroll's smile sent shivers down my spine.

"Where'd the previous owners go with the coins?" If only I could send the captain after them.

The barman was missing a lot of teeth. "Up in Nome, opening new whore houses. Mighty good businessmen."

Sharky grinned and gave his knife a twirl.

"What happens to this place now that the owner is dead?" I asked. "There is no next of kin, right?"

"Pends on whether Cap here knows of any. He sailed with you once, ain't that right, Cap?"

"Aye. He's got no family but ours."

He gaped at Captain Carroll. "Does that mean you'd be getting the Typhoon, Cap? And The Whale, too?"

I gasped and choked on the thick smoke in the air. What about Dr. Park's money in the bank? The shop? All the brothels? If so, he was a rich man in San Francisco.

And a likely suspect. Had Captain Carroll needed a different way to kill Dr. Park, since the mutiny charge hadn't stuck? He met my eyes and read them.

"Anything else, Mrs. Kelly?" he asked.

I swallowed. How long could I keep this going before he lost interest or patience? How was I going to get out of this place, even if he let me up from the table? The door seemed miles away, and beyond that lay Pacific Street. Even if I could retrieve my gun from the floor, what was that among so many thugs?

"What about the woman, then?" I asked. "Mrs. Alden?"

The barman scratched his head. "Who?"

"A woman came in here," I said. "Alone. A week ago."

"We like women."

"You don't like this kind of women. She was a preacher."

"One of them as marched out there? They want to tell us what to do? My own mother don't get away with that. She marched in here?"

"Somebody saw her. Talked to her." I turned to Captain Carroll. "It was the last thing she did before we found her under the wharf. Who killed her? Why?"

"Served her right."

"Answer the lady, Joe."

Joe's face closed up.

"She carried a Bible," I added.

Joe grunted. "Yeah, I saw her. Spitting mad, that woman. Nobody touched her."

Now we were getting somewhere. "Then how did she die?"

"Look, lady, I have work to do, all right? She came in raging at every man in sight and marched right up the stairs. Nobody laid a hand on her. Never saw her again."

"I don't believe you."

Captain Carroll laughed through his cigar smoke. "Then why are you asking the man?"

"I don't know!" I raised my voice in frustration. "You knew the owner. Was Dr. Park here, too?"

The barman put his hands on his hips. "It was the cocktail hour. Everybody making the rounds. He coulda been. Only he stops to collect the daily payout and has one drink. Then he leaves. Same thing every day. Never lingers."

"Did he ... consort with the ladies upstairs?"

"Some men aren't the type, ya know?"

"You mean he was..." Heat rushed to my face.

"Not on my watch," Captain Carroll said.

"He paid on time and he paid well," the barman said. "I don't care what he did."

I turned and glanced up the staircase. "Is the office up there?"

"I have work." He turned away, and I started to call after him, but one look from Captain Carroll stopped me.

"And if she was going up to speak with Dr. Park?" I asked.

"You think they're related?" His face was inscrutable.

"Maybe."

What a tangle. If she'd gone up to accost Dr. Park over money, I had no reason to think he wouldn't have strangled her in a rage. Perhaps they had a business arrangement go sour.

Perhaps Becky had been behind it all.

Chapter Twenty-Two

CAPTAIN CARROLL KICKED back his chair and rose. His empty beer glass left rings on the scarred table and he ground the stub of his cigar out next to it, adding a charred black spot.

"Off with you, men," he said. "The night's entertainment is over and your shift starts midnight."

"Give us an extra hour, Cap," said one of the men. "We found your girl." He put a large, clammy hand over mine and I yanked mine back under the table.

Captain Carroll chuckled. "Aye, that you did, lads. One hour. No more." He held out a hand to me as his men gave a cheer and quickly left us.

Folding my hands in my lap, I fixed my most condescending look on him.

"You'll not get a better offer," he said. "How about if I simply step aside and let you walk out alone?"

No one was watching us, but I had no doubt at all that I had the entire room's attention. I rose slowly from my chair, letting the feeling come back into my numb legs, every bruise on my arms and shoulders aching. My little black bag hung light and loose from my wrist, next to useless. The women's march seemed years ago.

"Now, my dear Mrs. Kelly," he said, taking my hand and drawing me close. "Let's not have any trouble."

His arms and hands were strong as iron bands around my waist and he drew me firmly toward the staircase instead of toward the exit. "I've a friend of my own that's been waiting," he said, "and I'll be damned if she goes missing." He hauled me up the first step. "As you seem to have no connections to anyone in this city, none'll care that you've dropped into the belly of The Whale."

He nearly carried me up another five steps. My struggles were utterly useless. The hall at the top was long and narrow, running in both directions and turned a corner at one end. The threadbare carpet was a nondescript color with years of accumulated stains. It was impossible to tell how many doors ran along the corridor as the gaslights were dim, but each was painted blue and depicted some sort of ocean scene.

Several men wandered about in various states of undress.

"Don't know yours," Captain Carroll said cheerfully, "but mine's Nora. Naughty Nora. Made her acquaintance last night, and she's promised me tonight, the glorious creature."

He continued to hum to himself until we came to the end of the hall and a door with a crude mermaid painted on it. Her massive bosoms put mine to shame.

"Fine art." He rapped on the door. "You aren't one of those do-gooders, so don't make a fuss. You might enjoy yourself if you've a mind."

My hand flew at his face, but he caught it with ease. "No

fussing. It's unladylike."

The door opened, and he pushed me in ahead of him. "We're here, my darling Nora! Make way for your captain!"

I stumbled briefly, then righted myself against a dirty wall papered in blue and cream chevrons. The light fixture was tarnished but shed a glow on the cramped room and its occupant. A tall bureau bristled with feminine potions and a variety of seashells. A Japanese screen in a corner bore several skirts and scarves and an ottoman held even more. Linens and drapes were faded blue and had not a speck of comfort attached to them.

"It's shipwreck for you, captain." A woman lounged across the bed on her stomach, chin in her hands, kicking her heels in the air.

Captain Carroll closed the door and gaped at her. As her only clothing seemed to be a drape of silk over her backside, I suppose I did, too.

"You siren." His speech slurred, and he leaned heavily on the bureau. "A shipwrecked sailor hasn't a chance. None 'tall."

Rising like a nymph from the ocean, the woman approached and stood boldly in front of him.

"You're late."

Dark wavy hair billowed down her back to the silk skirt tied around her narrow waist. Captain Carroll reached for it and the momentum pulled him face-first to the floor with a reverberating thud.

"You lost me a solid thirty dollars, you horse's ass," she said to Captain Carroll's back.

I eased toward the door.

"Don't try it," she said curtly. "This is your fault. I'll scream for Joe, and no one will ever see you again."

Considering she was without weapon, armor, or under-garments, I felt brave enough to say, "He's had too much to drink. I had nothing to do with it, and I'm here against my will."

She was already kneeling beside the captain, going through his pockets. He snored, his body limp as a baby.

"Save it. He had a beer." She pulled out his watch and let the chain run through her long fingers. "I told Joe to spike it. He was spending my time on you." She cut her eyes at me. "Lost me ten customers, waiting for his royal fatness. That, lady, is your fault." She reached into the next pocket. "Who are you, anyway? A little civilized for a captain's choice."

A black night with no stars was framed in the single open window, and it was impossible to tell which direction we faced.

"I marched on Pacific Street earlier," I said dryly. "The captain invited me in for a chat."

Her laugh was deep and throaty. "I'll bet he did. Well, you aren't getting a dime of it."

The woman was young. Perhaps in her early twenties. But the green eyes she turned on me knew more than I about the baser things in life. They were hard and glittered like glass.

"You think you're better than me?" she said.

Her tone warned me back a step.

"You have a house?" she asked.

I shook my head, and with a smirk, she went back to the captain's pockets. "Of course you don't. You're trapped by whatever pin money your husband or beau gives you or the rock-bottom wages of..." She glanced over her shoulder. "A bakery, maybe. Your body says you have an appetite."

A snicker followed, and I ignored it. Slowly, she took everything of value from Captain Carroll, adding coins and cufflinks to the collection on her bureau.

"Flora is buying a house," she continued, "on Kearny Street. It isn't much. But her appetites pay the mortgage every month and in two more years, she'll own it outright."

She rolled Captain Carroll over onto his back. His head lolled at my feet.

"What are you doing?"

"Collecting my wages and retiring for the night."

Diving into his jacket, she said, "Belle is saving up to buy this place. Can you imagine? But she's been here longer than I have. Hides her money where nobody knows about but me. I'm the only one she trusts on account of I keep my money there, too."

She rose, opened a bureau drawer, and pulled a pink embroidered robe from it. "This calls for a night off," she said, holding up the gold coin she'd just pulled from his vest pocket.

Slipping her arms into the robe, she cinched it tight and gave me a smug smile.

I blinked. Where had I seen it before?

"My life is dancing and gaiety, music and pretty clothes. I escort men to the opera. I flirt with the boys downstairs and give 'em a private audience if they slide the right amount of money down my corset."

She glanced down at her chest and laughed again.

"Some of the girls here are talented. They can play the organ or sing." She fondled a length of blue-green silk hanging from the screen. "Not me. All I have is my natural skill at fishing, and I'm very good at it."

In the time she'd given me to regroup, I'd decided I was in her debt for neutralizing Captain Carroll. The idea lasted until her next words.

"Now it's your turn," she said, pointing at my reticule. "We'll start with your adorable little black bag and go on from there." She held out her hand.

"You can't take that coin," I said, handing her the bag. "It's..."

"Mine," she finished. She rummaged in the bag while I took in the distance between myself and the door. It had not been locked, but the distance included a hall, a staircase, a saloon, Pacific Street, and a dash through Chinatown at midnight.

With a sigh, I said, "Nora, is it? How long have you worked here?"

"A few years," she said with a shrug. She dropped the coin into my bag. "I'm the best they've got. I make over thirty dollars a night and only have to work two or three hours a night to make it. Where else is a girl gonna get her hands on that kind of money?"

"There are plenty of jobs that don't involve theft," I snapped.

"And who would hire me, miss high and mighty?" Her smile was gone. "Domestic service? Surely you jest. That or less is what they'd deem me fit for. The work of an animal or an immigrant."

"It's honest work."

"I would not stoop to making beds for fifty cents a day," she scoffed. "Let the Japanese do it. And the Chinese can cook. Why would I become a kitchen mechanic?"

"You could marry," I offered, hating the words before they were out.

She stepped up and slid a skilled hand into my skirt pocket. "Listen to you." She moved into the next pocket. "Aren't you precious? Do you think anyone less than a cutthroat is going to offer a ring to someone like me?"

Her eyes were gorgeous up close, and they assessed my earrings for several long moments.

"Well, they won't. Girls like me have to take care of themselves. And the men in this city are all ugly and wicked no matter what they say. I've seen 'em all. I'm not staying in San Francisco." She finished with my pockets, disgusted with their empty depths. "When I have enough money, I'm leaving and never coming back."

The wall above the bureau was plastered with pictures cut out of magazines. Fashionable women. Handsome men. Postcards from seasides and fancy hotels and landscapes. Scraps of paper with scribbled notes and doodles. Ribbons.

"It isn't Christian to judge a woman for taking care of herself in a crazy world," she said. "I work for myself. I pay my taxes like any good citizen. I can move on any time I

DEATH AT THE WHARF

please and get a job in any town."

"If you live long enough to claim it."

She slammed my bag on the bureau, and a shell bounced to the floor. "Stop and stop there, lady. I've had my fill of preaching, prattling finger-pointers. I came straight out of an orphanage and let me tell you, this job is respectable, dignified, and independent compared to that hellhole."

I hadn't moved from my position against the wall, and it still wasn't safe to make a move elsewhere.

Nora paced back and forth around Captain Carroll's snoring girth.

"How dare you women go marching past my window shouting that I'm a vicious man-chasing whore! Or worse, I had no choice. Oh, poor me!" She seized a skirt from the Japanese screen and ran it over her cheek.

"Choosing this was easy. The orphanage? Any girl who loses her spirit is dead within a month. Every girl who keeps it is punished. And those can stay on at the orphanage to care for other incoming children." Her face grew distant. "Easy. Most of the babies are collected by the undertaker. Most girls beg to leave." Her voice drifted off.

"So you did," I said quietly.

"At least a domestic gets a cleaner place and better table scraps. But if we get sent back from a job that doesn't work out, whether or not it's our fault, we're sent here. To Pacific Street. Some of us come willingly. I know two girls who were attacked by a gentleman of the house they worked in. At least here, if a gentleman gets rowdy, Joe can kick him out. We have respect here. Safety. Someone who cares whether we live or die."

It occurred to me that I was in a brothel, alone, without money or resources, and absolutely no one was coming for me. There was no one to know whether I lived or died. And I had no way to know if they cared.

Taking in a deep breath, I shifted to the other side of the room, if only to shake off the notion.

Nora ignored my small bid for courage.

"And those who are unwilling?" I asked. "You cannot convince me everyone here is happy with their lot."

"They don't last long." She paused in front of her bureau and studied the cluttered wall. "But at least they go out fighting."

"Perhaps all women, in whatever lot they're in, are simply fighting for a better one."

She snorted. "Like you marching women?"

"Maybe everybody wants a say in their life. In their world."

"Like the vote?"

"That too."

She laughed and, for a moment, was a young, carefree version of a girl who'd forgotten what that was.

"This is as close to a vote as a woman will ever get. A man votes with his pants off. More wives should take that into consideration."

I hadn't heard her. Stunned, I stared at her face.

This was the girl from the tintype. The card in Mrs. Alden's Bible.

"Ask a fisherman how big his fish is. I dare you." She

held up the fabric in her hands. "This is one of the cleverest ideas I ever had. Men pay twice as much for a mermaid; did you know that?"

"I have your picture card," I said. "I found it."

She blinked. "You what?"

"You know Mrs. Alden."

"Who?"

"All your talk about the marching women," I said, "and you knew the very worst one."

"What are you talking about?" She carefully laid her mermaid tail back over the screen.

"A woman marched in here last Saturday at the supper hour. She was alone and fighting angry. Joe watched her come storming in and go up the staircase."

She'd frozen. A cool, hard glaze came over her face as she listened.

"I think she was going up after Dr. Park. The man who owns this place. But I don't know where his office is."

"His office?"

"I think they argued, and he strangled her. She was found beneath the wharf, tangled in a net."

Her perfect, dark eyebrows came together in a frown.

"Mrs. Alden was her name," I said. "And I want to know how she got your picture card in her Bible."

She moved to the door and blocked it. "I don't know the lady," she said.

Captain Carroll snored softly between us.

A desperate thought crossed my mind, and I spoke before I could change my mind.

"Do you know Rebecca Smith?"

Nora shook her head. "You're in the belly of The Whale, lady. We don't know anybody's name."

She glanced at the wall I'd recently vacated. A row of hooks ran along the top. But the wall was blank.

Another scan of the room told me the mermaid theme had been thoughtfully applied, from the wallpaper to the boudoir decor.

"Did you have a net hanging here?" I whispered.

She reached behind her back and locked the door.

Chapter Twenty-Three

"NORA?"

I watched her face as thoughts flew past it. She knew about Mrs. Alden's death. It was her net wrapped around the body. Her card in Mrs. Alden's Bible. She was absolutely caught out.

The question was, what would she do about it? I was as completely at her mercy as Mrs. Alden must have been.

But this young thing could not have possibly strangled a woman like Mrs. Alden. No more than she could best me. What Mrs. Alden had surely had in fighting rage, I made up for in weight and foresight.

Nora no longer had the advantage of surprise.

But who was her accomplice?

I tried again to capture her attention. "Nora. Who killed Mrs. Alden?"

"I swear it," she said. "I do not know the man."

"But you know it was a man who killed her?"

She nodded quickly. "Don't get the wrong idea. There's plenty of that goes on in The Whale. Not my business. It'd be my life if I noticed."

"It's your net around the woman. Did you sneak up

from behind and tangle her so Dr. Park could finish her?"

"No! I never touched the net!"

Captain Carroll snorted, and we both jumped.

This wasn't getting me anywhere. "How can I prove Dr. Park killed Mrs. Alden?"

"Don't try," she pleaded. "The man took my net. I wanted nothing to do with it."

"Don't you know him? The owner of The Whale?"

"No. I don't deal with men. Only Joe. He handles my money."

"You work nearly exclusively with men," I pointed out. "And you won't convince me you weren't part of this murder. The top whore covering for the owner? Seems logical to me."

My only advantage was that Dr. Park was dead. There was only Nora left.

Until she called Joe.

"He's dead, you know," I said. "Dr. Park. He can't hurt you for telling the truth."

She rubbed her arms. "I have no idea who killed the lady. I don't know who he is, and that's on purpose. He left me a mighty big pile of money to keep my mouth shut."

"If he did it and he's dead, where's the harm?"

"If someone else did it, and he's alive, he'll find out," she snapped.

I took in a deep breath and said, "Move away from the door."

She stepped aside.

"The deadbolt."

She shook her head. "It isn't to keep you in. It's to keep him out. How do you suddenly know all of this? Who are you, and why do you want me dead?" She looked down at the captain. "Why did he bring you in here?"

"My name is Mrs. Kelly. I'm working with the police, trying to find out who killed Mrs. Alden and Dr. Park."

She looked me up and down. "Why?"

"Because a friend of mine got involved."

"She dead?"

I closed my eyes and rubbed them. "I don't know."

"You're not one of those marching do-gooder women out there?"

"No."

"You didn't entertain the captain downstairs and then come up for some fun?"

"You can't tell?"

"I entertained him last night," she said. "I know he was coming up for more and you sidetracked him. Does he know about the killing, too?"

"Yes. But has no idea you might be involved."

"I'm not!"

"Prove it." I shoved aside the pile of laundry and lowered myself onto the ottoman. My feet ached.

She wrung her hands. "If he finds out I talked, he'll kill me."

"He can't harm you if the police protect you. Come with me and tell Detective Fisher what you know."

She jumped. "No police!"

"But you can't stay here. It isn't safe."

"This is the only safe place I've ever been."

"You don't leave?"

She crossed her arms. "I lie about the ocean all the time. I've never even seen it."

The irony of our situation struck me. "And I find clues all the time. I know things without ever meaning to."

"Are you a witch?"

"I've been called a water witch. I think that's close enough." I sighed. "If you won't come with me, you'll have to tell me everything that happened. Anything you can remember. Maybe he left a clue without realizing it."

"Why should I risk it? She was a marching, hypocritical, do-gooder church lady."

I raised an eyebrow. "How do you know?"

She swallowed.

"Unless your plan is to kill me, sooner or later I am going to tell the police about you."

"You can't prove nothing. The police leave us alone here."

"I can have you jailed as a thief."

"I'll run first."

"And leave your job?"

She scowled at the open window. The night was pitch black, and I stifled a yawn. My stomach growled, and I ignored it. Swallowing anything in this building was completely out of the question.

Nora turned to her bureau and opened the drawer again. She emptied it onto her bed, then repeated until the drawers were empty. "I'm getting dressed," she said.

"Sensible of you." I hadn't considered hauling her the block to the police station in her unmentionables.

She scrabbled beneath the bed and began to rummage through the room, and I leaned back against the wall to watch. It had to be into the wee hours of the morning. I'd nearly gone a full day and night, and my body fought between the sleep I'd missed and the feeling it was already time to rise and head for the bakery.

It was apparent that Nora had to dig deep in order to find a decent skirt or dress. She'd have to look like the respectable citizen she claimed to be if she wanted anyone to believe her.

My eyes closed while I waited, and I sank against the wall.

"Stop hitting me," I said with my eyes still closed. "I won't move. Work around me."

"Wake up," Nora said in my ear. "You have to move."

She grabbed my shoulder and shook hard.

Swiping at her, I sat up and discovered Captain Carroll's hand in mine. Jerking awake, I looked into Nora's eyes and she chuckled. "I couldn't help it. You fell asleep."

I was on the floor. Nora was fully dressed and her hair done up in a proper twist. Her skirt was bottle green but a perfect match to the high-necked, starched, white shirtwaist she paired with it. With the gloves and hat she wore, she could have marched on the street herself.

She also could have killed me.

She rose from her knees and fussed with a large valise as I hauled myself to my feet and felt for my earrings.

"It's time to go," she said, grabbing a shawl. "Joe has a wagon in the back alley for us."

A chill came in from the window. Dawn glowed apricot, vermillion, and lavender through the clouded sky.

Nora trailed a finger over the flotsam hung on the wall.

"We don't need a wagon," I said. "The station is an easy walk from here." I shook my head at Captain Carroll. "How long does that drug last?"

"Long enough for a man to be shanghaied." She picked up her bag. "I was going to let him sleep it off in the street."

"Won't he come blazing after you for drugging him?"

She laughed. "Sometimes I charge extra for it."

"What?"

She threw the deadbolt and pulled the door open. The barman stood in the narrow hall, smoke and liquor fumes rolling from his clothes and the filthy apron around his wide waist. He pushed into the room and it was immediately claustrophobic. I circled him as he knelt over the captain with a large tarp.

"Gently, Joe," Nora called from the corridor.

I joined her. "What is he doing?"

"We're taking the good captain home."

I spun to face her. "We're going to the police station."

"Keep your voice down. The girls need their beauty sleep."

Joe had rolled Captain Carroll in the tarp and, with a grunt, managed to hoist him over his shoulder.

Nora moved down the dark hall, and I hurried after her.

"We have to talk to Detective Fisher!"

She swept down a staircase, and I had to keep moving or be barreled over by the men behind us.

Nora stepped into the alley and said, "This is business, Mrs. Kelly. You drive us to his ship, and I'll tell you everything I know. Then you leave us there. Forever. You tell nobody. I need to disappear."

Joe dumped Captain Carroll into the bed of the wagon next to a small trunk. Nora added her valise.

"Tell the police," I said. "Then disappear."

She shook her head. "I won't step a foot into that place and if you take me there, I'll tell them you killed the captain here and run, screaming down the street."

"They wouldn't believe you."

"They would stop long enough to look in the wagon," she smirked. "Take it or leave it."

I was looking at a very resourceful girl. She could pull it off. And I needed her story.

Sensing victory, she turned to the barman. "Thank you, Joe." Nora stood on her toes and kissed him. "I'll never forget you."

"Be a good girl, Miss Lenora."

We climbed into the wagon, and I took the reins. Nora pulled her shawl tight against the chill and I drove us down the alley. Joe watched us until we turned a corner and entered the street.

"Where are you going?" Nora asked. "The water is that way. Even I can see it."

"You want to take Captain Carroll to his ship? Well, they're docked all the way down in the Potrero. Near Irish

Hill. I used to live there."

Her eyes grew wide as we drove straight down Dupont and joined all of Chinatown in their morning oblations.

"Settle in for a ride," I said. "This is the fastest way there." I only hoped it was fast enough for the sleeping hulk in the wagon behind me. Heaven only knew what might happen if he woke up now.

The sky warmed with suffused light as the sun rose ahead of us.

"What's that you said?" I asked.

"Red sky in morning, sailor take warning." It didn't sound encouraging.

Dodging the early morning traffic, I pulled onto Market Street and quickly onto Third Avenue without a glance at the Palace Hotel. Somewhere in that kitchen, Pearl was covering for me. My only hope was to present the world's most decadent tiramisu in exchange for keeping my job.

And soon.

We were definitely moving against the oncoming wave of merchants and grocers. Delivery boys in loaded wagons headed into the city from Butchertown and the Potrero frowned at us and I had my hands full trying to move out of their way.

Nora didn't say a word when we passed the noisy train depot, but my mind filled with memories. My first impressions of this bustling city and the welcome of a husband and his family had lasted mere hours.

After that, I'd made San Francisco my home on my own terms.

"Wait!" Nora grabbed my arm. "What's this? Where are we going?"

Third Avenue became Kentucky Street, but only after traversing the Long Bridge. I turned the wagon onto the wide wooden planks, sharing the clattering bridge with horsecars, pedestrians, and buggies. There were no rails. Just a wide-open expanse of pungent water on both sides, the muddy shallows that opened into the larger Bay.

Nora clutched the side of the wagon and nearly put dents in my driving arm.

"It's just the Bay," I said. Her fear would have been comical had I not known about her sheltered life. I didn't have the heart to mock her. "Why don't you tell me what happened that day in The Whale? We're nearly there."

Her eyes never left the water. She swallowed and said, "I heard them. From my room. The woman and the man had a fierce argument."

She inhaled sharply as we swerved around a buggy and I prompted, "But you didn't see them?"

"I peeked out at some point because they wouldn't shut up. She was ranting about money."

"I knew it!"

Nora hadn't heard me. "The woman was one of those marching types. I hated her on sight."

"Just because a woman has a strong opinion—"

She shook her head. "Because she was a big, fat hypocrite. Apparently, the man took off with their money and she wanted it back. Left her pregnant and penniless, she said, and demanded his pay."

"But she wasn't," I murmured.

Had she been lying to him? Why?

"What I want to know is why a do-gooder like her is in a whorehouse like mine, yelling at a man about being pregnant! I'll bet her simpering church ladies don't know about it!"

"So the man killed her?" I wasn't sure I wanted the details.

"He grabbed her and threw her to the floor. He was on top of her and had his hands around her throat before he looked up and saw me peeking."

"Oh!"

She lowered her voice. "It isn't the first time I've seen murder done, Mrs. Kelly." We took a minute, and she released my arm. "When he shoved into my room, I figured it was over for her."

"You did see him!"

"That don't mean I know who he is! He was real ugly about it. Knocked me around so I would be sure to take him seriously. Took my net. Left a stack of coins."

"Nora."

"I watched him wrap her up." She shuddered. "It was like watching a spider work. He dropped something in the hall and I saw it was her Bible."

"Oh."

The sun lit the water in shimmering ripples. It utterly distracted her.

"I snatched it up and shoved one of my cards in it. Ran after him and crammed it into the bundle." She blinked. "I guess I wanted her church friends to know the truth about her. Foolish, I know. I reckon he wasn't taking her back to church."

"He took her to the wharf," I said. "Tied her underneath in the water. I think he was hoping a fisherman would take the blame." We turned off of the bridge onto Kentucky Street. "That's where we found her."

A train passed in the distance.

"Mrs. Alden had a secret," I said, fighting the pang of loss as we entered the Potrero area. "If what my friend said is true, she claimed she was a widow, but really had a husband somewhere. Could this man be him?"

Something didn't match up. Dr. Park, so far as we knew, had only been in San Francisco for three years.

And Mrs. Alden had known him. Had they had a liaison that extended beyond a financial one?

"They were married?" she asked with a look of disgust.

"And he's been missing for nearly twenty years," I murmured.

I'd been married. Once. This was our street.

"Guess she found him." Nora shook her head.

"I think she's been patrolling Pacific Street all this time. Waiting for him."

I felt so lost here.

She cut her eyes at me. "Looking for a missing husband? Did she have his picture?"

I snapped back into the present. "How did you know that?"

"Joe found it. On the floor. He laughed and threw it away."

Chapter Twenty-Four

"WHEN, NORA? WHEN did he find it?" I pulled the horse to a stop.

"A few days ago."

"This whole time, you had his picture." It was defeating. "We could have found him right away."

"I didn't have it," she said peevishly. "Joe did. Joe said the woman never gave it a rest. Always waving that blasted picture in his face, asking had he seen the man. Joe reckoned he'd been long dead." She blew out a breath. "Careful what you ask for, is what I say."

I let those words hang in the air for a minute.

"What I mean is, Dr. Park and Mr. Alden can't be the same man. The picture would have helped."

"Oh." She gazed at Irish Hill, one of San Francisco's humbler rises. Its craggy backside left little room for the few buildings huddled on and about its slopes. Smoke from the Union Iron Works and the smelting foundry drifted past, swaying laundry on lines and curling along staircases tacked onto the outside of narrow, two-story wooden buildings.

Kentucky Street went for miles, but this length of saloons, homes, and shops teemed with memories.

"That's Dogpatch," I said. "Haven't seen my in-laws for a while." I turned the horse away from Kentucky Street toward the point, and we crossed over the train tracks on Illinois Street.

"At least they claim you," she said tartly.

"Sorry." The moment of silence was for both of us. "I'm not certain they do." They'd have weddings and business ventures and extortion and fistfights by now that I knew nothing of.

I wondered if they told stories about me.

We looked quickly over our shoulders as a muffled shout came from the wagon bed.

"Here it comes," Nora muttered. "Are we there yet?"

"Nearly." I gave the horse a slap with the reins. "So, the question is..." I stared out at the Bay.

Schooners, sails furled against four heavy-timbered masts, rocked on the water in the distance. Tugboats chugged along, gentle ripples in their wake.

"Which one killed her?"

Nora shrugged, trying to take in the view in every direction at once.

"Joe would have recognized either of them." I frowned. "And he only mentioned Dr. Park. It has to be him."

We smelled the Arctic Oil Works before we saw it. Even in the wee hours of the morning, a whisper in the air carried odors of timber and tar, coal fires and oil, dead fish and dried blood. The inescapable stench of smoked blubber hung permanently in the air over the moored ships and refinery.

As the point came into view, I slowed the wagon. Train

tracks ran on the inland side, along the front of the walled buildings, with a deviated line going directly into an arched stone entry. Smoke belched from the try works chimney stacks to the right, and the tops of massive metal tanks stood in a row on the left side of the works. I headed down toward the jetty that flanked the storage tanks, far from the fires, and the working interior fell out of sight behind the tall perimeter fencing.

"So, if Dr. Park killed Mrs. Alden over money and a pregnancy, who killed him two days later with a lance bomb?" I asked.

"Someone avenging her death?"

"Or someone who wanted them both dead." The thought of Becky's duplicity cut me deeply. "My friend is the tie between them. And she ran away when I confronted her about it."

"Guilty."

"You don't have to sound so gleeful."

"Well, it wasn't the church ladies. But look at the water, Mrs. Kelly! Isn't it glorious?"

Nora seemed to be shedding the horrors of her life as fast as the rising sun.

The jetty was a long, cleared road with the refinery walls on one side and a uniform pile of rough stones piled along the other. It ended at a broad, T-shaped, wooden pier with two massive brigantines moored to either side of it.

Three fishermen had abandoned their tiny boat to bob in the glittering shallows and had an open net spread out between them, slowly drawing their catch toward the sand at the foot of the jetty.

"It's exactly how I pictured it," Nora said, leaning eagerly forward.

Another shout from the tarp sent us wheeling down the jetty toward the ships.

"Are you going to stow away?" I asked. "All winter?"

"I can't show my face in San Francisco again. Not with a murdering bastard after me."

"Once we find him, you'll be safe."

The pier rumbled beneath us, and I slowed, maneuvering around crates and equipment. Our path grew narrow, and I had to stop between the ships while there was still room to turn the wagon around and leave.

"You don't want to find him," she said. "You don't want that man anywhere near you." She hopped out of the wagon and straightened her hat. "And, as fun as this is, Mrs. Kelly, I don't care. I have my own fish to fry."

The tarp was definitely struggling.

"Make yourself scarce," she said, clambering into the wagon bed with the rolling tarp. "I'm about to tell him what a horrible person you are."

"What?"

She smiled. "Nothing personal, but this is my job now. I kept my end of the deal. Which boat is his?"

My head swiveled between the brigs, and I pointed. "That one. The *Hidalgo*."

There seemed to be no one particularly guarding the place, but stacked crates and coiled rope were everywhere. I strained my ears for voices or running steps.

"Thanks. Every fisherman is a sucker for a good story. I'll tell him you did this." She grabbed the edge of the tarp. "And I rescued him."

I didn't budge from my seat. "I need the wagon to get back!"

"Take it after we're gone."

She tugged, and the tarp erupted. Captain Carroll rolled out and was much the worse for wear. His hair stood on end, his face was gray and clammy, one eye swollen yellow and green, and his suit rumpled. He struggled to sit upright, and I kept the horse from shifting as the wagon rocked.

Kneeling next to him, Nora took one of his fat hands and cried, "Captain! You're alive!"

Captain Carroll bent forward and vomited.

Nora had the sense to release him and gather her skirts out of the way. "I was so frightened!" she squeaked.

He was far from finished, however, and she had to move her valise onto the seat next to me and sit almost behind him. The tarp took most of his abuse and I planned to dump it into the water on my way back out.

If only they would leave.

"Oh, you poor dear!" she said, placing a hand on his shoulder. "Let's get you to your ship!"

"My ship!" he bellowed. "Hang the ship! Why aren't I in the boarding house? Where's Mrs. Petrie? Where's Sharky?" He looked wildly about and his eyes rolled up in his head.

There was a thought. I looked up and down the pier again. I didn't want to meet Sharky or any of his men out here.

"Darling!" She lightly slapped his cheek. "Captain..."
She looked at me.

"Carroll."

"Captain Carroll! Wake up! Come back to me!"

"What's this?" He rallied and pushed away from the
soiled tarp. "Tangled up!" He took hold of the side of the
wagon and dragged himself to his knees.

"That's it!" Nora said. "Let's get you out of here!"

"How did I get here?" he roared. "Why am I in a wagon?" He threw a leg over the side.

Nora scrambled over the opposite side and ran around to
assist. We were almost done.

The wagon rolled another foot as Captain Carroll hoisted himself over the side and nearly fell into Nora's waiting
arms. "Lay off, there!" He struggled away from her and
gripped the wagon with one hand, testing his legs.

"You were drugged!" Nora said. "Poisoned! I went after
you and saved you!"

"Saved me?" He ran a shaky hand over his paunch.

"Yes!" She gave me an exasperated look. "From, from the
men who were trying to shanghai you!"

"Shanghai."

"I couldn't let them! My darling captain! They wouldn't
believe me when I told them we were married!"

I sat there not believing it myself.

"And who might you be?" He squinted in her face.
"What's this all about, then?"

"It's me, my darling. Your lovely Nora." She put a tender
hand on his hairy cheek. "Your bride!"

He growled, and I leaned away from them. "My what, now?"

Nora tugged impatiently at her glove. "Sweetness..." A huge diamond ring gleamed from her finger. "You proposed to me and I accepted."

He stared at the ring for so long, I thought he might have had an aneurism.

"Don't know you," he mumbled. "No idea who you are."

He shook his head and Nora put a hand on his pants in a place that no female in broad daylight would dare.

His eyes grew wide, and he leaned within an inch of her adoring face. Knowing how bad his breath must be, I gave her full credit as an accomplished actress.

"Don't you remember me, dearest?" she asked. "We've had such fun together. I could never live without you. You are my life. And you promised me a tour of your ship." She glanced up. "The *Hidalgo*, is it not?"

He blinked at his ship, and a long whistle sounded in the refinery.

Her hand wandered and captured his attention once more.

"You mean..." He was trying so hard to understand.

Her disguise was too good. She huffed and said, "I'm the mermaid. From last night?"

His frown slowly melted into a smile. It was like watching a child receive a Christmas gift.

"Why, I've caught myself a big 'un!" He laughed, as if it couldn't be true.

I, knowing full well it couldn't, said, "Can you take the trunk?"

"Naughty Nora." Captain Carroll stood upright, although his face remained ashen. "It is you, is it?"

"Yes, my love. Forever." She threw her arms around him and kissed him full on the mouth.

I had to look away and focus on keeping my bile down. "The baggage," I muttered, staring down the pier.

"Those scoundrels would have taken you," Nora continued. "There was a huge fight. We barely escaped."

He kept an arm around her waist. "You have the spirit of five women," he said proudly.

"The trunk," I repeated.

They both turned to look up at me, he in fresh confusion and she in continued irritation. I shrugged. She was the actress. I had no idea what my line was supposed to be, but I needed to get out of here.

"Yes," Nora said with authority. "Bring it along." She reached up for her valise and thrust it into Captain Carroll's hands. "Thank you, love." Her hand nestled into the crook of his arm, her diamond winking in the sunshine.

"Do I know her?" His bloodshot eyes took in the entire wagon. "I'm sure I do."

"She helped," Nora said, tugging him toward the ship. "She's nobody. She's leaving."

I certainly was, and as fast as possible. Nora led her captain slowly away and caught him when he nearly stumbled. Climbing down from the wagon, I reached for the trunk and pushed it toward the back of the wagon. It was far too heavy for me to lift, and I wondered what, exactly, Nora had deemed worthy to carry forward into her newly married life.

The tarp dropped off the back to the pier and the trunk made a satisfying thud on top of it. Nora could come back for it herself. I was finally free of The Whale, no thanks to Captain Carroll.

I was going to drive back and tell Detective Fisher everything.

And then I was going home.

I hesitated. No, I thought. It wasn't home anymore. I'd be looking for a new one.

If I hadn't paused, I wouldn't have heard the steps that came to a sudden halt. Holding perfectly still, I waited for them to continue. Captain Carroll and Nora were speaking to each other, walking in the direction of the *Hidalgo*, but someone else had approached from the jetty, I was sure of it.

Slowly, I scanned the area. On the far side of a stack of crates, another pair of eyes blazed into mine. Only the top of his head was visible, but the cap pulled low and the face hidden behind the crate could not hide the line running down his temple. He stood between me and my way out.

What was he doing here? How had he followed me? Why?

I gathered my skirts and ran to catch up with the others.

Captain Carroll's voice boomed across the pier, and Nora's animated voice answered. They stopped in front of the brigantine and admired it. Two men standing at the gangplank greeted the captain, and he barked at them. More for show, I thought as I placed myself directly behind Nora, than necessity.

"She's been through hurricanes and war," he said. "But never had a skirt aboard."

I caught my breath and looked back, but we were alone.

"There's a first time for everything," Nora said gaily.

His men scowled at him, but Captain Carroll ushered Nora forward. "Meet the love of my life, my dear. My pride and joy. The only woman I've ever been faithful to."

The toughs from last night's table recognized me and what they assumed about the three of us, I did not want to know. I kept my eyes down and followed Captain Carroll's voice onto the ship.

"A tour won't hurt," he was saying. "But we're staying in the boarding house. Once a man's been aboard a ship for three years running, he wants to tread a bit of firm ground."

He appeared to be coming to terms with his new life in a hurry and, all things considered, it could have been worse. I, on the other hand, appeared to be the stowaway. I leaned over the ship's side, scanning the pier for the man I'd dubbed Whiplash.

"I need a drink," Captain Carroll said, moving aft. "So long as we're here, we'll eat something before I check in on the Oil Works." He caught my eye. "You. She says you two saved me?"

My dress looked like I'd slept in it. My hair straggled below my hat. My corset pinched in places that screamed for relief. And I was faint with hunger.

"Yes." Whatever her story was, I was forced to continue for now.

"Must've been quite a battle," he mused.

We passed the helm and the tiny galley, empty and stale, and dropped down a steep flight of steps. They opened into his quarters and Nora frowned at me as I entered, but I didn't care. I was done with my part of the deal. I nearly bumped my head against the low timbers. The room was small and cramped, but the baskets of fruit and bread on the center table took all of my attention.

"Normally, there's only the shipkeeper aboard when we're docked," he said, helping himself to an apple. "But I've a couple more for security, as you noticed." He polished the apple on his wrinkled vest. "I'll have to pay them, but it's worth it to keep that damn Shorey in check."

My ears pricked up.

"Shall I tell you about the time we came upon cannibals? The land was supposed to be deserted, and so it was once we finished with it."

Nora leaned in and whispered, "You'd better get rid of that wagon before he tries to take me out of here!"

Chapter Twenty-Five

CAPTAIN CARROLL WAS long-winded, and I watched nervously as his vigor slowly returned during the telling of his tales. He poured us all a cup of wine and I drank it gratefully. It was a deep, red, aged cabernet from Italy, so he claimed, but the nuances were lost on me. Nora sat on his knee and laughed in all the right places.

I sat in the only other chair. I needed to get off his ship. It was only a matter of time before the captain collected the last of his scattered thoughts and recalled last night's conversation.

Detective Fisher had already gone over the brigantines, looking for evidence. He'd questioned both captains and their crews several times. There was nothing keeping me here except Whiplash.

"The *Hidalgo* is a one-hundred-seventy-five-ton brig, my dear. She's been places and seen things most men only dream of."

Nora laughed. "Like mermaids?"

"No, lass, not until today. But if ever she broke on the rocks, it's them I'd blame."

The sudden thought brought a frown to his face and

Nora said quickly, "Have you seen polar bears? And reindeer? Igloos?"

"Aye. And scurvy and icebergs and fog and mutiny."

Nora scrambled. "Oh, how thrilling!"

"No, little Nora. It isn't. But sometimes the sea tests a man past his limits." His face darkened. "*Hidalgo's* seen pirates, and that's a fact."

"Do tell!" Nora seemed determined to wring every word from the man. Was she hoping he would nod off again and forget to kick her out?

He poured himself another cup of wine. "Captain Shorey." He nodded. "Black-hearted pirate if ever there was one."

Nora squealed.

"Wouldn't be surprised if he was behind my ambush last night. Were the men black as pitch?"

She wrestled with the answer and said, "It happened so quickly! We'd only said our vows when they attacked. Everything was black as pitch, darling."

Taking it as confirmation, he pulled her closer. "The man will stop at nothing to ruin me. We were in the Arctic, with room in the hold for one last catch before retiring for the season. Lookouts in the crow's nest called a sperm whale not twelve furlongs out, and we launched the whaleboats."

"A big one?" Nora asked.

"Aye! The biggest we saw all summer! But Shorey was off the port side and he saw it too. His men took to their boats and came for it at the same time."

"Oh, no!"

He grunted. "'Twas a race, and my only thought was to thrash him if his men made the beast sound before we could stick an iron into him. My lads got there first. Raymond McKee stood at the bow and got a harpoon in, and Sharky was screaming all hands stern for their lives and the beast raised his tail and took their boat down with him."

Nora's eyes held a sufficient amount of horror.

"Stove it proper, and the line was lost. Johnny Manta's boat was near enough to take up Sharky and young Peter, but the lad was done in. Saved a lock of his hair to send to his mother."

Captain Carroll pointed to a tall, narrow desk built top to bottom with drawers and cubbies.

"A whale might never be seen again," he continued, "but this one, this one came back for more. Johnny was pulling Dickie up when Shorey's men arrived, and the beast thrashed so fierce, the boats ran one into the other. I lost sight of who was where in the foam, but the long and short of it is that Shorey's men got another iron into the whale and the boat took off, smoking loggerheads, after it."

"You mean they got the whale?"

"We launched first! Means we spied it first! We had first blood, and the man didn't call off his boats."

Captain Carroll was working himself up, and I didn't envy Nora's seat.

"If the line had fouled or the hit not taken or the sleigh ride roughened to the point my men had to cut and run, there'd be no argument. But, by thunder, Shorey's men pushed our boats aside, threw curses and punches, took the whale, and turned their backs to us."

"How rude!"

He blinked. "My dear, if I'd been anywhere near a cannon, the man would not be moored on the other side of this pier. He lost me two boats that day. The first would not have happened had my men not had to be in such a hurry to claim the beast. The second tipped in the scuffle afterward and we never did find poor Dickie. One dead and one to Davy Jones and two whaleboats sunk with full tackle."

"How sad."

"Once we were back aboard and accounted for, we waited for the flurry, me growing angrier by the hour."

"Flurry?"

"Death throes. The men wield a lethal blow once the beast tires, and I wondered whether they could finish the job or not, thinking maybe we could take another go at it. Some don't. Some die trying."

He sounded so hopeful. I looked around the cabin with new eyes. This ship was a predator, not a lady.

"Eventually, the beast turned fin out, and we left once the bow header was securing the tail. Never was so furious. But I knew Shorey must remain in place to process the carcass, and that's where I turned it to my advantage. I'm not one to rest on my laurels." He tapped his nose and winked at Nora. "We sailed for San Francisco full ahead."

"I'm so glad you did!"

He finished his wine and reached for more.

"He took my whale. But I got here first. Means we took top prices for our barrels."

"You're rich!" Nora gave a little bounce on his lap.

"Hardly. But we traded time for space. We had flensed our last whale into blanket pieces aboard and cut that into horse pieces, but instead of rendering it ourselves, I left it for the try works here, you see. Our barrels more than made up for the blubber."

Everything he'd said had gone into one of Nora's ears and right out the other side without making a dent in her understanding. If they made eyes at each other one more time, I was going to go mad.

"I don't own her, of course," Captain Carroll said, running a hand along the table. "But someday I may. Grown too fond of the girl. She's saved us many a time, I'll tell you."

And he might have if I hadn't interrupted.

"Where is your first mate? The rest of your crew?" Their bunks were off to one side, narrow doors open. Vacant.

I was gratified to see him turn and look at me in surprise, as if he'd forgotten my presence. "The voyage is over. You didn't think we'd spend a single minute longer on the brig than that, did you? They're free to roam and have a fat purse to roam with!"

It was a relief to hear we were alone on the ship. "So you have no idea where they are?"

He tipped his head. "You asked about the murders."

He remembered.

"Don't think you'll catch me out," he said. "I keep tabs on them and if they fly the coop, I gather new men on the way back out to sea. If they'd done murder, I'd know."

I imagined he would.

"My mates linger on a while," he said. "To unload cargo and work with the oil works and sort the pay packets." He shrugged. "Only got in a couple of weeks ago, but the majority is done."

He turned back to Nora. "A petticoat wife? How?"

She put her cup down and her hands up his broad shoulders. "Last night, you said you loved me. It was your idea. You refused to leave without me."

"Did I, then?" He screwed up his face, trying to remember.

"You were tipsy," she admitted, "but forceful." She ran her fingers through his whiskers. "Called for a preacher, right out of The Whale's window. I nearly died, laughing."

"And there happened to be one walking past?"

She laughed. "Of course. Don't you recall the march?"

His eyes wandered back to mine.

"I had you pegged as the smartest man I've ever met," she said. "The minute I saw you, I knew. I can't wait to sail the seas with you."

"Well then, my pretty wife. It's done by others I know. It was Sharky insisted we dock this far south, but we might skip coming this way to lay up at all." He winked at her and lowered his voice. "We may overwinter in Herschel Island. Get the jump on everybody. But you didn't hear it from me."

"Lovely, darling," Nora said, giving his heavily whiskered neck a nuzzle. "But where shall we overnight?"

That was my queue. I stood and put my cup down. "I'll go fetch the trunk. Thank you for your hospitality, Captain Carroll."

Neither moved as I hauled forth and never had the foul air seemed so fresh. I could not leave the ship fast enough. Every rope and piece of tackle seemed steeped in death and the decks slick with blood. I pictured the peaceful waters of the Bay rising higher than the masthead in storm and clutched the rail in both hands.

On the other side of the pier, the *Alexander* stood proud, chains and hooks and giant brickwork ovens with vats matching those next to me. Much as I tried to talk some sense into myself, it was a fact on the dairy farm back home that we didn't hunt our cows. We didn't butcher any unless they were near the end of their life. And they weren't the size of a barn and trying to kill me and my family.

It was my first time on a ship, but I was not enchanted. Sailing was not the freedom I'd imagined, but a close-quartered prison from which land or death was the only escape. It was a violent world that floated above fathomless, merciless depths and the sheer magnitude of it made me close my dizzy eyes.

When I opened them again, I saw Becky.

Rubbing both eyes with my hands, I looked again. Where there had been a woman a moment ago, there was only the tackle I'd seen on Captain Shorey's deck. I rubbed my eyes again, but she did not reappear. Was it the flutter of a sail? A trick of the fickle light? My lack of sleep?

I hadn't had that much wine.

Smoothing at my dress, I looked over every inch of the pier below. The mates were still guarding the *Hidalgo* and there were more people along the jetty, but the pier, for all of its flotsam, seemed quiet. Our wagon was right where I'd left it, and the horse had a hoof tipped and head drooped in slumber. The refinery echoed with internal machinations and smoke belched from the smokestacks on the far side of the narrow point.

The *Alexander* appeared abandoned.

But what if…

Ah, me.

I hurried down the gangplank and passed the men before I could lose my nerve. If Becky was on the *Alexander*, it could only mean one thing. She'd hired one of Captain Shorey's men to murder Dr. Park.

"No."

The word brought me up short. Aunt Mary was firm.

"But…" The memory came. Detective Fisher said the witness claimed the murderer was a white man.

But if she hadn't, then what was she doing on board?

I stood on the pier, wavering. The road back to town stretched straight as an arrow along the jetty toward safety.

Dashing up to the wagon, I slid the whip from its socket. Then, taking the horse by the bridle, I turned him and gave him a solid slap on the flank. He headed inland at a trot. If anyone waited behind a crate for me to exit, the horse gave me a couple of minutes of distraction.

Looking left and right, I headed for the *Alexander's* gangplank. The lack of guards only increased my apprehension. After what Captain Carroll had told us, my expectations of Captain Shorey were in the gutter.

Perhaps my eyes had played tricks on me. If there was no

one on board, a quick tour of the decks would tell me so. But if Becky was here against her will…

I couldn't leave without knowing. The police were miles away. And so, it appeared, was everyone else.

Creeping along the deck, I walked softly over the planks. I took my time, gradually working my way around the tackle and peering into stowed boats and small windows. The silence mocked what I knew the ship's history to be. All the scrubbing in the world couldn't take away the odor of death.

I peered briefly into the galley. Passed trunks and cases and trapdoors that I left alone. The naked masts were skyscrapers, rising to heights only reached with narrow rope ladders. I let the whip trail the deck behind me.

With each step, I grew more uneasy. I was alone, but the ghosts of whaling men and the thrashing of leviathan seemed to rise with the cries of the gulls overhead. Standing at the far end of the ship, I stared out at the Bay once again and wondered if I'd ever have the courage to even cross it on the ferry.

The whip was ripped from my hand so quickly, my glove tingled. I spun to see Goliath throw it into the Bay.

He had me cornered.

Captain Shorey's arms were crossed, muscles rippling from his rolled shirt cuffs, his stance wide, his face grim, and fury snapped in his black eyes as he looked down on me.

My mouth opened, but nothing came out.

"I've had elephant seals aboard," the giant said. "Ugly buggers. Walrus. Sea lions."

I cleared my throat.

"I've had a squid the size of a locomotive fall on this deck from the belly of a whale."

A strand of hair blew into my face.

"But never." Here he leaned down to stare properly into my face. "Never have I ever had a skirt aboard the *Alexander*. Least of all a white woman!"

Sunlight bounced from his bald head and the gold hoop in his ear gleamed. I'd never known a man to have such little use for hair from the neck up. The nervous giggle rising from my stomach would likely seal my doom.

"What are you doing on my ship?" he bellowed.

"I saw her." I pulled my shoulders back and my chin up. "I know she's here."

"She? No women are allowed on board. The ocean does not share."

"I don't believe in superstition. But I do believe in pirates. Where's Becky?"

"I sailed with a cargo ship once. Bananas. Only ten men survived."

"Bananas? You're serious?"

"The worst luck ever to befall a ship."

"Besides a woman?"

"Get off my ship."

"I'll tell the police. They'll come back and search again."

"Go right back to the detective and tell him you trespassed."

"If Becky was here willingly, she'd come to me. I think you've locked her up."

He wiped a sleeve over the top of his head. "Are you

mad, woman? What are you doing here?"

"I've come for the truth," I said, folding my arms. "And I won't leave without it."

Chapter Twenty-Six

"FISHER!" CAPTAIN SHOREY roared, and I threw my hands over my ears.

"Where is the detective?" He turned in a circle, searching. "Where is he? He will be just as furious that you wandered off."

"He isn't here."

"Of course he's here. A woman doesn't wander the boat yards alone. Where did you leave him?" He looked over the side, down at the pier.

"In the middle of a riot on Pacific Street."

Squinting at me, he said, "I do not have time for politeness. Not today."

Captain Shorey was a dangerous man, and I had no idea why I was bluffing. The man had no qualms about taking the property and lives of others in his pursuit of fame and fortune.

If he and Becky were in league, I'd just placed myself in their way. But if I could keep my chin up long enough to make a dignified exit, I would hurry and do it. Criminals were second on my list of people to avoid, right after ghosts and barely ahead of detectives.

"You were there on the wharf," he said. "Both times. If death follows you, you'll lead it right back out of here!"

I couldn't let that pass. Not when he put it like that, superstition or no.

He grabbed my elbow roughly and hauled me across the deck. "Becky!" I cried, "Becky, where are you?"

"Fisher!" he yelled. "A man has a business to run!"

I threw an arm around a mast and immediately regretted it. He came to a stop, but not before I'd nearly wrenched my arm from the socket. "Wait! Just tell me the truth. Where is Becky?"

"Who is Becky?" he boomed.

"You will use up all the air with that volume." I tugged at my elbow, but he didn't relinquish it. "It's a simple question. It's why I came up here. I know what I saw. I saw Becky on your ship and all I want to know is if she's all right."

He let me go, but I kept a firm and aching arm around the mast.

"The girl I was with when we found the dead woman," I said. "You spoke with her. She nearly fainted."

"I just told you we don't allow women on board my ship," he growled. "And you are telling me you aren't the only one?"

"I saw her. Only a short while ago. Here." I waved my hand at the ship.

"You brought a friend to snoop around with?"

I wouldn't have thought it possible for his fury to grow even higher.

"Ahoy!" The call carried over the pier from the *Hidalgo*.

"Ahoy, *Alexander!* Could you stuff your words back down your infernal throat? Stow it, I say!"

Captain Carroll and Nora stood at the bow of the *Hidalgo*. Nora's skirts billowed softly in the breeze and she waved to me. I thought they made a pretty picture once enough distance was applied.

Captain Shorey whirled on me. "What is happening? Who is that? Is this a conspiracy? Are women attacking the ships? Did Carroll send you?"

I fought the impulse to smile. After all, I was in neither captain's graces. But at least I had witnesses.

"I think my friend Becky hired someone on your crew to run a lance bomb through her business partner. A Dr. Park. Or Parker, as he was known once."

His thick eyebrows rose and put deep wrinkles into most of the top of his head. "You what?"

"They say it was a white man who did it, but witnesses are notoriously unreliable. All I know for certain is that a man did it. Someone with nearly superhuman strength and fury."

I eyed him pointedly.

"The police have already gone over the ship and my crew. I've had to explain to the owners, over and over again, that we've done nothing wrong, either on land or sea, and sneaking a woman aboard on top of everything else is tantamount to a real thrashing!"

These last words were lobbed at the *Hidalgo* with the fury of a cannonball, and I could tell Captain Carroll took them as such. He puffed out his chest and frowned and spoke to Nora while glaring back at us. My window of opportunity was slamming shut.

"Who did it, Captain Shorey? And where is Becky?"

Although I braced, when Captain Shorey yanked me forward again, I released the mast. I was surely going to lose an arm to this man, one way or the other. He dragged me around a crate and hoisted me like a rag doll. In the time it took to draw breath enough to scream for help, we'd landed below deck and he dropped me unceremoniously to my feet.

"There!" he said, pointing. "There is the only white skin aboard the *Alexander*. 'Tis him you saw and no woman. I'll have no more of your nonsense!"

The young man paused and turned to us with an expectant face. "Yes, Cap?"

He was more boy than man, slight and pale, of good Irish stock, and we'd caught him working a heavy mop and bucket.

"This is Dickie." The boy stood taller. He obviously respected the captain. "Pulled him from the water after Carroll left. He's berthed with me, now."

"After he left?" I searched through Captain Carroll's story. "This is one of the boys lost when the whale destroyed the boats? He's supposed to be dead."

"He is," Captain Shorey said. "To Captain Carroll."

Dickie looked from me to his captain and back.

"But Captain Carroll would want to know he didn't die. Such a tragic thing." I thought of mothers who expected their sons home from a long voyage and received, instead, nothing but a lock of hair and whatever was in the pay packet.

I looked at the boy. "At least he owes you your wages."

"I paid him," Captain Shorey said curtly. "With his life. And he's grateful."

Dickie grinned.

"You won't be telling him. I'm only proving that you mistook the lad for a lady, so you'll close your mouth while I tell your detective a thing or two about knowing when his job is done."

"I am not here with Detective Fisher."

"Then Carroll did send you!"

"He did not!"

"He's not to know I've got Dickie here! You'll swear to it!"

"Why would I do that?" I stopped and brought my voice down to where it belonged. It was like being locked in the pen with an angry bull. "Goodness," I whispered.

Captain Shorey huffed. "Dickie. Take off your shirt."

"Cap?"

The boy and I shared a look that told me at least one of the men standing here knew their place when a lady was present.

The captain's jaw thrust forward and the boy removed his shirt with alacrity.

"Turn about there, Dickie."

Deep scars ran the length of his back, from the nape of his neck to below his belt. They were horrifyingly familiar. His back was thick with them.

"Are those…" I felt faint.

"Thank ye, Dickie. That's all. Back to the mop."

"Yes, Cap."

"The lad was caught up in mutiny charges," Captain Shorey said. "On the *Hidalgo*. Lashes means he was caught in the wrong place at the wrong time, but the charges didn't stick."

I reminded myself to breathe. "I know about that. But ... a boy?"

"Comes in all shapes and sizes," he grunted. "But no, this one was caught in the net with larger fish."

"So, your rescue of him was providential?"

For the first time, I heard something like a chuckle from deep in his chest, but it didn't manifest on his grim face. "No. Just necessary. His own men chose to leave him behind."

"But they must not have known!"

"They turned their oars on him. Tried to knock him out so he'd drown the faster."

Dickie put some energy into his task and kept his face turned away from ours.

"But why?"

"It was enough information to sail with me," he said. "Every man must account for his lashes. After that, a man's work speaks for itself. Dickie's been a good lad, and I'll keep him and his business as he pleases."

"You believed him? That he was innocent?"

"Aye."

"And he trusts you to keep his life a secret? Even with Captain Carroll a stone's throw away?"

Dickie looked at his captain.

"Aye. And you'll be doing the same."

Dickie went back to work as Captain Shorey pointed at the high, narrow steps. I gripped my skirts out of the way and took the rail with my other hand, eager to pull myself back into daylight and away from the vision of what forty lashes could do to a child's flesh.

Captain Shorey came up behind me and pushed. Even as I scrambled in embarrassment, I realized skirts were not only awkward on a ship, but dangerous. No wonder we were considered bad luck. If a storm rocking a ship was anything like me trying to stay upright on Mr. Paiva's little fishing boat, I'd be against it myself.

Removing my bustle from Captain Shorey's broad shoulder as swiftly as possible, I put a reasonable space between us, smoothing at my hair and doing a miserable job of it.

"Satisfied?"

"Yes."

"Now tell me who is with you."

"Nobody. I'm here alone."

He gave the pier another cursory glance. "You mean we are both looking for people who aren't here?"

"Apparently. But it doesn't make sense."

His face twisted in thought. "No. It does not. Why would you come out here alone?"

I sighed and shook my head. Where would I begin? There was no one on the *Hidalgo's* deck.

"You called me a pirate," he said, staring at my earrings.

"You accused me of murder."

The corner of his mouth twitched. "As it was, you pulled a dead woman out of the Bay and I've done nothing. I must stand by the idea that if one of us is a murderer, it must be you."

"And as there is an accusation by our neighboring ship's captain," I countered, "that you've dabbled in smuggling, I must stand by the idea that only a pirate would be caught with stolen gold coins."

His mouth flat-lined. "I trade exotic imports from place to place. I do not smuggle them."

"You don't know anything about a stash of gold coins?"

The wrinkles were back, and they carried an air of sarcasm. It chafed that Detective Fisher had been right all along. Becky was likely halfway to Vancouver by now and laughing all the way.

There was no point in poking the bear anymore. I was weary and sore and had hopefully out-waited the man behind the crates. The sun was directly overhead and the glare off the water made me squint as I peered down the jetty.

The horse and wagon were truly gone. I'd have to walk, at least as far as a cable car. I had a hand on my skirt pocket before I recalled that Nora had it all.

My muttered curse earned me a side eye from Aunt Mary.

Captain Shorey already had a hand to my waist, ushering me toward the gangplank.

"My crew hails from the West Indies. Jamaica. Haiti. Guyana. We sell more than whalebone and blubber. If

Carroll is crowing over a week's head start here, it's over nothing."

"He said you stole his whale. He blames you for the death of his men. The men with Dickie."

He stopped. The vile words he muttered under his breath were not in English.

"I did no such thing! My crew must toe the line twice as much as any sailor out there! Honor and respect on the sea is everything! My reputation is untarnished and I'll see it stays that way!"

I took a step back.

"His men used a bomb lance. They are made in New England, where the *Hidalgo* hails from. We don't use them unless we must. Look!" He pointed to the tackle in the stern. "A Greener gun. British. Fires harpoon from a bow-mounted swivel cannon. A bomb lance explodes deep inside the whale. Destroys it before it can dive below the ice. Ruins the whale if your aim is off." He drew in a mighty breath. "This was a sick whale to begin with. The bomb went off, and the whale began to sink. A fifty-foot humpback if it was an inch. It was a salvage operation and Carroll knew it. He pulled his men back, but not before they'd traded blows with mine."

I wondered what had really happened out there. Which captain was at fault? Whose story was the truth?

But all I asked was, "How can you tell it was sick?"

He looked at me as if noticing me for the first time. "I took it in. After wasting valuable time, Carroll's crew left. We fastened it starboard and threw down the cutting stage and started work. We knew it was too big to finish before the sharks took their lot, but the head was intact, plenty of spermaceti. The junk was ruined. But it didn't matter. We found ambergris."

"What?"

"Ambergris is in the intestines. Only in sick whales. Very rare. And very valuable."

I did not want to know the details.

"My crew earned every penny. Even young Dickie. The deck is always slick with blood and oil, but I never lost a man overboard." He squinted at me. "There's plenty of piracy and poaching in whaling, but not by me or my crew. What I want to know is, how is the man getting rich here?"

"Captain Carroll?"

"He was here first. He got top dollar. But I have more spermaceti and the ambergris. Took in almost five hundred gallons from that last whale. He should never have abandoned it. It brings in three to five times more than the regular oil."

"Oh." I had no idea about whale oil.

I had no conclusions about the captains. Each was adamant, and each offended. Neither seemed connected to the murders, but I actively disliked them both, anyway. I turned for the gangplank.

"You lied to me!"

"Captain Shorey," I said, gathering the last shreds of my dignity, "I have no wish to argue further. I cannot get off your ship fast enough."

He pointed a finger at the jetty. "You came with that detective and snuck up here to satisfy a woman's curiosity."

He ran a hand over his face. "And I've done that, no doubt. Take your trouble and calamity with you."

I peered beyond his finger to see Detective Fisher step from a wagon with a large valise in his hands. He walked through an open gate and vanished into the Oil Works yard. The gate shut promptly behind him.

Captain Shorey's fury was a sight to behold.

"Off with you! I'll have a word with that fool detective involving women in his work."

I sent up a prayer for Detective Fisher as I was dragged from the ship.

Chapter Twenty-Seven

"**T**HAR SHE BLOWS!" Captain Carroll stood in the center of the pier, Nora at his elbow, clutching her valise. "I pegged you for a coward, Shorey! Thought ye were sounded!"

Captain Shorey never paused. Dragging me by the elbow, he hauled me from the *Alexander* and marched over the pier without a glance.

"I've no time to chinwag," Captain Carroll said as we passed them. "Business to do!"

Our footsteps went from pounding over the wooden pier to crunching along the dirt jetty. Captain Shorey reached the Arctic Oil Works back gate and shoved. Nothing happened. Releasing my arm, he applied both hands, but it held firm. He shook the gate bodily, and it rattled the fencing on both sides.

Captain Carroll chuckled as he approached sedately, Nora on his arm. "Don't tell me you're here without the key?" He held a key up. "Allow me."

Wild-eyed, Captain Shorey stepped aside, breathing heavily through his broad nose. Captain Carroll turned the lock, pocketed the key, and slid the gate open.

The two collided, trying to enter first, shoving with shoulders and scowling furiously at each other. Nora and I followed and tugged the gate shut behind us.

We were in the boneyard. The entire open-air court was full of drying baleen. Thrusting up to fifteen feet in the air, bundles of whalebone stood curing in the sun, smelling to high heaven.

"You didn't clean it properly," Captain Shorey said. "Your men are lazy."

"The stench is off your boat, Shorey," Captain Carroll said. "Your men don't know a mop from a hole in the ground."

"I took better prices for mine," Captain Shorey said, wheeling on him. "Because mine were cleaned correctly."

"You're a cheat and a thief!" Captain Carroll peeled off his coat. "That whale was mine!"

"You're a rancid, swindling, smuggling, sorry excuse of a right whaler!" Captain Shorey rolled up his sleeves and began to circle.

Considering we were in a narrow corridor in a forest of whalebone, it seemed a foolhardy thing to do. I grabbed Nora's hand and pulled her farther in. There was no rhyme or reason to the place. No path or obvious exits. Just wall to wall towers of frilled baleen.

This was my chance. We needed to find Detective Fisher or make our way to the oil works office for help.

Nora tugged me to a stop. "We can't leave them!" she said. "Captain Carroll is all I have!"

"Captain Shorey will hurt him," I said. "We need the police."

"You and your infernal police!" She dropped her valise and turned me loose. "I have to save him!"

She darted into the fray, and I ran a few steps on. I passed stacks of baleen, laid down in a pile. I passed two barrels upended with a board to use as a sawhorse and a bandsaw sat unused next to it. Where were the workers? I went farther in and came abruptly to a wall. It should not have been so quiet. The captains' insults echoed overhead, along with Nora's shrieks, and I stopped.

Where was everyone? I looked back over my shoulder, worried. By the time I found my way out, someone was going to die. Crashes and grunts and blows grew louder as I traced my steps back, thinking evil thoughts about Detective Fisher. Where was he when we needed him? Infernal, indeed.

The entry to a huge warehouse yawned open at my next turn. The odor stopped me in my tracks. Wide vats boiled and steamed and baleen floated in them like giant strands of spaghetti. Beyond them in the back, barrels were stacked clear to the ceiling.

"Hello!" I shouted. "Anyone!"

The place was empty. Full of apprehension, I plunged back into the baleen forest.

I arrived to find the two captains circling each other, panting, with their meaty fists raised. Captain Carroll had refreshed his black eye and Captain Shorey's nose bled. Their shirts were fouled with dirt and blood, and torn where they'd come into contact with the baleen. Nora stood aside with Captain Carroll's coat in her arms, pleading with them to stop.

She met my eyes and shook her head in despair.

"Listen to me, Carroll." Captain Shorey spit blood on the ground. "Something's wrong with the barrels."

"You'll see me in Davy Jones' Locker before you'll stop spreading rumors!" Captain Carroll swiped a sleeve over his face.

"Rumors come from observant eyes. Just check up on it. This once. And I'll never mention it again."

"I don't trade in human cargo!"

"I never said you did. That's someone else's rumors. And I'm not a smuggling pirate."

"Then how'd you get that huge payout? Yes, I've seen the receipts in the office! What did you sell, Shorey? Your soul?"

"Ambergris!"

"The last whale?" Captain Carroll's face reddened, and he threw another punch that Captain Shorey dodged.

I'd crept closer to Nora. "Let's get out of here," I said.

"But the captain!" She never took her eyes off him as she circled them. His coat was slowly being reduced to pulp in her hands.

Captain Shorey lowered his fists. "I will tell you something. You are a fool. And the only way to prove it to you is to take you into that warehouse and show you."

Captain Carroll kept his fists up but straightened. "I will give you five minutes, Shorey. Professional courtesy. And then you will never speak to me or about me again."

"Done." Captain Shorey held out his hand. Captain Carroll stared at it, then spit in his hand and shook.

The two stalked away, completely absorbed in their feud.

Nora started to follow, and I said, "Wait. Once they're done, Captain Carroll will come looking for you, right?"

She nodded morosely.

"Then let's wait somewhere else. This place gives me the shivers. Detective Fisher left a wagon on the jetty. That's my ticket out of here. Come on."

I made my way to the gate while Nora collected her valise. She hugged the coat to her, saying, "He had some business or other here. And then we were going to wherever it is he lives." She sniffed as I closed the gate behind us. She was quite dazed. "Home, he said. He bought it. Can you believe it?"

"You aren't there yet," I warned her.

"No, but I'm glad you two showed up when you did. He'd just discovered we had no wagon." She climbed up to the seat and dropped the valise in the wagon bed. "And my trunk is dumped in the middle of the pier."

"Oops."

"Why are sailors so moody?" She straightened the coat in her lap. "You'd think they'd be so happy to be back on shore and alive that they'd be agreeable as lambs."

I shrugged and kept my eyes on the gate.

When it opened, I ducked behind the wagon.

"Where'd you go?" Nora asked. She bent over the wagon seat to look at me and I shushed her.

"I'm sure they have facilities in the office," she whispered.

I crouched low, looking under the wagon to watch two legs exit the boneyard and the gate slide closed. The legs moved toward the pier, a valise swinging next to them. Keeping the wagon between us, I moved around to the horse's head as the man moved swiftly to the pier.

"Now that I think about it," Nora said, "there would be no reason for them aboard a ship, would there?"

I ignored her giggle. What was he doing here? And wasn't that Detective Fisher's bag?

"Stay in the wagon, Nora. I'll be right back."

"What? Where are you going? Mrs. Kelly?"

I was already moving. Sharky was on his way to the *Hidalgo*. Where had he been? I hated to imagine coming face to face with the man, alone in the boneyard. But it was apparent he had been on a mission. He was by himself. Had ignored the fight his captain was in. And carried a stolen bag.

He passed the two sentries without a word and boarded swiftly.

Had Captain Carroll arranged for a distraction while his first mate ... did what?

Shifting from crate to crate, I went far enough onto the pier to verify Sharky's location without being seen.

"Mrs. Kelly!"

I spun, my heart in my throat, to see Detective Fisher on the deck of the *Alexander*.

"Stay there!" he called down, and vanished.

How had he gotten up there? Why? I was good and truly done with men snapping in my face. I hadn't done anything to warrant his commands. And he'd just betrayed my location to Sharky and everyone else on the pier.

I cowered behind the crates as voices approached, but it

was the two captains hurrying down the pier, deep in conversation.

"It may be," Captain Shorey said gravely. "Do you want help?" The blood on his shirt had darkened and stuck to his back.

Captain Carroll tenderly rubbed his jaw. "First mate ought to know. I'll ask him first." His eye was rapidly swelling shut.

"Very well. I'm aboard the *Alexander* if you need me."

Captain Carroll extended his hand. "Thank you, sir."

"An honor."

The two parted, each to his ship, and I stood there looking for flying pigs.

"Don't just stand there! Run!" Nora took my hand and yanked me from my hiding place.

"What? What is it?"

"The police! They're raiding the oil works! Hurry!"

"They're what?"

"Coming after us!"

"Are we in trouble for trespassing?" I asked, skirts flying. "For the fight? They know me, Nora. I'll talk to them." And in the process, give Detective Fisher a piece of my mind.

"They all have their guns out!" We ran up the gangplank after Captain Carroll. "And they're looking for you!"

The two sentries swiveled their heads after us, wide-eyed.

"How do you know?"

"I heard them say so, silly!"

Crossing the deck, we dropped swiftly into the captain's cabin.

"Sweet holy Jesus." Nora froze, and I nearly crashed into her at the bottom of the staircase.

Captain Carroll and Sharky were in a heated debate. Sharky leaned over one side of the table with his hands on it, and Captain Carroll faced him, speaking in low, fervent tones. Sharky slowly looked up and made eye contact with Nora.

She leaned hard into me, and he winked.

"The barrels are marked," Captain Carroll said. "Our mark is clear on some and sloppy on others. Who did the marking?"

"Young Peter, Cap." Sharky returned to the conversation, but it was as if his glance had turned Nora to stone.

Captain Carroll grunted. "May he rest in peace. But it was you I placed in charge of the unloading. You've got the tallies?"

"It's all in the log." He thumped on a ledger in the center of the desk. "I know our own barrels, Cap. Why did you let Shorey get under your skin? He's a lying scoundrel. He's probably on his ship right now, laughing up his sleeve at us."

"Shorey is an honorable man." Captain Carroll shook his head. "Captains have responsibilities to each other that outweigh personal grudges. The sea owns us all, mate."

Sharky's face went from incredulous to outraged. "But ... Cap..."

"Now. Why is the count higher in the warehouse than I know can fit in my cargo hold? I believe in miracles, and happy to have my hand out, so long as it's honorable."

"Cap. Could there be a clerical error? It happens, you

know. They'd never have mishandled us in Seattle."

"And we'll go only there from now on." Captain Carroll stiffly rolled his shoulder. "There are a third again of our barrels parked in that warehouse than we brought in."

"It's dark in there. How can you figure that with just a sweeping look?"

"You're right. I can't. I want you to take another tally. Today. Right now."

"Cap." Sharky straightened. "With all respect, we don't need to do that, sir. The works've already paid out. The deal's done. They're going to finish processing, and we'll scour and reship the empties for the next voyage. We're right in the middle of it."

"You'll get the men out there and do a complete barrel count. I want to see if they match up to what's on the books."

"They do."

"Captain?" Nora's voice shook with the effort of saying the single word.

Captain Carroll turned at her interruption, but his smile quickly became a grimace. "Nora, dear. I'd quite forgotten you, forgive me." He looked down at his shirt and put a finger to his eye. "I'm afraid I've made a clumsy impression. I never look like this. On land, that is."

"Sir—"

"Business will do this to a man. You mustn't be afraid. Come here, my darling."

Sharky's countenance shifted once again. "Cap! Do you know who that is?"

Nora kept her head down and moved swiftly into Captain Carroll's embrace, blood, sweat, and all.

"I do indeed, Sharky! Meet my bride!"

"Your ... she's a whore! A common tramp from The Whale!"

"Mind your language," Captain Carroll said. "This brave woman saved my life."

Nora kept her face buried in the captain's filthy shirt. She didn't see the shock, suspicion, and menace developing across the table.

"How? When?" Sharky fought hard to keep his tone in check.

I didn't have time for this. I expected to see Detective Fisher with every glance over my shoulder. What had I done to bring the entire police force down on me lately?

"Last night after you all left the Typhoon. I paid this lovely woman a visit. I was drugged, mate! Can ye believe it? An old salt like me falling for such child's play? She drove me to safety."

"After you married her?" There was no mistaking the sarcasm. "And did she tell you she knew me?"

"In the Biblical sense?" Captain Carroll barked a short laugh. "Mate, a girl like this is one in a million. I'll not hold her past against her any more than she'll do for me."

Nora shook her head, rubbing her nose against the captain's shirt.

Captain Carroll moved her gently away and ran a hand over his vest. "Pocket watch stolen. Everything stolen, blast them."

"I didn't." Nora's voice was small but insistent. "I didn't tell him anything."

"Everything, Cap?" Sharky's eyes narrowed. "Nothing left in your pockets?"

"I'll burn the place down," Captain Carroll muttered. "I can do that, now I own it I'll smoke 'em all out!" He winced and touched a gash in his shirt.

Nora turned a shocked face to Captain Carroll, and Sharky pulled out a revolver.

Captain Carroll was still feeling around in his pockets and didn't notice either of them.

"You've got work, Sharky," he said. "Best get to it, mate."

"Where's the coin?" Sharky aimed his gun at Nora's face. "Don't lie again, whore. I know you took it." He waggled the gun and met Captain Carroll's horrified eyes. "She's lying. She's your thief. You never married her. I'd put down good money that she drugged you, too."

The captain straightened and pulled Nora against him. "Sharky. Put the gun away. You have no respect for women."

"I didn't say anything," Nora whimpered. "I swore I wouldn't."

The reality of what Nora was saying finally got through to me.

Sharky held out his hand. "Good girl. Now give it to me. Prove your guilt. He might let you live."

"Sharky!" Captain Carroll's voice echoed in the small room. "Stow it! Now!"

I crept backwards, one step up at a time, trying not to

catch anyone's attention.

"Cap, I've done nothing but take care of you from the day I boarded. I'm loyal. Obedient. And you trust me to watch your back. And I'm telling you right now. This is one big lie."

Chapter Twenty-Eight

NORA TURNED IN Captain Carroll's arms to face Sharky. "I don't know what you're talking about!"

I was three steps up. If I took another, I wouldn't be able to see what was happening. I'd have to turn and run.

My skirts were in my hand when Sharky's gaze met mine. "Mrs. Kelly. Good of you to join us."

I blurted out the first thing that came to mind. "The police are raiding the oil works right now," I said. "Why?"

Captain Carroll's scowl would have melted paint off a barn. "Sharky. We're moored. But we're still at sea until you've been paid. And when I give an order to my first mate, I expect to be obeyed."

"Aye, sir." Sharky lowered the gun to his waist.

"Why are the police looking at these same barrels we're discussing, Sharky?"

"Must be Shorey's doing. He's a cheat. Tried to claim our barrels as his. They've caught him, then. Prison's too good for him, I say."

Captain Carroll gazed at him with one eye. "Are ye calling my wife a whore, Sharky?" It was impossible to miss the threat in his voice.

"No, Cap." Sharky's eyes narrowed. "I've never steered you wrong. You know that. But she's a liar. And a thief."

With a roar, Captain Carroll lunged over the table. Sharky raised the gun and fired. Nora was tangled up in the middle. I spun and took one step up before Sharky's hand dragged me back. I stumbled back against him as a figure darkened the passage above us.

"You have what you came for!" Detective Fisher shouted. "Let the lady go!"

I stood between them and both their guns were aimed at me.

"Captain! Captain!" Nora shrieked from the floor, where blood seeped from Captain Carroll's vest.

"Detective Fisher." Sharky's grip was a vise on my shoulder. "We're going to walk out of here nice and slow. You're going to get everyone out of our way. Tell your men to back away from the ship."

Detective Fisher didn't budge. He was bent forward so he could see us, and his back wouldn't last long in that position. His eyes were dark as flint and they were trained on Sharky's face. If I ducked, he might have a clear shot. But in this close space, the bullet could so easily hit any of the rest of us. Even he must see the advantages of letting us out onto the deck.

Sharky would be outgunned.

"You're trapped," Detective Fisher said. "I have men covering the pier and the oil works. You should have taken the bag and walked away."

Sharky shook me. "And I will. You should have followed

orders better. Now I have to bring Mrs. Kelly along."

He shoved me toward Nora.

"Don't shoot!" she cried. "Don't kill him!" Her white shirtwaist was bloody, and she threw herself over Captain Carroll, who grunted and said, "Darlin', not now."

"Pick up the bag," Sharky said, and shoved the barrel of his gun into my side. I took up the large leather bag that he'd stolen from Detective Fisher. Did I have it backward? Detective Fisher wanted Sharky to take it? It was heavy and awkward but immediately in Sharky's free hand.

"Sweetheart," he whispered in my ear. "If you try to run, I'll shoot you right through your pretty head."

I absolutely believed him.

Detective Fisher remained in place and Sharky said, "Why are you still here, Fisher? Move."

"You're on a point," Detective Fisher said, gun still aimed at us. "The refinery is locked up tight. Even if I push my men back, you're bottled in. There's no escape. Let the lady go."

"I'm a sailor, and you're a detective. We'll both do what we were born to do. There's no one on the sea side. You're dropping a whaleboat and I'm leaving in it."

"You won't make it out of the harbor."

"Unless your men can swim or sail, I will."

Sharky urged me toward the steps. "Nice and slow. Be a good girl and you'll make it out alive."

When Detective Fisher finally spared me a glance, I gave him a wan smile. It could be my last five minutes alive. Why waste them? His face remained deathly serious as he slowly

301

backed up and out of Captain Carroll's quarters.

Following carefully, I stepped onto the deck with Sharky close behind.

The only person in sight was Detective Fisher, his gun still raised and trained on my head. My smile vanished. Considering I'd done the same to him, I supposed we were even.

"Where are the others?" Sharky asked.

"On the pier."

Sharky wrapped his arms around me, the valise in my lap and the gun against my temple. "Toss your gun overboard, detective." His voice tickled my ear and his foul breath wafted past my face. I closed my eyes in a grimace.

A small splash loosened Sharky's grip.

"Let's go." Sharky pushed me forward, and I stumbled. "Drop that whaleboat there."

Detective Fisher went to the nearest boat and started pulling ropes as if he'd done it every day of his life. The pier was on the far side of the ship. No one standing there would see what was happening, let alone take a shot at Sharky.

The Bay rolled east, rippling in the afternoon light. Boats of every description were scattered over its surface between us and the rolling hills on the far side. Detective Fisher shoved the whaleboat and one end dropped below the rail.

Nausea bubbled in my stomach as Sharky laughed.

"It's not a one-man operation," Detective Fisher grumbled.

He looked up and caught my eye.

"A child could do it," Sharky said.

Detective Fisher continued to wrangle the boat and all I could think of was trying to get from the deck to a little bobbing boat on the Bay without falling into the water or landing on the boat and either breaking my neck or sinking it.

Sharky had his hands busy with the bag and the gun. Looking down, I could see the holster at his hips and the knife he'd toyed with at The Whale the night before.

Not a one-man operation.

"Where will you drop her off?" Detective Fisher asked. "Once you've passed the golden gates?"

"Seattle."

We both gaped at him.

Sharky laughed. "It's nothing. I should've never left Seattle. Had a good card racket going back in the day."

"You're not taking me in that tiny thing all the way to Seattle!" I said.

"Drop the boat, Fisher."

Detective Fisher met my eyes. I nodded. With a heave, he pushed the boat over and let the lines run. Sharky leaned forward to watch it drop. I had my hands on the hilt of his knife and whirled with it in a flash.

Sharky turned the gun on me and I took quick steps back, holding the knife in his face. "Let me go!" I cried. "Or I'll wait till you're rowing and jump with the bag."

For such a bold-faced lie, my words rang with conviction. I would be a puddle in the bottom of that boat, begging for mercy.

Detective Fisher stumbled away from the rails with his

hands in the air and said, "No one is following you!"

Sharky only hesitated a moment. "Aye. And see to it they don't." He backed to the rail with the gun still raised.

Detective Fisher had worked his way around and though I knew he was slowly coming up behind me, I didn't dare take my eyes from Sharky or lower the knife.

"Not that I'm worried," Sharky added with a wicked smile. "You've gone and gotten everything wrong. The wrong lady. The wrong ship. The wrong villain. A man could get away with murder in San Francisco."

"Don't think you will!" I cried.

He threw a leg over the rail. "Captain Shorey has the girl you're looking for. But you don't have the gold, do you?" He jiggled the valise. "So, he's going to be very, very upset with you and who knows what he might do to the poor thing."

Detective Fisher came up beside me, his face livid. "What are you talking about?" he roared.

"Idiots." He threw his second leg over the rail and tucked the gun into the front of his shirt. "Do you know what happens when dynamite gets old? Fragile stuff. Give my regards to my associate. May he rot in jail."

He dropped from view.

"This." Detective Fisher glanced at me. "This is exactly why I didn't want to work with you."

"He's getting away!"

He closed his eyes in defeat. "Count to ten, Mrs. Kelly."

"But—"

Placing his hands on my shoulders, he stared solemnly into my eyes.

We counted aloud, together. Then we broke apart and raced to the rail. Sharky had already rowed quickly into the Bay. I shuddered, recalling those powerful arms around me.

"Use the harpoon! Sink him!" I said.

"No need. Look."

Sharky's boat grew smaller. "What am I looking at?"

"The tug. There. The *Governor Tilden*." He pointed. "I have men on it. Come with me."

The chest bolted to the deck beneath the mizzenmast contained several items, including flags, but he pulled a gun from the side and swiftly aimed it skyward. It fired a blazing red flare into the twilight.

"It's the signal," he said. "It means our enemy is coming straight at them. And he is."

Amazed, I said, "I think that's the cleverest thing you ever did."

He tossed the gun back into the chest without comment and I turned for the captain's quarters.

"Nora," I said, "and Captain Carroll. They're hurt."

"Who's the other lady?" he asked, following me.

"Nora." I sped down the stairs. "She's the captain's wife."

"Captain Shorey is married?"

"No, Captain Carroll is!"

Nora looked up at us. "He's dying! Send for a surgeon! Please, Mrs. Kelly!" She held a blood-stained rag to Captain Carroll's chest.

"Avast, woman!" Captain Carroll remained prone, but his eyes were open and lucid. They were the only part of him that moved. "Get one of my mates down the gangplank like I told ye!"

He coughed and the blood spread.

"Nora, are you hurt?" I asked, kneeling down.

"I tried to stop him!" she cried. "I tried to move him out of the way!"

Her face had good color, and she moved and breathed with ease. Though she was covered in blood, it didn't seem to be hers.

"I'll fetch them," I told Captain Carroll.

"They know where the supplies are," he said as I rose. "Done many a surgery on a pitching deck m'self."

I slammed Sharky's knife into the table and left it quivering there.

"Dear God, run, Mrs. Kelly!" Nora was frantic, and I left with Detective Fisher in my footsteps.

Captain Carroll's voice followed us out. "Mutiny, damn him!"

I was down the gangplank and surrounded by officers when Detective Fisher took my arm.

"Ouch!" I pulled it away. "If one more man takes me by the arm again today, I'll punch him right in the nose!"

"Where are Captain Carroll's guards?" he asked his men. "The two who stood here earlier?" The guards were quickly pushed forward. "Your captain is in his quarters, shot. He needs medical care, and he's calling for you two. Don't botch the job or I'll hang you for murder."

The men ran up the gangplank and Detective Fisher sent two officers up behind them before turning back to me.

"What is that woman to Captain Shorey?"

"Who, Nora? Nothing."

"I know her from somewhere. Where?"

"The Whale."

The pier was an entirely different place. Officers were everywhere, talking, shifting crates, calling to each other as they watched the far-off pursuit over the water. The refinery belched and clanged, obviously back in business. Traffic on the jetty had been blocked at the far end, but the activity on the pier had garnered a thick crowd of onlookers, both on land and sea.

"Women like you don't come from The Whale," he said.

"Like me?"

"You know what I mean. Ladies. Why would I know her from The Whale?"

"She worked there. As a harlot."

"You think I'd know a harlot?"

"I think you would if you'd gone digging for information." I rubbed my aching arm and said, "Nora worked upstairs. She saw Sharky strangle Mrs. Alden. He paid her to look the other way and keep her mouth shut."

"Which is it? She's a harlot, or she's Captain Carroll's wife?"

By now, a sizable group had gathered around us. I recognized Sergeant Ross, Detective Fisher's boss. Officers Heyes and Wilson. Chief Crowley. Captain O'Meara. Sam.

"You have a tintype of her in dishabille!" I hissed.

I watched comprehension dawn on his face, and a snicker came from the crowd.

"She's both. Most of all, she's your witness, and you'd better hope she wasn't hurt, because she can send Sharky to the gallows for you."

"Well done, Fisher," Sergeant Ross said. "You knew exactly what to do with that note!"

"What note?" I asked.

A roar parted the crowd as Captain Shorey came striding up. "What is the meaning of this?" he asked. He'd changed his shirt for a fresh one, but his nose was swollen to twice its size. Finding me in the middle of a mob of police did not improve his foul mood.

"Am I under arrest?" he asked. "Why are you overtaking the pier and our ships?"

"Captain Carroll was shot," I said.

"Shorey, do you have a woman aboard your ship?" Detective Fisher asked.

"Sharky said you were cheating them with the oil barrels in the refinery," I said.

"Where do you store your dynamite?" Detective Fisher asked.

"Why are you going to be very upset at Detective Fisher?" I asked.

"Captain Shorey, you are under arrest." Detective Fisher pulled out a pair of handcuffs.

"Wait just one minute!" Captain Shorey boomed and put up his fists.

We all fell silent, and the crowd gave us some space.

"I'm the one with the questions," he said, turning to me. "Is Captain Carroll dead, then?"

"No," I said. "Not yet, I guess. They're taking care of him in his cabin."

He glanced at the *Hidalgo*. "And he claims I've cheated him?"

"No. Sharky did. Before he shot the captain and rowed off into the sunset."

"Mutiny?" Captain Shorey's word held contempt and fury.

"He claimed you were the real villain," Detective Fisher said, tapping the handcuffs against his leg. "Why?"

Captain Shorey straightened and dropped his fists. "Did he? And did he tell you the barrel marks were altered? The brands were filed from an A into an H. Saw them with our own eyes and you can go inside and look for yourself, detective."

Detective Fisher nodded, and two men left.

"Stealing my cargo is a very bad idea," Captain Shorey said, glowering.

"We are looking for a woman," Detective Fisher said. "Aboard your ship."

Captain Shorey glared at me. "And this is not her?"

Detective Fisher actually ran a finger around his collar. "No."

"How many women do you require to do your job, detective?"

This was met with a hearty round of chuckles.

"The note said a lady on a ship. I assumed it was Mrs. Kelly here, but I was told otherwise. That it was another lady on another ship, which can only be yours, which means, Captain Shorey, that there is, in actual fact, a different woman on your ship!"

I looked at him. "What note?"

Chapter Twenty-Nine

C APTAIN SHOREY CAME undone. "Is every skirt in San Francisco boarding my ship?" he bellowed.

"As captain," Detective Fisher continued, "I would expect you to know what this man, Sharky, was talking about. He said you had the girl I was looking for. I would anticipate your full cooperation in allowing us to board your ship. And I would insist that you explain the part about dynamite."

"I have no dynamite aboard. I have no woman aboard." Captain Shorey's voice was dangerous because of its sudden lack of volume. I stepped back a pace. If there was to be another brawl, I was well aware of what his fists could do.

Detective Fisher never flinched. "I have no reason to believe you are not in cahoots with this Sharky. He asked me to give my regards to his associate. That's you."

"Fisher?"

"Not now, Mr. Merrill."

"Right now, Fisher."

All eyes turned to Sam as he stood there, looking for all the world like an apologetic sardine next to a vengeful whale.

"The note," Sam said. "I have it."

He pulled a scrap of paper out of his pocket and pushed

his spectacles up his nose to read.

"The coins for the lady on the ship. Come alone. Drop them in the boneyard."

"I did," Detective Fisher said.

"It wasn't Mrs. Kelly the note referred to."

"We have just established that." Detective Fisher reined in his frustration.

"I must confess something." Sam straightened his tie and slipped the note back into his pocket. "I hope it doesn't besmirch my professional standing."

"What are you doing here, Sam? You were the only one left guarding the jail."

Chief Crowley grew tense and folded his arms.

"I've already let you down, Fisher." Sam looked beaten. "Yesterday, Miss Smith came to the station. Alone and frightened. She begged me to help her."

My knees went weak.

"What was she afraid of?" Detective Fisher asked.

"Mrs. Kelly." Sam darted a look my way. "It seems Miss Smith was accused of murdering her employer, Dr. Park, and felt that her arrest was imminent."

"So she turned herself in?"

"No. She stood by her innocence. It seems I was the only person she had left to trust."

"You are losing mine fast, Sam."

"I let her rest at the station. Told her she could stay un- til ... well, until she felt safe again, I suppose."

Chief Crowley and Captain O'Meara exchanged looks.

"It has to be her," Sam said. "When we found the note,

Miss Smith disappeared."

"Are you telling me that Sharky kidnapped Becky from the police station?" I demanded. It would have been after he left my interrogation. How else would he have known where the coins were?

"It's my fault he took Becky." I swallowed. "He was in The Whale when I said she ran the shop. He was probably planning to take me until he heard that."

"It's all my fault," Sam said. "I should have never left her alone. She was faint, and I left her lying down." He turned miserable eyes on me. "Her kitten was still there. She would never have left it behind."

The pier erupted with voices.

"Quiet!" Detective Fisher yelled. He took off his hat and ran a hand through his hair. "He leaves the note. He takes the girl." He pulled the hat firmly back on. "He brings her here." He glanced at Captain Shorey. "He hides the girl on the *Alexander* and waits until I show up with the coins."

He put his hands on his hips and I stared at the empty holster.

"He claims Captain Shorey is in on it, but the good captain claims otherwise."

Captain Shorey folded his massive arms.

"That leaves another accomplice." Detective Fisher looked up at the *Alexander*. "A hostage. And a bomb."

The shame I felt for the way I treated Becky burned clean away in the wrath I held for Sharky.

"A skirt? And a bomb? On my ship?" Captain Shorey roared. He turned to leave and several men hemmed him in.

"Let me at it! I won't let someone hurt the *Alexander*! Not while there's breath in my body!"

"Here now," Captain O'Meara said, grabbing the massive shoulder. "Don't give us trouble, captain. We're no more happy about it than you are."

"Shorey!" Detective Fisher said. "Tell me. What happens if your ship blows up?"

Captain Shorey could barely contain himself. "Besides the damage to my heart? The log lost. Proof of which barrels are mine in that warehouse. Months in dry dock for repairs." He paused. "Assuming she can be salvaged." His chest heaved. "No sailing when the ice breaks. Crews already gone. I'd be ruined at least a year, detective. Maybe for good."

"Sharky wanted you ruined," I said. "Not Captain Carroll." I turned to Detective Fisher. "He set Captain Shorey up to look guilty. But if you didn't arrest him, then dynamite is a solid backup plan. Sharky might have been content to let Captain Carroll take the profits and sail away, knowing the competition was ruined."

I looked at Captain Shorey. "After all, you took the last whale. But is that sin worth this level of revenge, captain? Sharky didn't stop with taking your barrels and destroying your ship. He demanded the coins."

All eyes went to Goliath. "I know nothing about coins."

"Then who is his associate?"

"Whoever it is," Captain Shorey said, "has been watching this spectacle. He's waiting with a woman and a bomb on my ship. What is he waiting for?"

"Sharky," I said. "He is waiting to see whether Sharky

escapes. I wonder how much he promised him?" I shook my head. "Sharky was never going to share. He was taking it all and his associate was taking the blame."

"What makes you think he's still here, then?" Detective Fisher asked. "Why wouldn't he have jumped ship?"

"How do we know he isn't sitting with a match next to the fuse right now?" Chief Crowley asked.

"What if the lady is already dead?" Captain O'Meara threw his hands defensively in the air. "I'm only saying there may not be a rescue."

"Heyes, your weapon." Detective Fisher held out his hand and Heyes put his gun in it.

"I'm coming," Captain Shorey said, flexing his hands.

"You are not." Detective Fisher checked the ammunition. "You can be heard coming a mile away."

"I'm going with you," I said. "Becky is my friend and I owe her."

"No." Detective Fisher slid the gun into his holster. "I'm going alone. It worked on the last ship I boarded."

Sergeant Ross nodded.

"I'll go with you, Fisher." Sam swallowed. "It's my fault."

"Sam, we're having a conversation when this is over. And you aren't going to enjoy it."

Sam looked away.

"Captain," Detective Fisher said, "I need to know where a woman, a bomb, and an associate could hide on your ship without immediate notice. Where do you hide things, Shorey?"

Captain Shorey was silent long enough to hold our interest.

"I do not trade in human cargo," he said.

"No time for being delicate," Detective Fisher pointed out.

"I've been in the wheelhouse. By the galley and my quarters all day. He's not aft."

"Where, Captain?"

"Try the forecastle. The crew's quarters. Check the hold below it. Between and below decks and the blubber room are all emptied."

I must have walked right overhead. Had Becky listened to my footsteps? To Captain Shorey's lecture?

Detective Fisher nodded. "If I don't come back, Ross?"

The men shifted on their feet.

"We can't know about the dynamite." Chief Crowley looked at Captain Shorey. "I won't risk my men."

"I'll give you ten minutes," Captain Shorey said. "Then I'll blow it up myself if it means catching the bastard who's in there."

"Done."

"Everyone off the pier!" Captain O'Meara shouted. The sound of boots reverberated from the wooden planks as everyone moved toward the jetty.

Captain Shorey walked next to Detective Fisher and Sam and I trailed behind them, searching the *Alexander* for signs of movement.

"Sam, he can't go alone."

"He makes the rules, Mrs. Kelly."

"I'm not leaving him."

"Mrs. Kelly?"

I dodged behind a pile of crates and tucked my skirts well in. A brief glance over my shoulder at the water was the only moment I gave any thought to the pursuit of Sharky. They would catch him, or they wouldn't.

"Mrs. Kelly." Sam wedged in next to me and crouched low.

"You're going to give us away!" I hissed.

He put a finger to his lips, and we held our breath as the pier became quiet. I counted to ten before looking around the crates.

Detective Fisher drew the revolver and walked up the gangplank. Captain Shorey remained on the pier, arms crossed, waiting.

The sun was low on the other side of the city and dusk deepened overhead. Soon, it would be too dark to see. Too dark to shoot. Much too dark to help.

"I know who the associate is," I whispered. "It has to be the man who attacked us on Pacific Street. He must be a sailor on Captain Carroll's ship, or how would Sharky know him?"

"Who?"

"I thrashed him with a whip. Right across his nasty face."

"Oh, my."

Another minute passed.

"He said the dynamite was old. Is it the missing part of the bomb lance, do you think?"

"I don't know. Weapons all over a ship like this."

I counted ten again.

"Becky can't stand the sight of blood." I straightened up.

"She's ill." Sam stood next to me.

With a mutual nod, we walked around the far side of the crates. Captain Shorey gave us a cursory glance, then stared back up at his ship.

"We're going aboard," I said.

"I'm saving Miss Smith," Sam said.

"I'm saving Detective Fisher." I smiled at Captain Shorey. "And you can come along and save us."

"Perfectly reasonable." He waved us ahead and followed quietly.

The *Alexander* didn't creak any more than it always did, but every step made me cringe. Captain Shorey strode confidently toward the large central hatch. "You can hear a step everywhere below deck," he said. "He might as well know we're coming for him." He yanked open the trapdoor to reveal steep steps going three stories deep with a straight drop down the center of them.

"I'll search from the bottom up," he said, and dropped without another word.

"Allow me, Mrs. Kelly." Sam went next. "I'll take the midsection."

The men were swallowed in the dim interior. I put a hand to the edge, but that was as far as I could force myself to go. Calling myself a coward, I backed away. The man from Pacific Street carried a personal grudge against me. He'd seen me in The Whale. He'd followed me here. No, I corrected myself. He'd come with Becky and waited for events to unfold. Only the fact that his superiors stood between us had kept me safe thus far.

And they were no longer relevant.

Detective Fisher was in the bow of the ship, and the others were in the middle. I turned for the wheel and the captain's quarters, knowing full well that Captain Shorey claimed to have been there all day, and I'd already taken a look at them earlier. But at least I had a plan.

I went directly to the open galley. Small, smelly, and starkly efficient, the kitchen's few pots and pans stowed in racks meant nothing to me. A flat rail tacked along the wall held every knife and cleaver a cook could want. I helped myself to a chef's knife and tested the blade on my thumb. The thin slice into my glove satisfied me and, heart in my throat, I turned to face the doors before me.

"There's nothing here," I reminded myself.

With that, I flung open the door to the charthouse, knife held high. Other than cubbies filled with scrolls, ink wells, navigation instruments, and pens, it was empty. I searched around the wheel and side cabin, finding only empty tin mugs, more equipment, and a pair of tall, roughly used boots.

All that was left was the captain's quarters. I hesitated at the top of the stairs. It was impossible to see what was down there or whether the layout was similar to the *Hidalgo's*. If it went through to the other sections of the ship or was contained at this end. Though I strained my ears, there was nothing but the sound of gulls crying overhead.

"Down you go."

The voice froze me in place.

A gun muzzle in the small of my back revived me enough to move carefully down into Captain Shorey's quarters. It was spacious without a central table, but a writing desk, chairs, and a wide, leather Chesterfield spoke of a man who enjoyed his comforts. The scent of cigar tobacco mingled with that of the pervading stench.

Detective Fisher sprawled across a Turkish rug, blood from a gash on his head mingling with the red in the patterns. Dead? Alive?

"Don't make a sound or you're next."

I stopped in the center of the room and turned around. He blocked the bottom step, and there'd been no other exit in sight.

"Boggs," he said, running a finger along the mark on his face. "You are as predictable as rain. Everywhere this man goes," he said, waving the gun at Detective Fisher, "you are sure to follow."

"Where's Becky?"

His lip curled at the sight of the knife in my hand. "The hatch is under the rug. A bit cramped. Not the most creative smuggler's hole."

"She's alive?"

"Until we finish this." He looked lovingly at the bundle of dynamite on the ledge next to him. Three sticks with their fuses joined at the end. Crystalized. "Cap cleared it all out. He'll have to buy fresh at the Giant."

We were all going to die if he so much as bumped it.

When I could speak, I said, "Sharky left you. He was

never going to give you a cut."

He shrugged. "I figured."

"Then why are you still helping him, Boggs?"

"Thought about blowing this thing and jumping ship." His smile shifted the whiplash into diabolical shapes. "But I saw you."

I backed a step in spite of myself.

"We have unfinished business, you and I."

Over the racing of my heart, I said, "I'll go with you. You don't need to hurt anyone else."

If I kept him talking, eventually Captain Shorey or Sam would arrive.

"That knife'll do," he said. "Come closer. Hand it over."

I stopped breathing. If I didn't move, he could as soon shoot me and then have his way. But if I did, it would buy more time for the others.

Which was louder? A gunshot or a scream?

Footsteps.

A single set. Slow. Stealthy. Overhead. We both heard them.

"Well then," Boggs said, and holstered his gun. "Another day, perhaps."

He pulled a match from his shirt pocket and struck it on his front tooth.

"Wait!"

The match lit all three fuses at once.

Bright sparks crackled as he said, "See you in hell, Mrs. Kelly."

Boggs turned and put a hand to the rail. Then curled

downward, falling sideways to his knees, and the scream on his face came out as a grunt. His wild eyes followed me as I dropped the knife, cradled the dynamite in my hands, and raced past him up the stairs. My mind registered the length of a pole in the stairwell. That one end of it had run clean through the middle of Boggs. That a figure at the top of the steps moved swiftly out of my way.

But there was no thought, no plan, no breath, as I tossed the bundle over the rail into the Bay. I fell on my face to the deck as the sound of thunder erupted and a spray of water drifted past.

Chapter Thirty

"B̲Y̲ G̲O̲D̲, M̲R̲S̲. Kelly." Sam bent over me.

I struggled and got to my feet. "Becky! Detective Fisher!" Already, I was moving back down the stairwell.

I passed Boggs without looking at him. Praying Detective Fisher wasn't lying over the hatch, I grabbed a corner of the rug and lifted it. The hatch was flush with the floor and solid wood, but the rug had to be moved another foot and Detective Fisher was dead weight.

"Help me! It's too heavy!"

Sam knelt with his shoulder next to mine and took hold of the rug.

"My cabin!"

Captain Shorey's presence filled the room as he stopped to stare at Boggs. In a flash, he saw what we were trying to do, and he dragged the rug from the hatch with one hand. Detective Fisher's head lolled with blood.

"She's in there," I said, but Sam was already lifting it.

Captain Shorey knelt at Detective Fisher's side and gently turned him over.

"Is he…"

Captain Shorey met my eyes. "No. Knocked out cold."

He went carefully over the detective, looking for other injuries, and I reached for the knife I'd tossed aside.

Sam pulled Becky from her dismal cell and held her head steady against his shoulder as I cut through the knotted gag. I continued with the bonds on her hands and feet and was unaware of the stream of oaths issuing from me until I looked up at Sam's shocked face.

"I'm sorry," I said. "Oh, Becky, I'm so sorry." I left Sam sitting on the floor with his feet hanging in the open pit, chafing Becky's limp hands, and went back to Detective Fisher.

"He's not awake, either?" I ran a careful hand over the massive goose-egg on his head. "Fisher. Ah, me. I'm sorry I was late."

Detective Fisher muttered a profanity.

I locked eyes with Captain Shorey. "Dynamite?" he said.

I nodded and sat down hard on the planks. There was so much blood.

"You saved my ship."

I looked back at Detective Fisher. There had been rather more at stake.

The pounding in my head became pounding on the ship as boots and loud voices came swiftly down into the captain's quarters. Boggs lay dead at the foot of the stairs, a hand clenched around the pole in his middle. The tip of its wicked blade extended from his back.

"Did you do that?" I asked Captain Shorey with a grimace.

He shook his head and rose, saying, "This one needs

bandages."

I glanced at Sam. It couldn't have been him. I frowned, trying to remember.

Men bent over Detective Fisher, firing questions at us. Chief Crowley, Captain O'Meara, and Sergeant Ross moved from person to person, trying to understand who had done what and how.

As if it weren't crowded enough, an officer stumbled down the steps with a struggling boy in handcuffs.

"We caught this one," Heyes said, "sneaking past, trying to escape! Do we haul him in, Ross?"

"No!" Captain Shorey's boom brought the room to a sudden silence. Without looking at me, he handed me a roll of bandages.

"Cap?" Dickie's eyes held terror and hope.

"That's my mate," Captain Shorey said. He put a massive hand on Dickie's thin shoulder. "He can tell you what you want to know."

Heyes looked down at Detective Fisher, then at me, worry clear on his face. I nodded reassuringly.

"Right," Sergeant Ross said, "talk."

Heyes removed the handcuffs and Dickie rubbed his wrists, aware of every eye trained on him.

"All of it, Cap?"

"Up to you, mate."

Dickie scanned the room and stopped on me.

"Thank you," I said softly.

His Adam's apple bobbed. "That there was Boggs," he said, jabbing a thumb over his shoulder.

Officers were already wrestling the body up the stairs.

Fighting the bile rising in my throat, I began wrapping the bandage around Detective Fisher's head.

"Boggs and Parker and me had a pact with Sharky," Dickie said. "Sharky had some valuables smuggled on the *Hidalgo*. A bloody fortune. He was gonna split it with us if we helped him take over the ship."

"A mutiny?" Sergeant Ross asked.

"Aye. Only Sharky didn't mutiny. And we got caught tryin'. Sharky blamed Parker, and we all went over the barrel and took our lashes 'cept Sharky. Cap made him the first mate instead of Parker, and when we docked, Parker took the valuables and ran."

"The gold coins?" I asked.

He nodded.

Captain Shorey was grim, but I could only imagine what Captain Carroll might think of this story.

Dickie looked around at the officers. "Sharky swore revenge on Parker, but we sailed that spring without catching wind of him. If I ran off, where'd I go? I stayed on and kept shut. Sharky was first mate."

Even Captain Shorey nodded.

"When Sharky talked Captain Carroll into running to San Francisco again, we knew why. I snuck in to talk to the cap and Sharky was there instead. He knew. On the next whaleboat out, he made sure I didn't come back."

"I fished him out of the sea," Captain Shorey said. "And now he's my mate. We never told Carroll."

"I can see why," Sergeant Ross said.

Becky started crying softly and when I turned, Sam had her in his arms, clucking over her like a mother hen.

"Sam?" He startled and nearly dropped her on her head. "Did Dr. Park have whiplashes all over his back?"

"You weren't supposed to know that."

I looked down at Detective Fisher, who hadn't revived yet, and tied off the bandage nice and tight.

"Sharky strangled Mrs. Alden when she demanded money," I said. "He was married to her almost twenty years ago, before she came here. Do you hear that, Fisher? She finally found him and he finally found Dr. Park. And Sharky killed them both."

"Mrs. Kelly?" Becky's voice was frail. "I do not snore something powerful."

Sam shushed her and held a mug to her lips.

"Sergeant!" An officer barreled down the steps. Several men, after being waved away by Sam, vacated the room.

"What is it?" Sergeant Ross gave Detective Fisher another worried glance.

"We caught the bastard, Sergeant Ross. Alive. But the bag. He threw it overboard. Before we could stop him. I take full responsibility. Sorry, sir."

The expletive from Detective Fisher caught everyone's attention.

"He's alive!" Becky said.

"That's all, officer." Sergeant Ross looked around the room. "The man in custody has at least two murders to his name, then, plus one attempted murder on the boat next door, and a charge of mutiny." He blew out a breath. "But who killed this old salt with the slash across his face?"

The room grew quiet.

"Nobody knows, sergeant," I said. "I was standing right in front of him when it happened."

"You threw the dynamite into the Bay?"

"Yes."

He considered this a bit.

"Mrs. Kelly?"

"Sam. What is it?"

"You were cursing."

"I apologize, Sam."

"In Chinese, if I'm not mistaken."

"You are. It was Cantonese, to be precise."

"I understood every word," Detective Fisher muttered. He hadn't moved a muscle and his eyes were still closed.

"Fisher, do you need help getting out of here?" Sergeant Ross crossed his arms.

"No, sir."

Sergeant Ross huffed and said, "Then I'll see you on the pier. Soon."

His barked orders accompanied scuffled steps overhead and mercifully faded away.

Captain Shorey still had his hand on Dickie's shoulder. They both watched me, deep in thought.

"Are those earrings new?"

I nearly punched him. Detective Fisher squinted up at me. "Get up if you're so thoroughly recovered," I said.

"I'm afraid I may lose my lunch. The ship is rolling too hard." His eyes closed firmly.

Captain Shorey raised an eyebrow.

I looked down at Detective Fisher. "What was so important about that bag?"

"It was every gold coin we took from Dr. Park's glove shop."

Becky gasped.

"You gave them to him?"

"It was that or you dead."

An uncomfortable silence hung in the air.

"Heyes said you were in the march," he said. "But you weren't. We found your buggy still parked on Montgomery."

"So. You missed me?"

"Apparently. Made an ass of myself in every establishment on Pacific Street. I didn't think they would admit to seeing you, but I had to try."

"I'm sure Joe didn't tell you. Then again, he didn't tell me, either. A fairly tight-lipped lot there."

He'd looked. It put me in a very forgiving mood.

"Light the lanterns," Captain Shorey said. "Inside and out."

"Aye, sir." Dickie scrambled to obey. The sunlight was nearly gone.

"Do you think you can walk, Miss Smith? You really should be home, recovering."

"Thank you, Mr. Merrill." Becky stood on shaky legs and leaned heavily on Sam. "You are the best detective in the whole entire world, Mrs. Kelly," she said. "Except when you think I've done it. Then, you are terrifying."

"Thank you," I said. Her misery was apparent. "I think.

Becky, I truly apologize."

"Well, I…"

That was as far as she managed. She'd seen the pools of blood and her eyes fluttered up in her head. Sam staggered.

"Allow me," Captain Shorey said. He scooped Becky up and Sam followed them meekly out, leaving me alone on the floor with Detective Fisher.

"Captain Carroll owns The Whale now," I said. "And all the rest of Dr. Park's properties. He's next of kin."

"Does he?"

"He received a single coin in an unmarked envelope the day Dr. Park died," I said. "He thought I'd sent it. Sharky demanded it from Nora today. I think Dr. Park must have known the *Hidalgo* was in port and tried to warn Captain Carroll."

"Or taunt Sharky." He squinted up at me again.

"Either way, it didn't end well for him."

He was silent.

"I've been thinking about what Becky said." I stared at my ruined gloves. "That Dr. Park had been kind to her. Perhaps he was trying to atone for his past life."

"Or he was exploiting her innocence as a foolproof cover to fence stolen coins."

"You always assume the worst in people!"

"It comes in handy in my career."

"You thought Captain Shorey had me."

"I saw you on his damn ship!" He winced. "And then you were everywhere else. Why don't you ever hold still?"

"You are not improving your headache."

"No."

After a pause, I said, "Do something for me."

His grin was lopsided. "I'm hardly in a position to be helpful just now."

"Don't be mad at Sam. He took care of Becky when no one else believed her."

"I'm still not convinced I do."

"What?"

"And Sam went against direct orders and left the station unmanned."

Captain Shorey reentered the room with a wide smile on his face and tin mugs in his hands. "My lady," he said, "I'm going to pour you some of my finest brandy." He went to the open hatch.

"I think I've ruined your rug, captain," Detective Fisher muttered.

Captain Shorey laughed, and the deep musical sound rolled through the cabin and warmed it.

"You are welcome to it, sir. Everything on my ship is forfeit to the lady, here."

Detective Fisher, deep in thought, looked back at me. "What do you normally keep in that hatch?" he asked.

"As far as you know," Captain Shorey said cheerfully, "my grog. I'll pour you some."

"Thank you, but my head is already spinning nicely."

"Then a cigar for later." He pulled a bottle from the hidden cupboard and opened it. "Will you join me on the sofa, Mrs. Kelly?"

It felt disloyal to leave Detective Fisher prone on the carpet alone.

"That was kind of you to help Becky, Captain Shorey," I said instead.

"One less skirt aboard." He gave me a meaningful look.

"I guess chaos tends to follow me," I admitted. "But I refuse to call it bad luck."

I accepted the mug he handed me with as much dignity as I could muster from the floor.

He raised his cup. "You are lady luck herself, Mrs. Kelly." He took a deep drink and settled himself on the Chesterfield while I sipped, feeling the heat rise in my face and grateful for the lantern glow that hid it.

Heyes came down the steps. "I'm here to escort Detective Fisher out," he said, looking back and forth between us. "Ross' orders."

"How is Captain Carroll?" I asked. Whatever the lovely liquid in my mug was, it was delicious. My shoulders relaxed and the ache in my arms softened.

"They say he'll live. Staying on his ship to recover. Him and his wife."

I turned a dazzling smile on Detective Fisher.

"Now what?" His wariness was delightful.

"Send Officer Heyes for Nora's bag."

All three men stared at me.

"Sharky had the wrong one. He threw a bag full of lingerie and love potions into the Bay."

Detective Fisher sighed. "I'm the one who was hit in the head, not you."

"When Sharky made me hand him the bag, I saw her initials carved into the handle. Other than that, her bag was exactly like yours."

Detective Fisher sat up. "You mean she took my valise from the boneyard? After the fight?"

"You mean you could sit up this whole time?"

Heyes ran up the steps again.

"And while we're on the subject," I said, "I want to know who the coins belong to."

He closed his eyes and ran a hand over his jaw with a groan.

"Because all the interested parties are dead or soon to hang, except Dickie, here." I gave Captain Shorey a meaningful glance. "I suppose it would have to be looked into. For Dickie's best interests, poor boy."

"Woman." Detective Fisher slowly and deliberately got to his knees. "Please."

"And there's dear Becky losing her place and position." I continued, "If anything, she's Dr. Park's next of kin." I sighed. "But it's a man's world, isn't it? No point in arguing the fact."

I drank the rest of my grog while Detective Fisher stumbled to his feet.

"If only there were some way to purchase the glove shop from Captain Carroll," I mused. "Becky and I could still keep house there."

My cup was empty, so I stood and shook out my skirts rather obviously in front of Captain Shorey.

"Thank you, Captain Shorey," I said, handing him the mug. "I hope to see more of you over the winter."

He stood and bent over my hand. "My pleasure, Mrs. Kelly." Our eyes met. "I'm certain we can arrange it."

Heyes came tearing down the stairs. "It's there, Fisher! Just like she said!"

Captain Shorey slid a cigar into Detective Fisher's jacket pocket. "Congratulations, detective."

Heyes cleared his throat.

Detective Fisher wobbled, put a warning hand out at Heyes, then pulled himself slowly up the blood-stained stairs.

Captain Shorey raised his mug as I followed. "Good night, Mrs. Kelly."

The night was brisk and lit with a million stars. The Bay mirrored them with the lanterns of innumerable boats.

Detective Fisher waited at the rail for me. "It's a wonder to watch you work, Mrs. Kelly. Have I thanked you yet?"

"If you call me a water witch one more time..."

"You are a damn good detective. There. Happy now?"

I took in a deep breath of ocean air. "You needed my help?"

"Desperately."

"And you'll let me help from now on?"

"Do you plan on finding more dead people?"

Aunt Mary listened intently.

"If they want to be found."

A movement on the pier, of black on black, shadows on rippling water, and a soft splash reminded me we were not alone. A cormorant bobbed back to the surface and floated, an ebony void in a quiet, twinkling sea.

I sighed. "Aunt Mary would like that."

The End

If you enjoyed *Death at the Wharf,*
you'll love the other books in the...

A Mrs. Kelly Mystery series

Book 1: *Shadows in Chinatown*

Book 2: *Death at the Wharf*

Book 3: *Murder at the Palace Hotel*

Available now at your favorite online retailer!

About the Author

Photo Credit: Jerusha Foltz

Award-winning author Jolie Tunnell brings the past to life in suspenseful historical mysteries with a hint of romance, bringing the flavor of the turn-of-the-century Wild West to the isolated mountains of Idyllwild and the writhing underbelly of San Francisco.

Her books gallop to the last page.

A Southern California native, she loves on her sprawling family, forces her freeloading tomcat to cuddle, and can drink her weight in Yorkshire Gold tea.

Thank you for reading

Death at the Wharf

If you enjoyed this book, you can find more from all our great authors at TulePublishing.com, or from your favorite online retailer.

TULE
PUBLISHING